5

Modern African Stories

by Ezekiel Mphahlele

*

THE AFRICAN IMAGE
DOWN SECOND AVENUE

Modern African Stories

edited by

ELLIS AYITEY KOMEY

and

EZEKIEL MPHAHLELE

FABER AND FABER
24 Russell Square
London

First published in mcmlxiv
by Faber and Faber Limited
24 Russell Square London W.C.2
Printed in Great Britain by
Latimer Trend & Co Ltd Plymouth

Acknowledgements

The Editors acknowledge with thanks the following authors and publishers for permission to publish and in certain cases to reprint the stories included in this anthology:

Flamingo Magazine and Christiana Aidoo for "Cut Me a Drink".

The *Radio Times* (B.B.C.) for "Ding Dong Bell".

Messrs. William Heinemann and Chinua Achebe for extract from *Things Fall Apart*.

Ato Bedwei for "Me and the Fish God".

Radio Ghana and Ghana Information Services for Peter Buahin's "This is Experience Speaking".

William Conton for "The Blood in the Washbasin".

R. Sarif Easmon for "Koya".

Cyprian Ekwensi for "A Stranger from Lagos".

Alex la Guma for "Coffee for the Road".

Victor Gollancz (Publishers) for extracts from Aldred Hutchinson's *Road to Ghana*.

Flamingo Magazine and James Matthews for "The Second Coming".

Casey Motsisi and *Drum* Magazine for "On the Beat".

Flamingo Magazine for "I Can Face You".

James Ngugi for "A Meeting in the Dark".

Dr. Davidson Nicol for Abioseh Nicol's "The Judge's Son".

Flamingo Magazine and Eldred D. Jones for "A Man Can Try".

Black Orpheus and Nkem Nwanko for "The Gambler".

Grace A. Ogot for "The Rain Came".

Gabriel Okara for "The Crooks".

African Universities Press and Frances Ademola for David Owoyele's "The Will of Allah".

Richard Rive for "Rain".

Can Themba for "The Dube Train".

Acknowledgements

Amos Tutuola and Faber & Faber for extracts from *Feather Woman of the Jungle.*

The Editors are also very grateful to Miss Thelma Rhind who was "only too pleased to type the whole collection for Africa".

Contents

Introduction *page* 9

1 *Cut Me a Drink*
CHRISTIANA A. AIDOO Ghana 13

2 *Ding Dong Bell*
KWABENA ANNAN Ghana 20

3 *Death of a Boy*
CHINUA ACHEBE Nigeria 28

4 *Me and the Fish God*
ATO BEDWEI Ghana 34

5 *This is Experience Speaking*
PETER KWAME BUAHIN Ghana 40

6 *Mista Courifer*
ADELAIDE CASELY-HAYFORD Ghana 50

7 *The Blood in the Washbasin*
WILLIAM CONTON Sierra Leone 60

8 *Koya*
R. SARIF EASMON Sierra Leone 68

9 *A Stranger from Lagos*
CYPRIAN EKWENSI Nigeria 80

10 *Coffee for the Road*
ALEX LA GUMA South Africa 85

11 *Machado*
ALFRED HUTCHINSON South Africa 95

12 *A Man Can Try*
ELDRED DUROSIMI JONES Sierra Leone 104

13 *I Can Face You*
ELLIS KOMEY Ghana 109

Contents

14 *The Second Coming*
JAMES MATTHEWS South Africa *page* 113

15 *On the Beat—Sketches of South African Life*
CASEY MOTSISI South Africa 124

16 *Grieg on a Stolen Piano*
EZEKIEL MPHAHLELE South Africa 129

17 *A Meeting in the Dark*
JAMES NGUGI Kenya 148

18 *The Judge's Son*
ABIOSEH NICOL Sierra Leone 162

19 *The Gambler*
NKEM NWANKWO Nigeria 172

20 *The Rain Came*
GRACE A. OGOT Kenya 180

21 *The Crooks*
GABRIEL OKARA Nigeria 190

22 *The Will of Allah*
DAVID OWOYELE Nigeria 194

23 *Rain*
RICHARD RIVE South Africa 201

24 *Feather Woman of the Jungle*
AMOS TUTUOLA Nigeria 209

25 *The Dube Train*
CAN THEMBA South Africa 223

Introduction

With the possible exception of Swahili, writing in black Africa first entered the field of cultural activity as a response to the presence of the white man. He it was, after all, who brought with him formal schooling and presented a challenge by his completely different way of life—and death.

In South Africa, Negro writing began in the Bantu languages. In 1884, we hear a Cape Province poet respond to the white man's presence in these tones, expressed in Bantu:

I turn my back on the many shams
That I see from day to day;
It seems we march to our very grave
Encircled by a smiling Gospel.

But the educated African was still a privileged person in those days in relation to the rest of his people. When, today, Dennis Brutus, the Coloured poet who has lived in South Africa for about thirty years, says,

Sleep well, my love, sleep well;
the harbour lights glaze over restless docks,
police cars cockroach through the tunnel streets;
from the shanties creaking iron-sheets
violence like a bug-infested rag is tossed
and fear is immanent as sound in the wind-swung bell,

we know things have become worse for the educated African in South Africa. Here oppression levels all: the educated man is pushed around much the same as the others, most often even more, because he is regarded as a menace by authority, especially if he is a writer, a teacher or a politician.

Introduction

Whatever present-day sloganizing may suggest, British colonialism in West Africa never released anything like the physical and mental agony that we see in white-settled countries like South Africa, Southern Rhodesia and Kenya. In spite of the humiliations the African civil servant was subjected to at the hands of his white superior, there was a relatively decent, fear-free home to go back to after work; he was not for ever harassed by the police, he wasn't moved from one place to another with whole communities, and he had a great deal of opportunity to rise above the illiterate or semi-educated masses. So with the teacher, and the lawyer, the doctor—to mention the main classes of educated men.

What, then, evokes the sense of challenge that is responsible for the spurt of literary activity that we have been noticing during the last decade or so in West Africa? British presence here can best be appreciated in its effect on individuals—on a vertical rather than a horizontal plane that takes in large masses of people. Some of these individuals have come to form an articulate front as writers. There are the Nigerians: Wole Soyinka, playwright and poet; Chinua Achebe, novelist; John Pepper Clark, poet and playwright; Gabriel Okara, poet; Christopher Okigbo, poet; Mabel Segun, poetess; Amos Tutuola, novelist; Cyprian Ekwensi, novelist; Onuora Nzekwu, novelist; David Owoyele and Nkem Nwankwo, fiction writers. Then there are the Ghanaians: poets such as Kwesi Brew, Awoonor Williams, Efua Sutherland and fiction writers like Kwabena Annan, Adelaide Casely-Hayford. Tutuola excepted, all these, including the Sierra Leoneans represented in this volume, are either products of the three oldest universities in West Africa, or have been influenced by their intellectual presence.

As individuals, they have become acutely aware of themselves as products of a Western education and Western institutions. The impact of these on them has been just powerful enough to make them look back, soberly and no longer ashamed as a group, into their past and the societies they come from. It is important to know that it is a sober retrospect which, although it may tend to idealize traditional beliefs, mores and rhythm of life, never romanticizes them. For have we not seen in French-speaking West Africa a poetry grow up which speaks the language of an *élite* and is preoccupied only with its sense of loss and other concerns which are not felt by the majority of Africans? And yet the prose writers of this same region, like the English-speaking ones, remain on the ground and even excel the latter in sheer breadth and depth.

In this volume, then, we have Christiana Aidoo's, Ato Bedwei's and Sarif Easmon's strong sense of local colour; Kwabena Annan's quiet but penetrating humour and Peter Kwame Buahin's bombastic kind; Adelaide Casely-Hayford's story of a man who has come to symbolize the younger generation's return to things African, much to the father's disgust; there is the conflict between the nationalism of a "been-to" and the practical sense of a sailor in William Conton's story; the colonial sex dilemma in Eldred Jones's tale. We are treated to Abioseh Nicol's well-measured prose; the restrained language of Chinua Achebe, which throws into bold relief impending tragedy that no one can stop; and then there are Nkem Nwankwo's pathos, the fatalism of David Owoyele's characters and Cyprian Ekwensi's sophisticated sense of detail.

Amos Tutuola is still with us and continues to weave myths around us in his peculiar fashion. The Kenyans, Grace Ogot and James Ngugi, explore the strange twists of irony that we experience in the fatalism of Africa: one brought about by the action of two young lovers who cheat the gods, and the other by the action of a young man whose soul has been soaked in the Christian aura of guilt.

We have already indicated how the South African socio-political life presents the kind of challenge that produces writers. The protest element here is strong. The tone and idiom here are quite different from those in West or East African writing. In Alex la Guma's story we see the ordeal of a mother as she runs into a police net while her children innocently demand coffee in a nagging refrain; James Matthews' highly self-conscious and brutal sense of irony is inescapable. As Richard Rive's and Alfred Hutchinson's imagery piles up layer upon layer, we come close to the bone of sheer physical and mental suffering. There is also Can Themba's unrelieved tension. Casey Motsisi who, incidentally, is the youngest of all represented in this volume, is the only South African here who can take time off to laugh at the whole grotesque southern scene.

These South Africans move in a literary world apart from that of the white writers in their country. Whereas the latter easily fall in the British tradition, the Africans take their cues from American Negro literature and from realists like Dickens and some of the Russians. Their writing is full of sensuous imagery, impressionism, anger, impatience, because they are always groping for a medium whereby they and their own immediate audience (they all began by being published at home, as distinct from the major West African fiction writers) can come to terms with a world of physical and mental violence, of dispossession, and with a world in which they are called upon to assert their human dignity.

Although we cannot seriously claim that we have evolved new styles as African writers, still less *un style négro-africain*—whatever its promoters may mean by it—we are doing violence to standard English. Furthermore, African writing in English shows a wide range of tones. The South African writer's attitude towards his audience differs sharply from that of the West or East African, because the former's audience is right at his doorstep, as it were. Again, there is interesting pidgin dialogue in English so evident in several of us. We can also claim to bring new experience to the language which enriches it; a dialogue that captures African speech idioms.

Perhaps when Africans direct their words less and less to an external audience, when the growth of literacy increases their immediate audience, new styles will emerge. On the other hand, there is a mitigating factor, which one can best phrase in the form of a question: can English ever hope to become the language of the common man in Africa to the extent that it can nourish the black writer's medium in a way that Dickens's was nourished? Is it not reasonable to predict that as long as English is, as it is now, mainly a political medium, an instrument of unity among various tribes and therefore a language of the *élite* only—as long as this is the situation—experimentation with styles must continue to be an intellectual pastime, a self-indulgence on the part of the writer who, naturally, feels weary of English English?

We present in this collection the newest of modern African writing. It was only on the insistence of the publishers that the editors included their own stories.

Cut Me a Drink

CHRISTIANA A. AIDOO

"When the memory of something hurts enough to swear an oath by, you mention it only in the 'cutting' of a drink. . . ."

—*An Akan Concept*

I say, my Uncle, if you are going to Accra and anyone tells you that the best place for you to drop is Avenida Circle, then he has done you good, but. . . . Hm. . . . I even do not know how to describe it. . . .

"Are all these beings that are passing this way and that way human? Did men buy all these cars with money? . . ."

But my elders, I do not want to waste your time. I looked round and could not find my bag. I first fixed my eyes on the ground and walked on. . . . Do not ask me why. Each time I tried to raise my eyes, I was dizzy from the number of cars which were passing. And I could not stand still. . . . If I did, I felt as if the whole world was made up of cars in motion. There is something somewhere, my uncles. Not desiring to deafen you with too long a story. . . .

I stopped walking just before I stepped into the Circle itself. I stood there for a long time. Then a lorry came along and I beckoned to the driver to stop. Not that it really stopped.

"Where are you going?" he asked me.

"I am going to Mamprobi," I replied. "Jump in," he said, and he started to drive away. Hm. . . . I nearly fell down climbing in. As we went round the thing which was like a big bowl on a very huge stump of wood, I had it in mind to have a good look at it and later Duayaw told me that it shoots water in the air . . . but the driver was talking to me, so I could not look at it properly. He told me he himself was not going to Mamprobi but he was going to the station where I could take a lorry which would be going there. . . .

Yes, my Uncle, he did not deceive me. Immediately we arrived at the station, I found the driver of a lorry shouting, "Mamprobi, Mamprobi!" Finally when the clock struck about two thirty, I was knocking on the door of Duayaw.

I did not knock for long when the door opened. Ah, I say, he was fast asleep, fast asleep I say, on a Saturday afternoon.

"How can folk find time to sleep on Saturday afternoons?" I asked myself. We hailed each other heartily. My Uncles, Duayaw has done well for himself. His mother Nsedua is a very lucky woman.

"How is it some people are lucky with school and others are not? Did not Mansa go to school with Duayaw here in this very school which I can see for myself? What have we done that Mansa should have wanted to stop going to school?"

But I must continue with my tale. . . . Yes, Duayaw has done well for himself. His room has fine furniture only it is too small. I asked him why and he told me he was even lucky to have got that narrow place that looks like a box. . . . It is very hard to find a place to sleep in the city. . . .

He asked me about the purpose of my journey. I told him everything. How as he himself knew, my sister Mansa had refused to go to school after "Klase Tri" and how my mother had tried to persuade her to go. . . .

My Mother, do not interrupt me, everyone present here knows you tried to do what you could by your daughter.

Yes, I told him how, after she had refused to go, we finally took her to this woman who promised to teach her to keep house and to work with the sewing-machine . . . and how she came home the first Christmas after the woman took her but has never been home again, these twelve years.

Duayaw asked me whether it was my intention then to look for my sister in the city. I told him yes. He laughed, saying, "You are funny. Do you think you can find a woman in this place? You do not know where she is staying. You do not even know whether she is married or not. Where can we find her if someone big has married her and she is now living in one of those big bungalows which are some ten miles from the city?"

Do you cry "My Lord", Mother? You are surprised about what I said about the marriage? Do not be. I was surprised too, when he talked that way. I, too, cried, "My Lord. . . ." Yes, I too did, Mother. But you and I have forgotten that Mansa was born a girl and girls do not take much time to grow. We are thinking of her as we last saw her when she was ten years old. But, Mother, that is twelve years ago. . . .

Yes, Duayaw told me that she is by now old enough to marry and to do something more than merely marry. I asked him whether he knew where she was and if he knew she had any children—"Children?" he cried, and he started laughing, a certain laugh. . . .

I was looking at him all the time he was talking. He told me he was not just discouraging me but he wanted me to see how big and difficult was what I proposed to do. I replied that it did not matter. What was necessary was that even if Mansa was dead, her ghost would know that we did not forget her entirely and let her wander in other people's towns and that we tried to bring her home. . . .

"These are useless tears you have started to weep, my Mother. Have I said anything to show that she was dead?"

Duayaw and I decided on the little things we would do the following day as the beginning of our search. Then he gave me water for my bath and brought me food. . . . He sat by me while I ate and asked me for news of home. I told him that his father has married another woman and how last year the *zkatse* spoilt all our cocoa. We know about that already. When I finished eating, Duayaw asked me to stretch out my bones on the bed and I did. I think I slept fine because when I opened my eyes it was dark. He had switched on his light and there was a woman in the room. He showed me her as a friend but I think she is the girl he wants to marry against the wishes of his people. I say, she is as beautiful as the sunrise, but she is not of our tribe. . . .

When Duayaw saw that I was properly awake, he told me it had struck eight o'clock in the evening and his friend had brought some food. The three of us ate together.

Do not say "Ei", Uncle, it seems as if people do this thing in the city. . . . A woman prepares a meal for a man and eats it with him. Yes, they do so often.

My mouth could not manage the food. It was prepared from cassava and corn dough, but it was strange food all the same. I tried to do my best. After the meal Duayaw told me we were going for a night out. It was then I remembered my bag. I told him that as matters stood, I could not change my cloth and I could not go out with them. He would not hear of it. "It would certainly be a crime to come to this city and not go out on a Saturday night. He warned me though that there may not be many people or anybody at all where we were going who would also be in cloth but I should not worry about that.

"Cut me a glass, for my throat is too dry. . . . When we were on the street, I could not believe my eyes. The whole place was as clear as the sky. Some of these lights are very beautiful indeed. Everyone should see them . . . and there are so many of them. "Who is paying for all these lights?" I asked myself. I could not say that aloud for fear Duayaw would laugh. . . .

We walked through many streets until we came to a big building where a band was playing. Duayaw went to buy tickets for the three of us.

You all know that I had not been to anywhere like that before. You must allow me to say that I was amazed. "Ei, are all these people children of human beings? And where are they going? And what do they want?"

Before I went in, I thought the building was big, but when I went in, I realized the crowd in it was bigger. Some were in front of a counter buying drinks, others were dancing. . . .

Yes, that was the case, Uncle, we had gone to a place where they had given a dance, but I did not know.

Some people were sitting on iron chairs around iron tables. Duayaw told some people to bring us a table and chairs and they did. As soon as we sat down, Duayaw asked us what we would drink. As for me, I told him *lamlale* but his woman told him "Beer". . . .

Do not be surprised, Uncles.

Yes, I remember very well, she asked for beer. It was not long before Duayaw brought them. I was too surprised to drink mine. I sat with my mouth open and watched the daughter of a woman cut beer like a man. The band had stopped playing for some time and soon they started again. Duayaw and his woman went to dance. I sat there and drank my *lamlale*. I cannot describe how they danced.

After some time, the band stopped playing and Duayaw and his woman came to sit down. I was feeling cold and I told Duayaw. He said, "And this is no wonder, have you not been drinking this sweet woman's drink all the time?"

"Does this make one cold?" I asked him.

"Yes," he replied. "Did you not know that? You must drink beer."

"Yes," I replied. So he bought me beer. When I was drinking the beer, he told me I would be warm if I danced.

"You know I cannot dance the way you people dance," I told him.

"And how do we dance?" he asked me.

"I think you all dance like white men and as I do not know how that is done, people would laugh at me," I said. Duayaw started laughing. He could not contain himself. He laughed so much his woman asked him what it was all about. He said something in the white man's language and they started laughing again. Duayaw then told me that if people were dancing, they would be so busy that they would not have time to watch others dance. And also in the city, no one cares if you dance well or not. . . .

Yes I danced, too, my Uncles. I did not know anyone, that is true. My Uncle, do not say that instead of concerning myself with the business for which I had gone to the city, I went dancing. Oh, if you only knew what happened at this place, you would not be saying this. I would not like to stop somewhere and tell you the end. . . . I would rather like to put a rod under the story as it were, clear off every little creeper in the bush. . . .

. . . But as we were talking about the dancing, something made Duayaw turn to look behind him where four women were sitting by the table. . . . Oh! he turned his eyes quickly, screwed his face into something queer which I could not understand and told me that if I wanted to dance, I could ask one of those women to dance with me.

My Uncles, I too was very surprised when I heard that. I asked Duayaw if people who did not know me would dance with me. He said, "Yes". I lifted my eyes, my Uncles, and looked at those four young women sitting round a table alone. They were sitting all alone, I say. I got up.

I hope I am making myself clear, my Uncles, but I was trembling like water in a brass bowl.

Immediately one of them saw me, she jumped up and said something in that kind of white man's language which everyone, even those who have not gone to school, speak in the city. I shook my head. She said something else in the language of the people of the place. I shook my head again. Then I heard her ask me in Fante whether I wanted to dance with her. I replied "Yes".

"Ei! my little sister, are you asking me a question? Oh! you want to know whether I found Mansa? I do not know. . . . Our uncles have asked me to tell everything that happened and you, too! I am cooking the whole meal for you, why do you want to lick the ladle now?"

Yes, I went to dance with her. I kept looking at her so much I think I was all the time stepping on her feet. I say, she was as black as you and I, but her hair was very long and fell on her shoulders like that of a white woman. I did not touch it but I saw it was very soft. Her lips with that red paint, looked like a fresh wound. There was no space between her skin and her dress. Yes, I danced with her. When the music ended, I went back to where I was sitting. I do not know what she told her companions about me, but I heard them laugh.

It was this time that something made me realize that they were all bad women of the city. Duayaw had told me I would feel warm if I danced, yet after I danced, I was colder than before. You would think someone had poured water on me. I was unhappy thinking about these women. "Have they no homes?" I asked myself. "Do not their mothers like them?" "God, we are all toiling for this threepence to buy something to eat . . . but oh! God! this is no work."

When I thought of my own sister, who was lost, I became a little happy because I felt that although I had not found her, she was nevertheless married to a big man and all was well with her.

When they started to play the band again, I went to the woman's table to ask the one with whom I had danced to dance again. But someone had gone with her already. I got one of the two who were still sitting there. She went with me. When we were dancing, she asked me whether it was true that I was a Fante. I replied "Yes." We did not speak again. When the band stopped playing, she told me to take her to where they sold things to buy her beer and cigarettes. I was wondering whether I had the money. When we were where the lights were shining brightly, something told me to look at her face. Something pulled at my heart.

"Young woman, is this the work you do?" I asked her.

"Young man, what work do you mean?" she too asked me. I laughed.

"Do you not know what work?" I asked again.

"And who are you to ask me such questions? I say, who are you? Let me tell you that any kind of work is work. You villager, you villager, who are you?" she screamed.

I was afraid. People around were looking at us. I lay my hands on her shoulders to calm her down and she hit away.

"Mansa, Mansa," I said, "do you not know me?" She looked at me for a long time and started laughing. She laughed, laughed as if the laughter did not come from her stomach. Yes, as if she was hungry.

"I think you are my brother," she said. "Hm."

Oh, my mother and my aunt, oh, little sister, are you all weeping? As for you women!

What is there to weep about? I was sent to find a lost child. I found her a woman.

Cut me a drink. . . .

Any kind of work is work . . . this is what Mansa told me with a mouth that looked like clotted blood. Any kind of work is work . . . so do not weep. She will come home this Christmas.

My Brother, cut me another one . . . any form of work is work . . . is work . . . work!

Ding Dong Bell

KWABENA ANNAN

Not having much development in our village, we all agreed when the Government Agent told us that we should do something about it. I remember the occasion very well. It was towards the end of March when the cocoa was all in, packed and sent to the coast, and Kwesi Manu had started his house again. Every year he would buy the cement, engage a couple of Northern Territories' labourers, lay out the blocks, and then run out of money. The walls had been built two years back; last year, he had managed to get the roof on, only to have it flung off again by the great Easter storm which did so much damage. The iron sheets were flung like a handful of pebbles across the street, knocking down Ama Serwah's stall. The old lady put Kwesi before the Native Authority Court for failing to pay for the loss, and this caused a first-class row which lasted us all through the rains.

The village certainly needed to be improved. The roads were laterite tracks from which the dust rose like thunder clouds whenever a lorry went through the place. Goats, chickens and sheep wandered about its alleys and slept in the doorways. We were always complaining of the difficulty of getting supplies from the nearby town, and to hear the women grumble you would think that it was unusual to walk a mile or so to fetch water from the pool. Still, we accepted the life; it had been lived a long time, as we all knew, and if there had been nothing to complain of we might have quarrelled much more often among ourselves than we do now.

We hadn't any local council either. The chief was well liked, and we saw no reason to change. There had been talk of joining us up with the next village to form a "local authority area". The Government

Agent was always on about it. But our neighbours were a grasping lot, always farming our land and trying to claim that it belonged to them, and we preferred our separate existence. I suppose it was this that made the Government down in Accra take up the idea of development. If we wouldn't join in a local council, it was because we were too set in our ways, and "development" would get us out of them. We understood all that. But when the Government Agent asked us whether we agreed to anything, we always said yes. It was easier in the long run to agree and never did any harm. And as a matter of fact, on this occasion, we forgot all about the idea until one Wednesday morning when the chief beat "gong gong" to call us together. When we reached the palace there was our Chief, *Nana,* and an educated clerk sitting in the compound. I call him "educated" because he was obviously a town man, in neat city clothes, with a black book under his arm and pencils sticking in his hair. It turned out that he was a new clerk in the Government Agent's office and had been sent to talk to us.

We listened to what he had to say, although we had heard most of it before: how we should think again about forming a local council, how we should pay the levy on time, why didn't we help the local teacher and send our children to the mission school, did we not know that the Government had forbidden the making of *akpeteshie* because it was dangerous to drink, why had we not cleared the bush right down to the river. It was much like the regular routine visit, which kept the Government satisfied and left us alone, with the local Native Authority policeman standing there ready to walk round the village looking for *akpeteshie,* and having a quiet drink of it with the clerk behind the court-house—until the clerk suddenly told us that the Government Agent had been so pleased when we had asked for his help that he was sending a Development Officer the following week to make a start.

We didn't quite know what to make of this, and it soon slipped our memory—the next day being Thursday when we don't farm, and a good week's supply of liquor is ready for use. I had business to do in Kumasi the following week-end—I usually stock up with a few cases of corned beef and sardines for the store—and did not get back until late on Wednesday morning. The first thing I saw in the village was a large black car with pick-axes. The whole village had turned out to see what it was all about, and as I came up a tall thin European in blue shorts and shirt was standing in front of the crowd lecturing them. He couldn't speak our language *twi* of course, but you could have told just by the way he waved his arms that he meant business. The Chief looked as pleased as he could, but I could see that he was worried, and the elders sat in stony disapproval.

"Great changes are taking place in the country," the European said, through a rat-faced interpreter. "Last week I was in Accra and everywhere I could see great buildings going up, good roads, good schools. And what can be done in Accra can be done too in the villages."

Well, I could have told him straight away that he was making a mistake. The one thing we detest hearing about is Accra and what the city crooks are doing with our money. Then before anyone could stop him, he was off about our neighbours: how co-operative they were, how ready they had been for his help, how they said they were going to extend the lorry park and the market. ("So that they can put their prices up," shouted a voice, but this voice was hushed down.) Then he got on to us. He was worried about the water and the roads. Of course we agreed. If you ask anybody in our town whether this or that is good, you will always be told that everything is as bad as it can be. We don't boast and we like to grumble. So by the time the European had asked us about the latrines and the roads and the rains, and whether the harvest was good, and how we liked the new mission school, he must have thought we were ready for all the development there was in the country.

The only time he got stuck was when he suggested that we line the streets with deep concrete gutters, and Tetteh Quarshie stood up and said no, that wouldn't do, he must have somewhere for his ducks to get food and drink. The European didn't quite know whether to take this seriously or not—and Tetteh stood there, bent with age and drink, clutching his cloth to his bony ribs and muttering like someone from the Kumasi asylum—so he left it and came to the point (which all of us could see he had fixed on long before he set foot in the town).

There was nothing wrong with the idea in theory. We were to dig out two or three wells by the forest path leading to the main road with the help of some "well-diggers", and a mason who knew how to case the sides with special concrete rings. We might have to dig twenty or thirty feet down, but there were plenty of rings and, when we were finished, the water in each well would stay sweet throughout the year. It took a long time to explain, but most of us soon grasped the idea. Only, we don't care to do things in a hurry. So the chief spoke for us all when, after politely thanking the officer for his trouble, he told him that we would discuss it and let the Government Agent know our decision. Up came little Francis Kofi with a basin of eggs which Opanin Kuntor handed to the clerk with a second round of thanks. And before the European knew what was happening, the meeting had broken up and he was being led to his car. Off it went in a cloud of dust, followed by the Land Rover, and we settled down again.

After this, of course, the letters began to arrive—Your good friend this, Your good friend that; His Honour was anxious to hear what we had decided; Could we agree to Monday week for the diggers to make a start?; and so forth. We sat quiet and said nothing. There is no post office in our town, and the effort of getting stamps and paper is usually enough to deter the Chief from correspondence.

Monday came and went, so did Tuesday and Wednesday; and on Thursday we collected as usual at Kofi's bar. By three in the afternoon, we had started on the *akpeteshie*, and at half-past four no one noticed the arrival of the Government Agent and his car until he sent his clerk stumbling and sweating down the road to ask for *Nana* and the elders.

"He is not well," said Kofi Tandoh.

"He has travelled."

"He is mourning for his sister."

"He has the measles." This came from a young idiot of a schoolboy who had edged his way into the group.

The clerk stood first on one leg, then on the other, and scratched his head. He knew as well as we did that after half a bottle of *akpeteshie* the Chief might as well have travelled for all the help he could give. I believe the clerk said as much to the Government Agent, a fattish European with a red face and pale eyes, who immediately flew into a rage, cursed the Chief and the village, and then ordered the constable with him to go and seize the still and what was left of the liquor. But he was unlucky. We usually have two or three kerosene tins cooling off in Opanin Kuntor's yard, but this time, with the cocoa season over and a good number of funerals under way, we were down to a few bottles only. By the time he had collected these, and we sat there without raising a finger in apology or protest, *Nana* himself appeared. He was far from normal and came roaring out of the palace apparently thinking that he was celebrating the yearly *adae* festival.

The Government Agent gave him one look and drove off without a word. We all went back to sleep. But the next morning we were worried. We had a hurried meeting at the palace, brought in the schoolmaster to advise, and agreed that something must be done to turn away the wrath to come. The only way seemed to be "development". So we sent Francis Kofi on a bicycle with a letter drawn up by the teacher, with *Nana* and the elders making their mark.

It seemed to meet the case, for two days later the Land Rover came back, with the European. The site was cleared and we took it in turns to dig. It was easy work and unmarred by any mishap, except on the second night the European was with us when old Nyantechie went out before the moon rose to obey the call of nature, stumbled over one of the concrete rings and pitched into three feet of well. This brought out the European, twice as brave as Lugard, from the schoolroom where he had settled himself. He found Nyantechie on the ground nursing his ankle, crept back to the school and was shot at by the local escort constable who hadn't seen him go out and who fancied himself as something of a hunter.

Still, by the end of the week, the three wells were finished, with a concrete parapet and a rough awning of palm branches to keep out the dirt. There was a shallow depth of water in each, and as a parting gesture we all queued up, with the European and his clerk, to try it. It tasted terrible. But then, it was rare in our village for anyone to drink water except the children, and they complained that the water from the wells had no taste. The women liked it all right, although I suspect that, being women, what they liked most was the opportunity it gave them of arguing who should have the first use of the buckets.

One might have thought that that was the end of it, with no great harm done and everyone turning back again to a normal life. But the village was uneasy. We didn't like it and wondered what might come next. Then Opanin Kuntor fell sick, and swore beyond reason that it was the well water which had brought him down. He told his maid-servant to fetch his water from the pool again, recovered quickly and went round the village triumphant, warning everyone of what they might expect. Gradually, however, matters righted themselves. And we had something to take our minds off the Government in the "out-dooring" ceremony of Kwame Tweneboa's child. This was a high occasion. Kwame was well over fifty, and although he had taken a second wife, neither had brought forth until now—and the woman herself was nearing forty. It called for a special celebration. We set to work, and Opanin Kuntor had the still going night and day in his yard. We had learned a lesson, too, from the previous occasion and decided to post sentries at the far edge of the village who would give the alarm should danger threaten: one shot for the local police, two for the Government Agent.

We slept well the night before the "outdooring". There wasn't a great deal to do on the farm so we ate and drank the day away, drank and gossiped into the night until the moon went down, when we went to bed and slept late. The next day, nearly the whole village went to pay their respects to the mother. The child, a boy, was named Osei Bonso after a famous ancestor of Kwame Tweneboa, and there was a good deal of friendly drinking, with the result that by mid-afternoon most of us were asleep again. The forenoon had been cloudy, with a leaden sky, driving us into the shelter of the neem trees which straddled the road, or to the shade of the compounds. Goats and sheep browsed in the bush, and a stray hen scratched lazily in the scrubby ditch by the school where you could see the children sprawled across their desks or asleep on the veranda.

Suddenly, there was the sound of a double shot; then, to our astonishment, two more. There was immediate confusion. The Chief was still asleep; so were most of the elders. They were shaken into some kind of order while Opanin Kuntor hurried off to hide what was left of the *akpeteshie*. The rest of us collected round the Chief's compound and held ourselves in reserve. There was the sound of a car, then another; the Government Agent pulled up outside the palace, and the driver signalled to a large touring car, which followed, to do the same. The Union Jack fluttered from the bonnet of the second car, and the driver—a uniformed constable—carefully chaperoned from the back seat an elderly European. Someone recognized him as the Regional Officer whom most of us knew to be next in power and glory to the Governor, if not to God Himself.

After the customary greetings had been made, with the Government Agent trotting up and down in attendance on the big man, we were told that the Regional Officer was interested in our town, that he had heard of our efforts to "improve the amenities of the district through self-help", and had been good enough to interrupt a tour of inspection to visit us. This was said by the Government Agent in such solemn, satisfied tones that it was clear that, by digging the wells, we had helped more than ourselves.

Nana and the elders received this with perhaps less enthusiasm than they should have shown; they were alarmed at the second visit of the Government Agent, distrusted his intentions, and were concerned—as we all were—by the possible fate of the still and the rest of the drink. So it was with relief that we heard the Regional Officer saying that he would like to see the wells, and we led the way down the narrow path. Of course, when we got there, the Government Agent, with great satisfaction, thought he would like a drink. One of the women lowered the bucket into the nearest well and hauled it up on the rope. The Government Agent dipped a calabash into the half-bucket of water and handed it with delight to the Regional Officer who took a good mouthful, swallowed, then tried to spit it out, choking and spluttering with an agonized grimace. The Government Agent stared in amazement, and we looked uneasily at each other.

"Try it," said the Regional Officer, and spat into the bush; "try it yourself," and he wiped his mouth with a folded handkerchief, still coughing and spitting, his eyes watering.

The Government Agent took a cautious sip, and a look of absolute disbelief came over his face. He turned, spat and shouted: "Salifu, come here. Taste this." The constable driver came forward and took a long draught. "Fine."

"What is it?"

"Gin, sir. Native gin."

"How the devil did it get in there?" said the Regional Officer.

We all tried it then, including *Nana* who stood between the two

Europeans. None of us said anything, however, for the few who guessed what had happened didn't care to tell. Eventually *Nana* spoke; and it says much for his presence of mind that he kept a serene countenance and a solemn note to his voice.

"Owura," he said, addressing the Regional Officer, "what has been done was necessary and right. The spirits are angry that we have left our forefathers' ways and the pool from which my father and his father's father drew their water. For this reason we have purified the well and placated the spirits with a little gin."

"A little!" exclaimed the Regional Officer. "What would it have tasted like if you had put in a lot?"

"*Akpeteshie?*" asked the Government Agent sharply.

"No, no," said the Chief, with a dignified air. "That is not allowed, although it would have been better and cheaper."

The Government Agent looked at the Regional Officer, who said nothing. Then they turned and walked back to the village. I could see that the Regional Officer was amused; and slowly his good humour spread. By the time we reached the village there was a pleasant, unspoken accord between the two sides. Beer was fetched, and a bottle of whisky; the health of the Regional Officer, the Government Agent, the Chief and Elders, the village, and Kwame Tweneboa, were drunk. Finally, the two cars moved off and we went back to the palace.

"How much did you put in there?" asked the Chief.

"*Nana*, it was three kerosene tins full," said Opanin Kuntor. "I was afraid. But I put the tins in complete. They must have leaked."

"Ah," said the Chief. "I'm sure they did."

Death of a Boy

CHINUA ACHEBE

(When a woman of Okonkwo's clan was killed in a neighbouring town, the elders demanded as compensation and as hostages a virgin and a young boy of fifteen. The virgin was given to the man whose wife was killed; the boy Ikemefuna into the charge of Okonkwo, who brought him up together with his own son Nwoye.)

So Okonkwo encouraged the boys to sit with him in his *obi*, and he told them stories of the land—masculine stories of violence and bloodshed. Nwoye knew that it was right to be masculine and to be violent, but somehow he still preferred the stories that his mother used to tell, and which she no doubt still told to her younger children—stories of the tortoise and his wily ways, and of the bird *eneke-nti-oba* who challenged the whole world to a wrestling contest and was finally thrown by the cat. He remembered the story she often told of the quarrel between Earth and Sky long ago, and how Sky withheld rain for seven years, until crops withered and the dead could not be buried because the hoes broke on the stony Earth. At last Vulture was sent to plead with Sky, and to soften his heart with a song of the suffering of the sons of men. Whenever Nwoye's mother sang this song he felt carried away to the distant scene in the sky where Vulture, Earth's emissary, sang for mercy. At last Sky was moved to pity and he gave to Vulture rain wrapped in leaves of coco-yam. But as he flew home his long talon pierced the leaves and the rain fell as it had never fallen before. And so heavily did it rain on Vulture that he did not return to deliver his message but flew to a distant land, from where he had espied a fire. And when he got there he found it was a man making a sacrifice. He warmed himself in the fire and ate the entrails.

That was the kind of story that Nwoye loved. But he now knew that they were for foolish women and children, and he knew that his father wanted him to be a man. And so he feigned that he no longer cared for women's stories. And when he did this he saw that his father was pleased and no longer rebuked him or beat him. So Nwoye and Ikemefuna would listen to Okonkwo's stories about tribal wars or how, years ago, he had stalked his victim, overpowered him and obtained his first human head. And as he told them of the past, they sat in darkness or the dim glow of logs, waiting for the women to finish their cooking. When they finished, each brought her bowl of foo-foo and bowl of soup to her husband. An oil lamp was lit and Okonkwo tasted from each bowl and then passed two shares to Nwoye and Ikemefuna.

In this way the moons and the seasons passed. And then the locusts came. It had not happened for many a long year. The elders said locusts came once in a generation, reappeared every year for seven years and then disappeared for another lifetime. They went back to their caves in a distant land where they were guarded by a race of stunted men. And then after another lifetime these men opened the caves again and the locusts came to Umuofia.

They came in the cold harmattan season after the harvests had been gathered and ate up all the wild grass in the fields.

Okonkwo and the two boys were working on the red outer walls of the compound. This was one of the lighter tasks of the after-harvest season. A new cover of thick palm branches and palm leaves was set on the walls to protect them from the next rainy season. Okonkwo worked on the outside of the wall and the boys worked from within. There were little holes from one side to the other in the upper levels of the wall, and through these Okonkwo passed the rope, or *tie-tie*, to the boys and they passed it round the wooden stays and then back to him; and in this way the cover was strengthened on the wall.

The women had gone to the bush to collect firewood and the little children to visit their playmates in the neighbouring compounds. The harmattan was in the air and seemed to distil a hazy feeling of sleep on the world. Okonkwo and the boys worked in complete silence, which was only broken when a new palm frond was lifted on to the wall or when a busy hen moved dry leaves about in her ceaseless search for food.

And then quite suddenly a shadow fell on the world, and the sun seemed hidden behind a thick cloud. Okonkwo looked up from his work and wondered if it was going to rain at such an unlikely time of the year. But almost immediately a shout of joy broke out in all directions and Umuofia, which had dozed in the noonday haze, broke into life and activity.

"Locusts are descending", was joyfully chanted everywhere, and men, women and children left their work or their play and ran into the open to see the unfamiliar sight. The locusts had not come for many, many years, and only the old people had seen them before.

At first, a fairly small swarm came. They were the harbingers sent to survey the land. And then appeared on the horizon a slowly-moving mass like a boundless sheet of black cloud drifting towards Umuofia. Soon it covered half the sky and the solid mass was now broken by tiny eyes of light like shining stardust. It was a tremendous sight, full of power and beauty.

Everyone was now about, talking excitedly and praying that the locusts should camp in Umuofia for the night. For although locusts had not visited Umuofia for many years, everybody knew by instinct that they were very good to eat. And at last the locusts did descend. They settled on every tree and on every blade of grass; they settled on the roofs and covered the bare ground. Mighty tree branches broke away under them and the whole country became the brown-earth colour of the vast, hungry swarm.

Many people went out with baskets trying to catch them but elders counselled patience till nightfall. And they were right. The locusts settled in the bushes for the night and their wings became wet with dew. Then all Umuofia turned out in spite of the cold harmattan and everyone filled his bags and pots with locusts. The next morning they were roasted in clay pots and then spread in the sun until they became dry and brittle. And for many days this rare food was eaten with solid palm-oil.

Okonkwo sat in his *obi* crunching happily with Ikemefuna and Nwoye, and drinking palm-wine copiously, when Ogbuefi Ezeudu came in. Ezeudu was the oldest man in this quarter of Umuofia. He had been a great and fearless warrior in his time and was now accorded great respect in all the clan. He refused to join in the meal and asked Okonkwo to have a word with him outside. And so they walked out together, the old man supporting himself with his stick. When they were out of earshot, he said to Okonkwo:

"That boy calls you Father. Do not bear a hand in his death." Okonkwo was surprised and was about to say something when the old man continued:

"Yes, Umuofia has decided to kill him. The Oracle of the Hills and the Caves has pronounced it. They will take him outside Umuofia as is the custom and kill him there. But I want you to have nothing to do with it. He calls you his father."

The next day a group of elders from all the nine villages of Umuofia came to Okonkwo's house early in the morning and, before they began to speak in low tones, Nwoye and Ikemefuna were sent out. They did not stay very long but when they went away Okonkwo sat still for a very long time supporting his chin in his palms. Later in the day he called Ikemefuna and told him that he was to be taken home the next day. Nwoye overheard it and burst into tears, whereupon his father beat him heavily. As for Ikemefuna, he was at a loss. His own home had gradually become very faint and distant. He still missed his mother and his sister and would be very glad to see them. But somehow he knew he was not going to see them. He remembered once when men had talked in low tones with his father, and it seemed now as if it was happening all over again.

Later, Nwoye went to his mother's hut and told her that Ikemefuna was going home. She immediately dropped the pestle with which she was grinding pepper, folded her arms across her breast and sighed, "Poor child".

The next day, the men returned with a pot of wine. They were all fully dressed as if they were going to a big clan meeting or to pay a visit to a neighbouring village. They passed their cloths under the right arm-pit, and hung their goatskin bags and sheathed matchets over their left shoulders. Okonkwo got ready quickly and the party set out with Ikemefuna carrying the pot of wine. A deathly silence descended on Okonkwo's compound. Even the very little children seemed to know. Throughout that day Nwoye sat in his mother's hut and tears stood in his eyes.

At the beginning of their journey the men of Umuofia talked and laughed about the locusts, about their women and about some effeminate men who had refused to come with them. But as they drew near to the outskirts of Umuofia silence fell upon them too.

The sun rose slowly to the centre of the sky and the dry, sandy footway began to throw up the heat that lay buried in it. Some birds chirruped in the forests around. The men trod dry leaves on the sand. All else was silent. Then from the distance came the faint beating of the *ekwe*. It rose and faded with the wind—a peaceful dance from a distant clan.

"It is an *ozo* dance," the men said among themselves. But no one was sure where it was coming from. Some said Ezimili, others Abame or Aninta. They argued for a short while and fell into silence again and the elusive dance rose and fell with the wind. Somewhere a man was taking one of the titles of his clan, with music and dancing and a great feast.

The footway had now become a narrow line in the heart of the forest. The short trees and sparse undergrowth which surrounded the men's village began to give way to giant trees and climbers which perhaps had stood from the beginning of things, untouched by the axe and the bush-fire. The sun breaking through their leaves and branches threw a pattern of light and shade on the sandy footway.

Ikemefuna heard a whisper close behind him and turned round sharply. The man who had whispered now called out aloud, urging the others to hurry up.

"We still have a long way to go," he said. Then he and another man went before Ikemefuna and set a faster pace.

Thus the men of Umuofia pursued their way, armed with sheathed matchets, and Ikemefuna, carrying a pot of palm-wine on his head, walked in their midst. Although he had felt uneasy at first, he was not afraid now. Okonkwo walked behind him. He could hardly imagine that Okonkwo was not his real father. He had never been fond of his real father and, at the end of three years, he had become very distant indeed. But his mother and his three-year-old sister . . . of course she would not be three now, but six. Would he recognize her now? She must have grown quite big. How his mother would weep for joy and thank Okonkwo for having looked after him so well and for bringing him back. She would want to hear everything that had happened to him in all these years. Could he remember them all? He would tell her about Nwoye and his mother, and about the locusts. . . . Then quite suddenly a thought came upon him. His mother might be dead. He tried in vain to force the thought out of his mind. Then he tried to settle the matter the way he used to settle such matters when he was a little boy. He still remembered the song:

Eze elina, elina!
Sala
Eze ilikwa ya
Ikwaba akwa oligholi
Ebe Danda nechi eze
Ebe Uzuzu nete egwu
Sala

He sang it in his mind and walked to its beat. If the song ended on his right foot, his mother was alive. If it ended on his left, she was dead. No, not dead, but ill. It ended on the right. She was alive and well. He sang the song again and it ended on the left. But the second time did not count. The first voice gets to Chukwu, or God's house. That was a favourite saying of children. Ikemefuna felt like a child once more. It must be the thought of going home to his mother.

One of the men behind him cleared his throat. Ikemefuna looked back and the man growled at him to go on and not stand looking back. The way he said it sent cold fear down Ikemefuna's back. His hands trembled vaguely on the black pot he carried. Why had Okonkwo withdrawn to the rear? Ikemefuna felt his legs melting under him. And he was afraid to look back.

As the man who had cleared his throat drew up and raised his matchet, Okonkwo looked away. He heard the blow. The pot fell and broke in the sand. He heard Ikemefuna cry, "My Father, they have killed me!" as he ran towards him. Dazed with fear, Okonkwo drew his matchet and cut him down. He was afraid of being thought weak.

Me and the Fish God

ATO BEDWEI

I quickly grabbed my slate and started running excitedly for home. There was a lot to tell Mother on my first day at school. As I was executing the final turn to our cottage I stumbled on to a group in a circle. There was a lot of confusion around. I became curious and wriggled my way through the group to see what was happening. The first thing I saw in the opening was a very large fish: in fact, it was the largest I had ever seen. After my curiosity had been filled to the full, I looked up at the lucky fellow who caught it. There was a constant grin on his face, with everybody in sight shaking his hand. I looked on enviously and resolved that as soon as I laid hands on a fishing-rod I would catch a fish which would make his look like a dwarf comparatively.

My chance came two years later, on my eighth birthday. But I regretted at that time that it ever came. It happened on one Thursday in November when the cocoa harvesting that season was said to have been at its peak. My father was very happy and told Mother in no mean terms that he felt extravagant. She promptly seized the opportunity to demand that a new lavatorine be fixed in our cottage as, according to her, it was disgraceful for an educated man and his family to go to a public lavatorine. Father, however, rebuked her for the "silly" suggestion and explained to her that what he needed was relaxation and something to efface the muck of the year-long fatigue. One would have thought that Father meant us to go on a holiday. But the phrase "going on holiday" is exotic in our vocabulary owing to the abundant if not superfluous sunshine which we experience in that western part of Africa. Nevertheless, Father made his point clear; he wanted to throw a party.

His intention seemed dubious at first as it was quite absurd to throw a party without a proper cause in the village of Nkwanta. He therefore had to invent a vital occasion calling for such merry-making. Fortunately or unfortunately, I was picked as the scapegoat. My father sent Kyeremeh, his nephew and heir apparent (according to custom), to all his friends and relatives, inviting them to his only son's eighth birthday party. Even my boisterous Uncle Kwcku who lived in the city was invited to the party, which was to take place the coming Saturday. I am, however, proud to say that my supposed birthday party was the first of its kind in the village at that time, even though I was really born in October and not November.

To make the occasion look more genuine, my father bought me a beautiful T-shirt as my birthday present. Mother, who had been nagging all the time of how she wished I was a girl, showed her disapproval in a very practical manner by buying me a doll. On that Saturday, I was in the room I shared with my father's nephew, Kyeremeh, when I heard Uncle Kweku's seven-year-old car approaching from the distance. I could always tell his car a mile off. The nearer it came the louder was the noise. At last, his car came to a standstill in front of our cottage. I saw father coming to welcome him and dodged back quietly into the house to get dressed as instructed.

Soon afterwards, I heard a lot of commotion in the hall and knew that the guests had arrived for my birthday party. I was at my best in my multicoloured T-shirt; at least that was what my mirror assured me. Majestically, I walked to the crowded hall hoping desperately to draw attention to me, but nobody knew I existed at all. All eyes were turned on the four-gallon tin full of home-made gin placed in the centre of the hall; so I just squatted on the floor somewhere out of sight.

I heard Uncle Kweku pouring the inevitable libation calling on the gods to wipe away any impending catastrophe that might befall them during their drinking session. Then the guests started drinking in full swing. About half an hour later, Uncle Kweku sighted me and waved; then started singing "Happy birthday" in English drowsily. Unfortunately none of the guests with the exception of my father knew a word of English and as my father was obviously not in the mood at that time, it therefore became a one-man show. My uncle stopped singing unceremoniously and drew Father aside. I saw him gesticulating with his hand and knew there was something afoot, as usual; so I strained my ears to catch what he was telling Father, ". . . you are so stubborn, Bonsu", my uncle was saying, "you are not cut out to be a farmer and you know it. I have a flourishing business in the city and of course I wouldn't mind at all to take you on as my partner. After all blood is thicker than water, you know."

"Look, Kweku," said my father heatedly, "you have been pestering me for the past three years to join your so-called firm and my answer has always been no. And it is still NO."

The finality in my father's voice made Uncle Kweku explode with anger. "You ungrateful bush rat," he said, "I sent you to college after Father died. I gave you the money to start your rotten farm."

At that moment my mother came and rescued my father from further humiliation. But Uncle Kweku was not deterred. "Great farmer," he sneered across the room and continued shouting profanely. The outburst was a usual habit of Uncle Kweku when he got boozed. Thus, the party continued without a hitch.

I began to think of my birthday presents; discarding Father to his fate in the process. First, the shirt from my father which I had put on for the occasion and the doll from my mother. I knew exactly what I was going to do with the doll. I would simply burn it and bury the ashes. I had expected her to buy me . . . well, something exciting but not a doll. I sat gloomily in my secluded corner and blamed Mother for my loneliness. I wanted to run away somewhere and cry; only I was told specifically by my father not to leave the room till all my guests had gone. My guests! The irony of it made my heart beat faster. I frowned when I heard Uncle Kweku's high-pitched voice above all others. Then I remembered I had seen him with a neatly wrapped parcel when he got out of his car.

"I wonder where it is now?" I thought. "Aw, forget it; he would rather buy gin to drink." I shoved the thought away somewhere and settled on counting the guests. I was on the fifth count when the thought of knowing what was in that parcel came creeping back. I stopped counting and began to crawl unobtrusively towards the far side of the room, and suddenly came upon my father's obsolete three-foot cupboard with a parcel on it. I tremblingly straightened to snatch the parcel from the cupboard but instead I hit something with my head which turned out to be Uncle Kweku's glass. He stood towering over me; the front of his shirt all wet with the contents of the glass. He swore and got hold of my collar.

"My boy," he roared, "that was very naughty of you. Oh! that reminds me; I have a wonderful present for you, but you won't get it till you have tasted a little of your old uncle's gin."

He replenished his glass and put it to my lips. I glanced around furtively and quickly took a sip.

"That's better," he said, "now let's open the parcel."

It was an unusual one, rather a bit too long and a bit too small in width. I was undoubtedly disappointed in advance. "What sort of a parcel is this?" I thought disgustedly. He finally unwrapped the parcel and to my surprise and joy I saw it was a fishing-rod. I quickly grabbed it from him and made straight for my bedroom. On entering, I shut the door and heaved a sigh of relief: "At long last I've got what for two years I've been longing for." My mind went back to two years ago. I saw the fish vividly, its owner grinning and feeling on top of the world; and imagined myself in his place.

I shook my head vigorously to shut out my day-dreaming and took the rod from its case. I manipulated it for some time; laid it beside my bedding, and got into bed. Tomorrow I would go fishing; I knew the particular stream I was going to fish in and I knew the particular fish I was going to catch. A tremor ran through me when I thought of the fish. The fish was called Obosom, the fish god, occupant of "Onkasa", the Silent Stream. It was the largest fish in the Silent Stream.

In our village there is a living testimony in the person of Agya Kwajo of the fish god's fury when angered. He dared venture to drink from the Silent Stream, and as a result got a perpetual bump on his forehead.

Suddenly I heard Uncle Kweku's car making a lot of racket as it started to leave. The house seemed strangely quiet after that. I wondered when he was going to buy a new car. But then, Father had said that he was almost bankrupt. That's the reason he's been pestering Father to join his firm in the city. The owls wailing in the distance broke the stillness of the night. I finally went to sleep and dreamt I had caught and eaten the fish god.

The next morning, on Sunday, I woke up about seven and found the cottage empty. My parents had gone to the farm. I quickly had a bite of something and went in search of Agya Kwajo. I located him, as usual, sitting underneath the big odum tree near the school park, with three old gossip-mongers, who rarely did any work, but lazed around talking about the villagers all day long. I greeted them and was invited to sit down.

They chatted away for over half an hour talking about the world at large with the gap narrowing gradually to individuals in our village. I coughed loudly to remind them I was around in case they wanted to talk about my parents. That stopped them. The break in their gossiping gave me the chance of telling Agya Kwajo about what was on my mind. At the mention of the fish god his face softened with a smile. He loved talking about his adventure; although there had been rumours that he got the bump under quite different circumstances.

"Oh, my son," he wailed, "you have touched a very delicate spot in my life." As he spoke, the bump on his forehead moved revoltingly and seemed ready to fall apart at any moment. I heard somebody calling me and knew that my parents had come home. At any rate, I had heard that story lots of times now and I knew it by heart. He would have told me the same thing again anyway. I excused myself to his disappointment and took off for home.

I almost changed my mind about catching the fish god, but then I asked myself where the blazes I was going to catch the biggest fish to become a hero. Furthermore, there was no river within easy reach of the village, the only possibility was the Silent Stream. Hastily, I grabbed my fishing-rod and sneaked out of the house.

I finally reached the stream and fitted a hook on the rod and without delay plunged it in. I saw a lot of small fish playing around the hook, but my target, the fish god, had not put in an appearance.

I remembered I had not fixed bait on the hook and was going to pull it out of the stream when suddenly the fish god popped up and, as if defying me, just swallowed the hook. I drew excitedly with all my strength till it was on the hard surface. Its calmness on the ground gave me confidence. I felt very heroic and stretched my hand to touch it. But, my gosh, I will always remember the terrific electric shock I got. I dropped the fishing-rod and turned to run, but, oh my! there is something wrong somewhere; the earth seemed to be moving round and round and round. The last thing I remembered was falling into a big black tunnel.

When I came to, I was in my father's bedroom surrounded by what seemed like the whole population of our village. I pinched myself to see whether I was still alive and went back to sleep. It was obvious they had found out about my mischief. The following day I learnt that the fish god died and as a result the villagers had decided unanimously to ban my parents and me from the village for ever. We packed off and joined Uncle Kweku in the city. With Father's financial backing, their firm grew into a prosperous concern; and to this day, they attribute their success to me.

This is Experience Speaking

PETER KWAME BUAHIN

I. THE INMATES OF MY ROOM

Should I blow or should I not blow my own trumpet? That is the question. It is very unfortunate, but it still remains a fact that the person who blows my trumpet has very unceremoniously left me. Not because he was not sufficiently paid but rather because he could not develop sufficiently strong and projecting cheers to make my trumpet heard amidst the din and bustle of Accra City life. And now, in his absence, I must willy-nilly sound this trumpet however faintly.

By way of introducing the first note, I am a man who always faces facts squarely and is frank even to the extent of being imprudent. I am very short when it pays to be short and I am very tall when it is useful to be tall. "All weather" is my nickname. I am an intricately complex mixture of all that it pays to be. I am a Bachelor of Arts (B.A.), first-class honours in ancient and modern Palmwinology; a master of all drinkables except coal-tar, cascara sagrada and turpentine; a Fellow of the Royal Institute of Alcohol; and Head of the Faculty of Immunity against Intoxication in the International University of Sparkling Bubbles. I am a man with green blood in my veins and with a more fertile brain than Erasmus's. In a word, therefore, I am a very important person who is now soliloquizing, with a mind in a cloudy puzzlement, to find out why the government did not make it possible for me to drive in any of the luxuriously modelled and fashioned cars provided for the VIPs during the celebration of our Independence.

I stay at Accra New Town, in a house where lizards and bats and mice enjoy such first-class but highly unharnessed democratic freedom that they freely and easily and impudently spit at and excrete on me, and even go to the sad extent of at times sharing my bed with me. I go out and come to meet them, carelessly relaxing in my bed, in a bossing attitude. Poor me, how dare I question them? It is just inviting them to multiply their trespasses. What is worse, our desires never harmonize, they are always at loggerheads, always conflicting and always quarrelling.

When I feel like taking my siesta, they feel like having sports. If they would be kind enough to allow me to lie on my back quietly, as an I-cannot-help-it spectator, whilst they do the high-jumping and the running and the pole-vaulting on the field beneath which I sleep, I wouldn't mind because that would mean training me to be more tolerant. But the pity of it all is, they don't. Sometimes the high-jumpers miss and the pole falls on me. At other times too, they themselves lose their equilibrium and fall heavily on me—thus bruising me with their weight and polluting me with their pungent smell. And of course, when such unhappy cases occur, I, the poor victim, have to run to the doctor to cure my bruises and see the ever-ready-to-squeeze-out-money storekeepers for some Milton to wash off their acrid smell. All this is a big agent of erosion on my economic resources.

At times, too, when there are no sports, Miss Sun, the residential bread-baker, bakes her bread and the oven being perpendicularly above my head, I am often more baked than the bread in the hot oven. It is impossible to convince this nagging woman to bake her bread at any other time except twelve o'clock.

Of course, with Miss Sun, I can say, "there is comfort in every situation however wretched." She never fails to give me ice cream in the evening, so that is a big consolation. But the lizards and the mice. . . .

Talk I must, and I did question and advise them to have some respect for my age, experience and learning, by stopping all that rank nonsense.

"You man, don't encroach upon our rights—don't dictate to us what we must do and what we must not do—know that dictators are out of place in a democratic world such as ours. You have rented the four corners of the room and we have rented the two sides of the roof —if you don't want the sight of us, and our unavoidable falls on you, then try to separate your four walls from our two sides of the roof by the thickest ceiling your academic degrees can devise—if you fail to do this, our best advice is, don't be silly."

Thus rebutted I humbly approached the landlord with the characteristic humility of a tenant and poured forth in a profuse strain the litany of the gross offences committed against me by the mice and the bats and the lizards.

The landlord, who has an epidemic terror for anything that sounds like "Expenditure", was not prepared to embark upon the project of ceiling my room.

And yet, suggestions and remarks, however much they may be rebutted in the beginning, sometimes bring home some rich curative effects in the end. My appeal to the landlord to get my room ceiled, which seemed as tasteless as a cube of sugar in the mighty ocean, in the long run effected something good. To escape belling the cat, the landlord suggested that I should rather employ a qualified steward, who could solve the heart-rending situation within a twinkle of an eye. This meant, of course, taxing my economic resources and not his. I had to choose between staying at the old premises and employing a steward whose salary would perpetualize my economic instability; and leaving the house to face that awful problem of finding a room in Accra which often compels honest people to shun recognizing old faces (when they are suddenly confronted) or to dodge all familiar faces (when they are the first to see such faces) for fear these faces might know that they are roomless Johnnie Walkers.

A beggar has no choice but there I was an exception. I had a choice and therefore chose the former, and employed a highly recommended and best capacitated steward, Mr. Cat.

In fact, Mr. Cat proved to be efficiency personified. Within just two days, the co-tenants at the naked roof had become as dumb and as noiseless as a blank wall and as still as still could be. The slightest self-assertion they displayed meant the loss of their individualities, and the felicitous augmentation of the honourable steward's morsels and capacities. His sharp whiskers were ever on tiptoe, his bright eyes were ever yearning and itching for action. His claws were ever sharp and ready to claw, and to tear to sumptuous morsels any mouse or lizard or bat who even posed as a pole-vaulter or high-jumper.

The few that managed to keep their heads by remaining actively passive were very bony. Their skin assumed a supernatural transparency, and their ribs could be counted. They were living skeletons, speeding precipitately towards annihilation.

Conditions began to take a happy turn—they grew from worst to worse, and then to bad—and so to good, and from good to better—but very unfortunately they never became perfectly V-shaped. Before I could score the superlative conditions of affairs, something very sad happened.

One fine Saturday morning, a very faithful precursor of a jolly good Easter day, when the sun filled the earth, with its charming and fascinating festive smiles, I decided to take that Easter Sunday smile with the broad smile of a banquet. I bought a guinea-fowl, for a guinea, and sent it to Miss Kind to make it appear at my Easter table.

I chose Miss Kind because I trusted her cooking capacities. Miss Kind, the Headmistress of Domestic Science in the Amalgamated School, displayed all her tactful dexterity and skill in translating my wishes into a concrete reality. Thus the long-expected Sunday arrived, accompanied by the well-toned guinea-fowl, gracefully clad in a rich brown swimming-jersey and swimming in a delicious pool of sauce, wonderfully seasoned, palatably and sweetly embellished with first-class spices and ingredients. Every nose that smelt the discharge of the highly scented and sweet odour of the dish was bound to grow wild with uncontrollable anxiety. My teeth began to water, my tongue instinctively began to jump about and even my eyes could feel, how exactly I don't know, the most categorically assured palatability of the dish.

I therefore determined to compose a befitting atmosphere for gourmandizing, and to break that day the record established at my table. I left the dish happily resting on the table, and made for the nearest canteen ("Eat All Canteen", it was), to buy "You are lucky today wine", to accelerate the already quick flow of my saliva, and to heighten my agile appetite. Meanwhile, Mr. Cat the steward was standing faithfully by—watching. Before I left, I asked him to chase away any intruder who might visit my dining-room in my absence. I traversed a distance of seventy-seven yards and still I could smell the sweet scent of my dish. If men were to serve their country with the straightforwardness and the conscientiousness and the anxiety with which I set off to get the "You are lucky today", we should enjoy such first-class rapidity in our progress that our world could be most accurately described as a social, cultural and political paradise. I got the bottle and I was on my home trip—I was fifty yards nearer and I did not smell anything. I blew my nose, thinking my nostrils were not clear. And still I did not smell anything. I drew nearer still and I heard nothing. This time I breathed in heavily and still no scent of the sweet dish.

I ran home as fast as my legs could serve me, and there I was—dish and everything gone. If you had been in my shoes, what would you have done?

With eyes sparkling with anger and disappointment, with a voice vibrating with painful disappointment and with a tongue suffering from the pangs of deprivation of such a *bonum delectabile*, I volleyed questions at my steward. "I found it to be a disturbing intruder, so I chased it out, as you directed me to do," was all the answer I got.

"Did I ever say so? And if yes, how can a dish be an intruder?" said I.

"It filled the place with its unharnessed odour, and fearing it might pollute the air, and therefore mar the happy-go-lucky mood of Easter, I just got rid of it." "How?" "Good heavens above; by simply removing it from the table and by keeping it where its odour would not be felt." I plucked up hope and quietly asked for the place where the dish had been kept.

"Goodness me, why brood over spilt milk, I have kept it in my stomach," said Mr. Cat.

"This is gross misconduct—I thought you could construct a line of demarcation between the intrusion of the mice and the innocent objects of my delight—I thought you were efficiency personified, not knowing that you are a helpless monument of harmful inefficiency. Truly, a fool will be a fool, whether he goes to school or not."

I made a very clever move to catch hold of that mighty and saucy steward, and thrash him as mercilessly as I could give vent to my anger. But he quickly took to his heels and I was left without a steward and back to my A.B.C.

So I decided to leave the house and find a better place to stay.

2. THE SEARCH FOR A NEW ROOM

I spent my Easter Monday moving from house to house, eagerly trying to find somewhere to settle.

Quite unexpectedly, I found myself behind a palatial building which was a living advertisement of the splendour and the beauty of modern scientific and architectural achievements.

I entered with a great air, and asked to see the landlord. I met him quite happily having a drinking bout. He wore a mighty moustache which had been purposely grown to play the role of a sieve when he was drinking thick palm-wine. His eyes moved as actively as the hungry eyes of an eagle, and the palm-wine had made him more eloquent than Dingle Foot, and more actively lively than an American. I noticed there were two types of people in that drinking bout—the quick and the dead. Either quick or dead they had to be. From the way the landlord responded to my good afternoon, I got to know that he did not understand a word of English. And I do not know why he took me to be a Ga speaker; he very seriously spoke Ga to me and his Ga was Greek to me. *Oblayo* was the only alpha and omega I understood.

He looked at me and I looked at him. The silent trade is actually out of application when one is after a room to rent, otherwise I must have applied my knowledge of it. In the long run, I got a gentleman to communicate my intentions to him and I became very sorry, for his *Oblayo* meant I looked too young—was unmarried and therefore girls (the *Oblayos*) would be haunting me if I came to stay there. I regretted I had told him beforehand that I was a bachelor, otherwise I might have told him that though I look young, I have a wife and two children.

Anyway there was much sense in what he said. He wanted a married man to stay there, so that the wife might take charge of the house, sweeping and lighting fires there. These two things are very dear to an old Ghanaian.

I saw my mistake. I shouldn't have said I was a bachelor. But before then, I was made to believe that stressing the fact that I was a bachelor would quickly find me a room to rent. But here this information did not work efficiently. There I was in a very big dilemma. Should I change my tongue or should I not change it? I asked my interpreter to tell the landlord that I wanted to modify what I had just said; that is, if I said I am not married, it does not necessarily mean that I am not engaged to a woman. I am, and I am going to get married. This week would see me a married man and so if he could—he might settle matters with me, and I would come with my wife the following week and that would fully qualify me to be his tenant. My wife would sweep the house, light fires there to make the *Asamanfo* happy, whenever they paid their visit.

Getting married that week became a *conditio sine qua non* for my occupying the two chambers and a hall of the first floor at the monthly rentage of £12. I knew I had not engaged any woman, so I planned with the constructive advice of bosom friends to visit a night club—where I could as quickly get a wife as I wanted to get married.

At last I came to the club. I increased my store of experience by many rich deposits of face-facts-in-the-face incidents. I stoutly called for a bottle of stout, and two bottles of beer. I lighted my Town Hall and began to play the big man. I had thrown in the bait and I was expecting a good catch. My expectations were answered.

As I enthusiastically sat stouting and beering my spirits, two attractive ladies made their advance towards me. My heart was filled with brightly smiling prospects. That was already the beginning of a good enterprise. They greeted me nicely and my heart leaped with joy.

One of them started to address me with a big *Ofane* and I beg your pardon, *Minuu Ga*, was my quick reply. They smiled and I returned a broader smile as I realized there was a world of meaning in their smiles.

While still standing, one of them opened a stream of heart-to-heart conversation with me. "Please, it seems I know you," was the next sentence. "Of course, sweet ladies, I have travelled the length and breadth of Ghana, I am a big aviator. I am sure it is quite true you know me and I am glad you have made this remark. I nearly made the same remark." They looked at me and smiled very confidentially.

They came up to my fancy. They were exactly the types of ladies who could call forth a young man's sensibilities. From the sparkling beauty of their faces—from their blooming rosy cheeks made more rosy by pancake—from their sweet lovely lips made lovelier by lipsticks—and from the superfine sweet fragrance which graced the air about them, I quite logically deduced the following:

That they were specialists in the fascinating modern plastering arts of "Pancaking and Lipsticking and Love-inviting." Doctors of Lavender-Sprinkology they were.

There they stood before me—their sweet eyes swimming in a jolly pool of love, and not a bit in a hurry to leave me. I essayed to invite them to sit down, but again I was seared by their appearances. They looked so very dignified that my much-boasted dignity did not seem commensurate with theirs. They bloomed and blossomed with dignity and grace and splendour. Very reasonably tiny-waisted, slim, flexible, smooth-skinned and in fine they were a wonderful tapestry skilfully woven with the interlacing threads of all that is existible in the thrillingly sweet province of Lady Beauty.

"Will you give me the honour, sweet ladies, of sitting down by me?" And scarcely had I ended the wording of my invitation than I saw these ambassadors of beauty sitting one on my left and the other on my right. Every repeated glance I cast unveiled a new world of beauty.

They were as bright as the sun, lovely as the moon and as terrible as they were flirtatious. With sweet fingers and with finger-nails glistening with masterly manicure, they rang glasses. I had the exclusive monopoly of paying for the drinks, and I executed that self-courted troublesome task with interlocking consistency. They had the privilege of constantly placing orders for this brand and that brand. It was indeed very expensive to bid them company.

Besides being great cosmeticians, they were highly qualified Fellows of the Royal Institute of Alcohol.

They drank with masterly poise all brands of drinkables—except cola, which was too strong for their weaker sex. The atmosphere was quite serene and aesthetic. Many more ladies, some of similar and others of dissimilar description, began to pour in.

A dance soon started. My two ladies who were so advantageously slim, so conveniently tiny-waisted and so tactfully flexible, quick-stepped and mamboed and calpysoed with characteristic flexibility and elasticity of rubber. So light-lipped that those delicate lips could wear nothing heavier than charming smiles.

Yes, I should not lose sight of the patent fact that Lido is not a garden of beautiful flowers only. According to the Akan proverb *Kurow biara Mensa wo mu* which being literally interpreted means—In every town there is a third born. I encountered some ladies whose descriptions were in conflict with those already described.

The *Mensas* (Third Born) of the night club so thick-lipped that their lips could easily suspend a fat bottle of beer in the air, and still render the force of gravity absolutely incapable of doing anything about it—a passive onlooker it must willy-nilly be. So bulky and so heavy and so superlatively the opposite of flexibility and elasticity that they moved about and danced with the flexibility of a big timber log. What a wonderful ocean of difference I witnessed in their typologies. But, however greatly they differed in appearances, they had, as correctly as facial expressions could dictate to me, a unity of purpose—and that was to be very "Sikaditious" and never to be in a hurry to get married to any young man who was sufficiently in a hurry to get married with the big "UT of purpose", namely a house to rent. They were all after a lily of the valley *affair de cœur*—a love-affair which is strictly a nine-day wonder. No amount of wording or bossing could convince any of them about the usefulness and the necessity for doing what Adam and Eve did. No lady in the catalogue was prepared to have a husband, even for a period of one week.

That is always the case—men are more often than not interested in women, and women in men. I was by no means an exception that way. I did not mind those of my sex and moreover I knew from experience that they could not help me; or even if they posed as helpers, they would only be developing the axe they might have to grind in so doing. At best, they would be arranging things for themselves.

I left the place completely broke—without any balm for the pangs of my wounded ambition. I abandoned the old idea of getting accommodation in that house whose walls welcomed only the married.

The apple was sour—after all, this was not the only building that observed good architectural norms—and therefore it was not the only beautiful building in town. After all, it was too remote. That was how I cheered up my sinking spirits.

Try, try, try again became my slogan, and I tried and tried and tried again. This time, I was ever on the alert to study circumstances before voicing out anything. At long last, news struck my inquiring ears about a house to let.

After what I called a serious study of the circumstances of the place—I drew the conclusion that a married person would have more chances of success than a bachelor. So I put on my big D.B. coat, lighted my big cigar, all to make me appear rather special, and I set out on my adventure. With a friend's child resting in my arms, I arrived at the house—this time I was welcomed by a landlady who looked superbly wicked and nagging. I told her what I had come there for, avoiding all premature information about myself.

And she asked me, "Is this your child?" and I said yes. And she said, "Is it a product of your unharnessed lust or is it a legitimate child?" And I said, "Be sure I wouldn't do anything that is illegitimate—that is to say, the child is a legitimate son." And she said, "May I therefore understand that you are married?" And I said, "There is no harm in trying." And she said, "You are married, and you want my room—anybody who is married is no friend of mine and therefore cannot be a tenant here." I was trying to scratch my head in protest when she proudly left me, to entertain the furniture if I cared.

Married or not married—that is the question—and the answer lies in your star and not in yourself, for whether married or not married, you can be given or be refused a room to rent.

Mista Courifer

ADELAIDE CASELY-HAYFORD

Not a sound was heard in the coffin-maker's workshop, that is to say no human sound. Mista Courifer, a solid citizen of Sierra Leone, was not given to much speech. His apprentices, knowing this, never dared address him unless he spoke first. Then they only carried on their conversation in whispers. Not that Mista Courifer did not know how to use his tongue. It was incessantly wagging to and fro in his mouth at every blow of the hammer. But his shop in the heart of Freetown was a part of his house. And, as he had once confided to a friend, he was a silent member of his own household from necessity. His wife, given to much speaking, could out-talk him.

"It's no use for argue wid woman," he said cautiously. "Just like 'e no use for teach woman carpentering; she nebba sabi for hit de nail on de head. If 'e argue, she'll hit eberything but de nail; and so wid de carpentering."

So, around his wife, with the exception of his tongue's continual wagging like a pendulum, his mouth was kept more or less shut. But whatever self-control he exercised in this respect at home was completely sent to the wind in his official capacity as the local preacher at chapel, for Mista Courifer was one of the pillars of the church, being equally at home in conducting a prayer meeting, superintending the Sunday school or occupying the pulpit.

His voice was remarkable for its wonderful gradations of pitch. He would insist on starting most of his tunes himself; consequently they nearly always ended in a solo. If he happened to pitch in the bass, he descended into such a *de profundis* that his congregations were left to flounder in a higher key; if he started in the treble, he soared so high that the children stared at him open-mouthed and their elders were lost in wonder and amazement. As for his prayers, he roared and volleyed and thundered to such an extent that poor little mites were quickly reduced to a state of collapse and started to whimper from sheer fright.

But he was most at home in the pulpit. It is true, his labours were altogether confined to the outlying village districts of Regent, Gloucester and Leicester, an arrangement with which he was by no means satisfied. Still, a village congregation is better than none at all.

His favourite themes were Jonah and Noah and he was for ever pointing out the great similarity between the two, generally finishing his discourse after this manner: "You see my beloved Brebren, den two man berry much alike. All two lived in a sinful and adulterous generation. One get inside an ark; de odder one get inside a whale. Day bof seek a refuge fom de swelling waves.

"And so it is today my beloved Brebren. No matter if we get inside a whale or get inside an ark, as long as we get inside some place of safety—as long as we can find some refuge, some hiding-place from de wiles ob de debil."

But his congregation was by no means convinced.

Mr. Courifer always wore black. He was one of the Sierra Leone gentlemen who consider everything European to be not only the right thing, but the *only* thing for the African, and having read somewhere that English undertakers generally appeared in sombre attire, he immediately followed suit.

He even went so far as to build a European house. During his short stay in England, he had noticed how the houses were built and furnished and had forthwith erected himself one after the approved pattern—a house with stuffy little passages, narrow little staircases and poky rooms, all crammed with saddlebags and carpeted with Axminsters. No wonder his wife had to talk. It was so hopelessly uncomfortable, stuffy and insanitary.

So Mr. Courifer wore black. It never struck him for a single moment that red would have been more appropriate, far more becoming, far less expensive and far more national. No! It must be black. He would have liked blue-black, but he wore rusty black for economy.

There was one subject upon which Mr. Courifer could talk even at home, so no one ever mentioned it: his son, Tomas. Mista Courifer had great expectations of his son; indeed in the back of his mind he had hopes of seeing him reach the high-water mark of red-tape officialism, for Tomas was in the government service. Not very high up, it is true, but still he was in it. It was an honour that impressed his father deeply, but Tomas unfortunately did not seem to think quite so much of it. The youth in question, however, was altogether neutral in his opinions in his father's presence. Although somewhat feminine as to attire, he was distinctly masculine in his speech. His neutrality was not a matter of choice, since no one was allowed to choose anything in the Courifer family but the paterfamilias himself.

From start to finish, Tomas's career had been cut out, and in spite of the fact that nature had endowed him with a black skin and an African temperament, Tomas was to be an Englishman. He was even to be an Englishman in appearance.

Consequently, once a year mysterious bundles arrived by parcel post. When opened, they revealed marvellous checks and plaids in vivid greens and blues after the fashion of a Liverpool counterjumper, waistcoats decorative in the extreme with their bold designs and rows of brass buttons, socks vying with the rainbow in glory and pumps very patent in appearance and very fragile as to texture.

Now, Tomas was no longer a minor and he keenly resented having his clothes chosen for him like a boy going to school for the first time. Indeed on one occasion, had it not been for his sister's timely interference, he would have chucked the whole collection into the fire.

Dear little Keren-happuch, eight years his junior and not at all attractive, with a very diminutive body and a very large heart. Such a mistake! People's hearts ought always to be in proportion to their size, otherwise it upsets the dimensions of the whole structure and often ends in its total collapse.

Keren was that type of little individual whom nobody worshipped, consequently she understood the art of worshipping others to the full. Tomas was the object of her adoration. Upon him she lavished the whole store of her boundless wealth and whatever hurt Tomas became positive torture as far as Keren-happuch was concerned.

"Tomas!" she said, clinging to him with the tenacity of a bear, as she saw the faggots piled up high, ready for the conflagration, "Do yah! No burn am oh! Ole man go flog you oh! Den clos berry fine! I like am myself too much. I wish"—she added wistfully—"me na boy; I wish I could use am."

This was quite a new feature which had never struck Tomas before. Keren-happuch had never received a bundle of English clothes in her life, hence her great appreciation of them.

At first Tomas only laughed—the superior, dare-devil, don't-care-a-damn-about-consequences laugh of the brave before the dead. But after hearing that wistful little sentence, he forgot his own annoyance and awoke to his responsibilities as an elder brother.

A few Sundays later, Tomas Courifer, Jr., marched up the aisle of the little Wesleyan chapel in all his Liverpool magnificence accompanied by a very elated little Keren-happuch whose natural unattractiveness had been further accentuated by a vivid cerise costume —a heterogeneous mass of frill and furbelows. But the glory of her array by no means outshone the brightness of her smile. Indeed that smile seemed to illuminate the whole church and to dispel the usual melancholy preceding the recital of Jonah and his woes.

Unfortunately, Tomas had a very poor opinion of the government service and in a burst of confidence he had told Keren that he meant to chuck it at the very first opportunity. In vain his sister expostulated and pointed out the advantages connected with it—the honour, the pension—and the awful nemesis upon the head of anyone incurring the head-of-the-family's ire.

"Why you want to leave am, Tomas?" she asked desperately.

"Because I never get a proper holiday. I have been in the office four and a half years and have never had a whole week off yet. And," he went on vehemently, "these white chaps come and go, and a fresh one upsets what the old one has done and a newcomer upsets what he does and they all only stay for a year and a half and go away for four months, drawing big fat pay all the time, not to speak of passages, whereas a poor African like me has to work year in and year out with never a chance of a decent break. But you needn't be afraid, Keren dear," he added consolingly, "I shan't resign, I shall just behave so badly that they'll chuck me and then my ole man can't say very much."

Accordingly, when Tomas, puffing a cigarette, sauntered into the office at 9 a.m. instead of 8 a.m. for the fourth time that week, Mr. Buckmaster, who had hitherto maintained a discreet silence and kept his eyes shut, opened them wide and administered a sharp rebuke. Tomas's conscience was profoundly stirred. Mr. Buckmaster was one of the few white men for whom he had a deep respect, aye, in the depth of his heart, he really had a sneaking regard. It was for fear of offending him that he had remained so long at his post.

But he had only lately heard that his chief was due for leave so he decided there and then to say a long good-bye to a service which had treated him so shabbily. He was a vociferous reader of halfpenny newspapers and he knew that the humblest shop assistant in England was entitled to a fortnight's holiday every year. Therefore it was ridiculous to argue that because he was an African working in Africa there was no need for a holiday. All his applications for leave were quietly pigeon-holed for a more convenient season.

"Courifer!" Mr. Buckmaster said sternly. "Walk into my private office, please." And Courifer knew that this was the beginning of the end.

"I suppose you know that the office hours are from 8 a.m. till 4 p.m. daily?" commenced Mr. Buckmaster, in a freezing tone.

"Yes, er-sir!" stammered Courifer with his heart in his mouth and his mouth twisted up into a hard sailor's knot.

"And I suppose you also know that smoking is strictly forbidden in the office?"

"Yes, er-er-sir!" stammered the youth.

"Now hitherto," the even tones went on, "I have always looked upon you as an exemplary clerk, strictly obliging, punctual, accurate and honest, but for the last two or three weeks I have had nothing but complaints about you. And from what I myself have seen, I am afraid they are not altogether unmerited."

Mr. Buckmaster rose as he spoke, took a bunch of keys out of his pocket and, unlocking his roll-top desk, drew out a sheaf of papers. "This is your work, is it not?" he said to the youth.

"Yes, er-er-sir!" he stuttered, looking shamefacedly at the dirty ink-stained blotched sheets of closely typewritten matter.

"Then what in heaven's name is the matter with you to produce such work?"

Tomas remained silent for a moment or two. He summoned up courage to look boldly at the stern countenance of his chief. And as he looked, the sternness seemed to melt and he could see genuine concern there.

"Please, er-sir!" he stammered, "may-I-er-just tell you everything?"

Half an hour later, a very quiet, subdued, penitent Tomas Courifer walked out of the office by a side door. Mr. Buckmaster followed later, taking with him an increased respect for the powers of endurance exercised by the growing West African youth.

Six weeks later, Mista Courifer was busily occupied wagging his tongue when he looked up from his work to see a European man standing in his doorway.

The undertaker found speech and a chair simultaneously. "Good afternoon, sah!" he said, dusting the chair before offering it to his visitor. "I hope you don't want a coffin, sah!" which was a deep-sea lie for nothing pleased him more than the opportunity of making a coffin for a European. He was always so sure of the money. Such handsome money—paid it is true with a few ejaculations, but paid on the nail and without any deductions whatsoever. Now with his own people things were different. They demurred, they haggled, they bartered, they gave him detailed accounts of all their other expenses and then, after keeping him waiting for weeks, they would end by sending him half the amount with a stern exhortation to be thankful for that.

Mr. Buckmaster took the proffered chair and answered pleasantly: "No thank you, I don't intend dying just yet. I happened to be passing so I thought I should just like a word with you about your son."

Mr. Courifer bristled all over with exultation and expectation. Perhaps they were going to make his son a kind of under-secretary of state. What an unexpected honour for the Courifer family. What a rise in their social status; what a rise out of their neighbours. How good God was!

"Of course you know he is in my office?"

"Oh yes, sah. He often speaks about you."

"Well, I am going home soon and as I may not be returning to

Sierra Leone I just wanted to tell you how pleased I should be at any time to give him a decent testimonial."

Mr. Courifer's countenance fell. What a come-down!

"Yes, sah," he answered somewhat dubiously.

"I can recommend him highly as being steady, persevering, reliable and trustworthy. And you can always apply to me if ever such a thing be necessary."

Was that all! What a disappointment! Still it was something worth having. Mr. Buckmaster was an Englishman and a testimonial from him would certainly be a very valuable possession. He rubbed his hands together as he said: "Well, I am berry much obliged to you, sah, berry much obliged. And as time is short and we nebba know what a day may being forth, would you mind writing one down now, sah?"

"Certainly. If you will give me a sheet of paper, I shall do so at once."

Before Tomas returned home from his evening work, the testimonial was already framed and hanging up amidst the moth-eaten velvet of the drawing-room.

On the following Monday morning, Courifer Jr. bounced into his father's workshop, upsetting the equilibrium of the carpenter's bench and also of the voiceless apprentices hard at work.

"Well, sah?" ejaculated his father, surveying him in disgust. "You berry late. Why you no go office dis morning?"

"Because I've got a whole two months' holiday, sir! Just think of it—two whole months—with nothing to do but just enjoy myself!"

"Tomas," his father said solemnly, peering at him over his glasses, "you must larn for make coffins. You get fine chance now."

Sotto voce: "I'll be damned if I will!" Aloud: "No thank you, sir. I am going to learn how to make love, after which I am going to learn how to build myself a nice mud hut."

"And who dis gal you want married?" thundered his father, ignoring the latter part of the sentence altogether.

A broad smile illuminated Tomas's countenance. "She is a very nice girl, sir, a very nice girl. Very quiet and gentle and sweet, and she doesn't talk too much."

"I see. Is dat all?"

"Oh, no. She can sew and clean and make a nice home. And she had plenty sense; she will make a good mother."

"Yes, notting pass dat!"

"She has been to school for a long time. She reads nice books and she writes, oh, such a nice letter," said Tomas, patting his breast-pocket affectionately.

"I see. I suppose she sabi cook good fashion?"

"I don't know, I don't think so, and it doesn't matter very much."

"What!" roared the old man, "you mean tell me you want married woman who no sabi cook?"

"I want to marry her because I love her, sir!"

"Dat's all right, but for we country, de heart and de stomach always go togedder. For we country, black man no want married woman who no sabi cook! Dat de berry first requisitional. You own mudder sabi cook."

That's the reason why she has been nothing but your miserable drudge all these years, thought the young man. His face was very grave as he rejoined: "The style in our country is not at all nice, sir. I don't like to see a wife slaving away in the kitchen all times to make good chop for her husband who sits down alone and eats the best of everything himself, and she and the children only get the leavings. No thank you! And besides, sir, you are always telling me that you want me to ba an Englishman. That is why I always try to talk good English to you."

"Yes, dat's all right. Dat's berry good. But I want make you *look* like Englishman. I don't say you must copy all der different way!"

"Well, sir, if I try till I die, I shall never look like an Englishman, and I don't know that I want to. But there are some English customs that I like very much indeed. I like the way white men treat their wives; I like their home life; I like to see mother and father and the little family all sitting down eating their meals together."

"I see," retorted his father sarcastically. "And who go cook den meal. You tink say wid your four pound a month, you go able hire a perfessional cook?"

"Oh, I don't say so, sir. And I am sure if Accastasua does not know how to cook now, she will before we are married. But what I want you to understand is just this, that whether she is able to cook or not, I shall marry her just the same."

"Berry well," shouted his father, wrath delineated in every feature, "but instead of building one mud hut you better go one time build one madhouse."

"Sir, thank you. But I know what I am about and a mud hut will suit us perfectly for the present."

"A mud hut!" ejaculated his father in horror. "You done use fine England house wid staircase and balustrade and tick carpet and handsome furnitures. You want to go live in mud hut? You ungrateful boy, you shame me, oh!"

"Dear me, no sir! I won't shame you. It's going to be a nice clean spacious mud hut. And what is more, it is going to be a sweet little home, just big enough for two. I am going to distemper the walls pale green, like at the principal's rooms at Keren's school."

"How you sabi den woman's rooms?"

"Because you have sent me two or three times to pay her school fees, so I have looked at those walls and I like them too much."

"I see. And what else you go do?" asked his father ironically.

"I am going to order some nice wicker chairs from the Islands and a few good pieces of linoleum for the floors and then. . . ."

"And den what?"

"I shall bring home my bride."

Mr. Courifer's dejection grew deeper with each moment. A mud hut! This son of his—the hope of his life! A government officer! A would-be Englishman! To live in a mud hut! His disgust knew no bounds. "You ungrateful wretch!" he bellowed. "You go disgrace me. You go lower your pore father. You go lower your position for de office."

"I am sorry, sir," retorted the young man. "I don't wish to offend you. I'm grateful for all you have done for me. But I have had a raise in salary and I want a home of my own which, after all, is only natural, and"—he went on steadily, staring his father straight in the face—"I am as well tell you at once, you need not order any more Liverpool suits for me."

"Why not?" thundered his irate parent, removing his specs lest any harm should befall them.

"Well, I am sorry to grieve you, sir, but I have been trying to live up to your European standards all this time. Now I am going to chuck it once and for all. I am going back to the native costume of my mother's people, and the next time I appear in chapel it will be as a Wolof."

The very next Sunday the awful shock of seeing his son walk up the aisle of the church in pantaloons and the bright loose over-jacket of a Wolof from Gambia, escorting a pretty young bride the colour of chocolate, also in native dress, so unnerved Mista Courifer that his mind suddenly became a complete blank. He could not even remember Jonah and the whale, nor could his tongue possess one word to let fly, not one. The service had to be turned into a prayer meeting.

Mista Courifer is the local preacher no longer. Now he only makes coffins.

The Blood in the Washbasin

WILLIAM CONTON

The father sat alone and quite still in his canoe. Only the splash, splash of the waves against its bottom broke the silence. On one side the beach and the low-lying land behind it formed a narrow white and green ribbon, stitching the blue sea to the blue sky. On the other side the infinity of the horizon lay unbroken.

He wore only a loin cloth, and a discoloured clay pipe parted his lips. His head was bent forwards, and his hands held the fishing-line loosely. He was lost in thought, it seemed. They were pleasant thoughts. His son, whose letter had been read to him yesterday, would be home now. It would be a brief home-coming—only a few hours; but it would be full of honour. And yet he could not accept the invitation to go to Freetown and watch the ship come in. He was ten thousand times happier sitting here in his canoe. Mechanically he baled water out, and the sunshine reflected by the disturbed pool between his leathery feet lit a glow of happiness on his creased face.

The mother had risen early that morning, long before dawn. She was not going to see the ship come in either. However, she wanted to get her cooking and housework over as quickly as possible, because she had been told that the new television set in the village would show pictures of the ship and of her son and she did not want to be late for them.

He was her only child; and although she was the senior wife, and had every right to demand help from the children of the other wives, she preferred to do all her housework and cooking herself, now that her son had left home. First she lit her palm-oil lamp and made her way down to the stream for her bath. Then she returned to her hut, carrying a bucket of cold, clear water from the stream for the day's cooking. She went to his hut and roused her husband. Next she stoned and pounded the rice by the rose light of a flamboyant dawn, lit a fire, and put the rice on to boil. She then gathered her washing and went down to the stream again.

By this time her husband's compound was alive with activity. The other wives' huts had come to life one by one, and young children's voices shrilled. There was only one topic of conversation in each of these huts, and it was also the main topic throughout the village—Kelfah's ship. Those children who were old enough to go to Freetown on their own were dressing quickly and soon following the narrow path out of the village and towards the main road, where they sat on boulders waiting for the bus to Freetown. Because it was the only bus that day, they prayed it would not be full.

Kelfah's mother returned from the stream with her washing, which was spotlessly done, as always. She took the rice off the fire, took her husband some cassava and fried fish prepared the previous day, and watched him place the food, together with his fishing-tackle and bait, into a plastic bag, and set off for the mouth of the stream, where his canoe was beached. As he moved away from her she said, "Kelfah arrives today." He replied, "I have not forgotten, you will watch the pictures today, and I shall listen to you this evening."

And so she had returned to her hut to make her palm-oil sauce with potato leaves and dried fish, and had then hurried across the compound to the crowded barri where the television set was already talking loudly and dancing with bright pictures.

The son, Kelfah, knew as soon as he had laughed that he had sinned.

It had been a bad voyage from the start, this, the first voyage of an Elder-Dempster mail-boat from Liverpool to West Africa in the charge of an African master. First there had been the dock strike on Merseyside and the fierce anxiety before and after his decision to take her out without the help of tugs. The pilot had done a brilliant job; but the responsibility for the decision and any possible consequences which followed from it had remained Kelfah's and had placed a telling strain on him. He had watched this manœuvre from this bridge dozens of times; but the difference between watching it as a subordinate and doing so as master was immeasurable. He knew that if anything went wrong the fact that this was the first time an African had had command of a mail-boat would be enough to ensure the most extensive publicity for the mishap. However, all had gone well, and his handshake with the departing pilot in the estuary had been eloquently grateful.

Then there had been the matter of the seating plan for the captain's table. Ama had been in his state-room when the chief steward brought the draft plan, just before they sailed. She had taken offence at once at the fact that she was not placed on his right. "But Ama dear," he protested, "I expect the chief steward is trying to get people mixed up by race as well as sex. I have got a European woman on each side of me whilst you have a European man on each side of you. I am sure he is doing it in the interests of good race relations, not to do you out of your rightful place by my side. He's not that kind of chap at all."

"I don't care. I want to sit near you not only because I am your cousin but because I enjoy talking to you more than to any European or anyone else on that table. Don't you want me to enjoy my meals?" Ama's lips were trembling and Kelfah knew that this usually meant trouble ahead. He hesitated. He need only press the bell to call back the chief steward and, with a few pencilled arrows on the draft, rearrange the whole plan.

But Kelfah was weak. And, like most weak men, he hated his weakness to be seen. Had it occurred to him as soon as he saw the plan to alter it he might have done so, but to make the alteration now would make it clear to the chief steward that he was doing so at Ama's insistence. He could not afford to have his officers think him so pliable.

So with considerable effort he had told Ama that the seating could not now be changed, and Ama had taken all her meals in her stateroom, silently furious. At meal-times, when he should have found relief and distraction from the responsibilities of his command, her empty seat, directly across from his at the oval table, reproached him pitilessly, and he kept glancing nervously towards the entrance in the hope, vain as he well knew, that she might appear.

Then, to make his spirits heavier still, had come the storm. It was not that his seamanship was unequal to the test. His long and careful training, during more than twenty years at sea, had given him more than enough experience to handle his ship in any storm likely to blow up on this run. But he had a desperate anxiety that not even the smallest thing should go wrong on this his first voyage as master. It led him to try to oversee himself the minutest details. For the eighteen hours that the storm lasted he did not leave the bridge, keeping in constant touch with all parts of the ship, and with Liverpool. When the storm ceased and he did at last go below, he knocked first at the door of Ama's state-room. She refused to open to him; and as he threw himself fully dressed on his bunk, it seemed that the weariness of his body had all of a sudden overwhelmed his spirit too.

Yet he could not sleep. Taut nerves prevented heavy eyelids from closing. A sense of guilt towards Ama, a sense of responsibility for his ship, alternated in smothering his consciousness; and without wishing to do so he found himself fighting them both, using up more and more of his nervous energy in doing so, and driving sleep ever further away.

But even now he did not really feel any alarm. He had trained himself, like any sailor, to go without sleep for a long time. He put on the wireless, found a concert of classical music, and tried to allow himself to "unwind".

He had to get up three or four hours later to attend a champagne party given by one of the VIPs at his table, a Cabinet Minister. To his surprise he found Ama there. The host had ordered far too many bottles of champagne and by the time Kelfah entered the bar, the party was already noisy. The noise dropped respectfully as he came in, and he felt for a brief moment, a return of his self-assurance. He went straight across to Ama, who was talking to an elderly university professor who had spent thirty years on the "Coast", and was known to be a chronic alcoholic.

Ama was clearly bored by the old man; yet she answered Kelfah's greeting only very curtly, and then turned half away. "My God, how these women take things to heart," Kelfah thought. The professor was talking about the storm, and he answered mechanically. Gradually, the group around him grew larger. The old professor alternately drank champagne and talked nonsense, both at great speed; but few people in the group took much notice of him.

Two hours later the party had run down, with the host starting to go round urging his remaining guests to "have one for the gangway". The small chop had run out long ago; everyone who had come to meet people had gone, leaving the host with those who had come to drink—and Ama and Kelfah. He could not think why she was staying so long. She still ignored him. She hardly spoke or drank but just stood and listened to the increasingly silly and noisy chatter around her. He stayed only because she did, because he felt instinctively protective towards her, however unreasonable he might think her attitude towards him.

The professor was addressing him in a loud voice, spilling champagne all over his tie as he did so: "Captain, we are all *terribly* proud of you, you know! You are from Freetown, I suppose?"

Ama turned and looked at Kelfah defiantly. They had both gone to secondary school in Freetown, but had been born in Sherbo, into a very old and proud family, and had gone to primary school there. The professor clearly expected to find that the first master of a mail-boat should come from Freetown, and had almost suggested by his tone that Kelfah had no right to come from anywhere else. Kelfah hesitated. The man was drunk, and perhaps it did not matter much what he replied. Ama's eyes were turned full on him, as if challenging him to conceal his origins. He shrank before their strong, steady gaze.

"I went to the Methodist Boys' High School," he said evasively.

"Ah, then you'll enjoy this story," said the professor, jumping to the wrong conclusion and draining half a glass of champagne as he did so. "When I was a youngster in the Navy during the war I was on a cruiser anchored for one day off Bonthe. There was an old fellow in a canoe alongside with a big catch of fish which he was trying to sell us. He had a particularly fine grouper, at least as long as my arm; but he was being difficult about its price. A mate of mine had a harpoon gun, and we had been practising with it on porpoises in the Gambia river the previous week. The devil got into me and to win a bet I took the gun and aimed at the grouper in the old boy's canoe. I did better than hit two birds with one stone—I harpooned fish and flesh with one shot. The harpoon went through the grouper, the old boy's calf, and the bottom of the canoe. Devil of a mess. The ship's carpenter, armourer and butcher all had to be called to help clear it up after we had raised the canoe with its bloody contents up on deck. That old boy cursed me, my parents and my grandparents for the whole of the hour it took to release him. Wonderful energy for a chap that age."

Ama smashed her glass down on the bar, as one or two people laughed. It was then that Kelfah laughed. It was a mirthless laugh, hollow, grating; the laugh of an embarrassed man, a tired man, a weak man, reacting with the crowd. Then he saw the look in Ama's eyes. This time it was not defiance, but hatred. She had remembered at once; her father and his father were sons of the same father whose death they had often described. He had died of gangrene in Bonthe hospital during the war, a week after having been shot through the leg by a rusty harpoon fired into his canoe by some playful sailors.

A fire of hatred blazed higher and higher in Ama's eyes, and the circle of listeners was now deathly silent and still. Ama turned and ran out of the room, and Kelfah followed her at once. He pushed his way into her state-room behind her and closed the door.

It was only then that he noticed that she had cut her finger when she broke the champagne glass. She went straight to the bathroom washbasin and put the bleeding hand under the tap. Keeping it there, she turned round to face him. He had expected her eyes to be red and moist, but they were hard and steely.

"That man told you that he killed one of our tribe, our own grandfather and you laughed with him."

"Ama, I did not link our grandfather with this man's story at all until I saw you looking at me like that. I have had a bad time since we sailed—that strike, that table plan, the storm. I feel tired, Ama, very tired. I was hardly listening to the man's story. I laughed mechanically when the others laughed. You must believe me."

"I don't. You are no longer one of us. You have become one of them. All you have done since we sailed proves it. You have taken on a white man's uniform and a white man's attitudes. You have betrayed us. You know you have a sacred duty to kill a stranger who has killed one of us. And yet you laugh with him. By the blood which that man drew from my grandfather, and by the blood which you have caused me to lose today, I am going to ask our gods to curse you, that murderer, and this ship. When she was launched, the Christian God was asked to bless her and all who sail in her. I ask the gods of the Sherbo to curse her and all who sail in her."

Kelfah felt kindling in his brain the same fire he had seen his ill-fated laugh light in her eyes. He tried desperately to quench it.

"Ama, what are you doing? Do you know what you have just said? I am your cousin, a Sherbo like you. Neither my job nor my uniform nor any words of yours can change that. If your curse is heard you will not escape either. Can't you see that?"

He was close to panic; his cheeks sagged, his eyes widened and he put out a hand against a bulkhead to steady himself. The water running off the hand was now almost clear. Ama turned off the tap, dried her hand and, without looking again at her cousin, walked out of the state-room.

During the rest of the voyage to Freetown, Kelfah's health broke down completely. Yet he would not go to the surgeon. He avoided meeting anyone except the officers on the bridge. He ate hardly anything, had hardly an hour's sleep in four nights. And the fire in his brain grew bigger and bigger, torturing him, blinding him. On the eve of their arrival he looked so wrecked that the first officer ignored all his assurances that he was all right and brought the surgeon to the bridge. Kelfah was ordered to bed at once. Every hour that night the surgeon called to see him. He refused to take a sedative but in the early hours of the morning, finding that he was still tossing restlessly, the surgeon had him held down and forcibly injected.

At first the sedation seemed to work normally. Kelfah slept off but woke at dawn as the ship drew abeam of Cape Lighthouse at the entrance to Freetown harbour and the engines slowed. Finding himself alone, he dressed hurriedly, unlocked a drawer, took out a pistol, loaded it, and slipped it into his pocket. He combed his hair and carefully inspected himself in the mirror. Then he went up to the bridge. His brain felt cooler, but filling it was the overpowering desire to take his ship safely to her berth himself today, to show the thousands of his fellow-countrymen he knew were waiting on the Queen Elizabeth Quay that a Sierra Leonean could bring a great vessel not only safely thousands of miles, through storm and calm, but also gently, gently against the old rubber tyres which waited to cushion her berthing. He was determined that no one on that ship, whether doctor or sailor, should prevent him from bringing his ship softly, smoothly, silently against those yielding cushiony rubber tyres.

The officers on the bridge were clearly surprised to see him; but quickly fell into their proper places in the chain of command, as he took over control. The coxswain obeyed his orders mechanically and only the tinkle of the engine-room signal broke the silence on the bridge. The great white ship slipped slowly past the waterfront of the centre of the town, and slowly the decorated quay came into view, with its great crowd.

The coxswain obeyed an order which brought the ship's bows round until, raked and sharp, they pointed at the centre of the crowd. A slight movement to his left made Kelfah turn, and he saw the doctor with Ama. They had come on to the bridge, he in search of his patient, she . . . she . . . why? he asked himself. What did she want, coming here without permission at this moment of all moments. Why? Why? The question repeated itself in his throbbing brain with a steeply increasing loudness—and then he caught sight of her bandaged finger and suddenly something seemed to explode deep down in him; and not a fire but a raging inferno now seemed to spring to life in his brain. He signalled full speed ahead, leapt forward, knocked the astonished coxswain aside and seized the wheel. He swung round and without a word, drew his pistol and held it rock steady pointing at his incredulous officers. Obediently, the great engines turned faster and faster, and the great ship lifted her bows and gathered speed.

The doctor was the first to speak. "Don't be a fool, man. Put that gun away." Only the rising note of the breeze through the shrouds and of alarm spreading through the ship and quay answered him. The engine-room rang up for confirmation of the signal. Kelfah confirmed with a steady hand. "Full speed ahead." Beyond the Cape, his father and his mother watched. Down below, the professor slept the deep sleep of alcoholism. On the bridge Ama collapsed. But her gods merely smiled. . . .

Koya

R. SARIF EASMON

Koya was being groomed for stardom—in a harem. It was her birthright and she entered upon it with a precocity that sometimes astonished and at times even alarmed her elders. She was the sole arbiter of her own dignity, a mysterious personal protocol that decided whether *the* Koya could do this, or if Koya could *not* do this. Wherefore Koya was as much a problem to herself as she was a porcupine of prickly contradictions to her friends of her own age. Hardly yet a slip of a girl, she was just turned nine years.

With a grace all her own, Koya curtsied in native style as befitted a well-trained Susu girl, and rose up in front of her mother.

"*N'Kha sigga, N'ga Fatmatta* . . . May I go now, N'ga Fatmatta?"

Fatmatta *Gbaylie*—meaning Fatmatta the fair, a soubriquet the tribe had bequeathed her as a compliment to a complexion like that of a peach browned by eternal sunshine—looked down with approbation and a smile on her only child. Her oval face, very, very beautiful, held a look of immense satisfaction and pride—almost of self-worship—for the child was almost a true copy, post-dated by eighteen years of her own elegant self.

"Yes, you may, Koya." The mother's eyes seemed to absorb much of the sunshine in the great backyard, so that the browns of her eyes appeared to go several shades lighter as her love and her pleasure in her child beamed out of them. It was a light that transformed everything within her and now so irradiated her face that even the slight down-turning of the corners of the lovely pink lips disappeared, removing the one blemish to her features. "Well, well," putting the last deft touch to the knot in Koya's headkerchief, "ain't we beautifully turned out today!"

Koya smiled. In her *taimlay* and *lappa*, all silk and pink, she was as colourful as summer, elegant as a figure in a Watteau painting—if Watteau had painted such scenes as Gauguin saw in the tropics. From her headkerchief to the red Mouké slippers on her feet, she irradiated pleasure. She looked a fairy in that sunshine but her smile stamped her as of the world: it was a smile of sophistication and it made Koya look not so much like a child dressed for a party as a scaled-down model of a woman of the world.

The smile showed teeth white and narrow, brilliant against pink lips and her burnt-honey complexion. But the smile quickly disappeared from her face as she listened to her mother's last instructions:

"N'Koya is *my* daughter," Fatmatta was smiling still, trying to mix honey with what bitterness a parent must from time to time measure out to her child, if that child is to take her place in the world without undue distress. And as usual when she was imparting the inherited wisdom of the aristocrats of the tribe, she fell to addressing Koya in the third person: "She must not forget that. Nor must she forget the quality of the distinguished person she is to marry when she grows up. She must not let me down *again*!"

All the sunshine drained out of the little girl's face. Under the headkerchief her brow contracted and relaxed many times, and she bit her lip before she returned:

"Ah, Nga Fatmatta!" her lips trembled. And had the woman not been so determined on her worldly education, she would have perceived she was crowding too much sail on the little vessel before her. "And I try *so* hard to be like you!"

"Of course, dear! Of course!" Fatmatta conceded. "But . . . but . . . I have not been able to forget the last time. . . ."

Koya visibly wilted. Her eyes fell to the ground. . . .

For she had not forgotten either. She was so uncomfortable she unconsciously slipped one foot out of a slipper to press a toe into the earth. It had happened a fortnight before. . . .

"Koya," N'ga Nenneh had ordered, "b-b-blow the f-f-fire up."

Though far from being as elegantly dressed as she was today, Koya was still the slickest of the seven young girls around the kitchen in N'ga Nenneh's home. And she had jibbed at the order. She did not like the smell of wood smoke; nor the echoing, weak feeling in the head when she rose from the fireside of three stones carrying the pot tripod-fashion off the ground.

"Maseray," Koya turned to the little girl beside her and doled out her most bewitching smile. "Maseray, do blow the fire up for me...."

"*Say mah yahinkhee*.... D-d-d-drat the-the child!" N'ga Nenneh's stammer ran on a parallel course with her notoriously short temper—and all the children knew well just how much stutter preceded the descent of her hand on their backs if her orders were not promptly carried out. "How d-d-do you exp-p-pect to c-c-cook in your o-o-own home, Koya, if you c-c-can't do-do-do these little things f-f-for yourself?"

The fireside was in the shade of the mango tree some distance from the grass-thatched kitchen. It being the dry season, the women of the harem cooked out of doors. It was pleasant enough in the sunshine; there was a clump of bananas at the far end of the compound against a background of greenery, conspicuous in which were scores of oranges nearly ripe. Several coco-palms, two or three papayas were elegantly dotted among the oranges. Nearer, two or three chile bushes were still green with fruit though their leaves were dusty with rice winnowings, standing as they did hard by three native rice-mortars, with half a dozen pestles lying about the ground.

Koya glanced uncomfortably at all these—anything, indeed, rather than towards N'ga Nenneh, whose order she liked no more than she liked the weight of her right hand. Yes, the sunshine and the scene were pleasant enough, if she could only keep out of the wood smoke.

Her eyes finally rested appealingly, pleadingly on Maseray.

Maseray grinned back. The vast gap in her teeth made the grin look equally comic as uneasy. Her eyes switched to N'ga Nenneh. The vein in the woman's throat was already throbbing. She was a small, wiry woman with a slightly pock-marked and rather ageless face. Small as she was her husband Bah Saidu, had a wholesome respect for her temper—and all the girls brought for training to the three women of the harem knew that she ruled the roost over everybody. Hence, much as little Maseray would have liked to oblige Koya, she could do no more than shift uneasily from one foot to another and grin back sheepishly at her friend.

"K-K-Koya," the sides of N'ga Nenneh's nose were already quivering, "w-w-will you b-blow the f-fire or not?"

Koya pouted. She regretted sorely that her mother, Fatmatta, was such an indifferent cook. N'ga Nenneh, on the other hand, was by far the best cook in town, if not in the whole tribe. For which reason it was part of Koya's grooming to come for cooking lessons. Pouting, she weighed the pros and cons of disobeying N'ga Nenneh. She sighed—and went down on her knees beside the fire stones. . . .

Puffing her cheeks out, Koya blew and puffed till the flames licked higher and higher between the firestones to gloat and glory round the sides of the pot.

When she rose from the fireside her eyes were streaming with water. But neither N'ga Nenneh nor Koya's companions could say whether it was from the wood smoke or whether she was crying out of a sense of outraged dignity.

Ten minutes later, N'ga Nenneh finished cutting up okra for the main savoury dish of the day. She had sat on the earthern mound in the kitchen to do this and now she moved nimbly out of the hut to wash her hands outside.

Thus it was that Fate planned little Koya's revenge on thc *cordon bleu*. The irony of the situation was that Fate did not consult Koya at all; and, furthermore, quite against character, Koya had undertaken to do some work about the kitchen without having been ordered to do so.

No doubt it was her appreciation of the beautiful that compelled her to the task. It was a very large dish she was washing in a calabash. It lay there, glowing translucently as the sun shone through its delicate thinness. Of course Koya had scrubbed it with the *sappo*—native scrubber—well-soaped. And when N'ga Nenneh actually came upon her the child had forgotten she was working and was running her fingers over the beautiful pink and blue floral designs on the side of the dish.

"La-illah-il-Allah!" N'ga Nenneh cried, as befitted a good Moslem—and a *Chernoh* at that! "K-K-Koya, set that d-d-dee-dish down a-a-at once! Careless Koya! You're b-b-bound to b-b-br-break it."

And so N'ga Nenneh bore down swiftly on Koya and with a sigh of relief stooped over dish and calabash on the ground. "This d-dish", she said, lifting the gorgeous oval out of the calabash and smiling proudly, "is am-among my most p-p-prized p-p-possessions. I b-brought it t-t-to this house as a-a w-wedding pre-present—l-long before you w-w-were b-born, careless K-K-Koya!"

If she had given all her attention to the dish instead of partly to Koya; or if she had not unluckily forgotten she'd been cutting okra, all would have been well. But unhappily okra is probably the world's most slippery edible vegetable. And before one could say "knife" the dish shot out of N'ga Nenneh's hand towards Mother Earth. She made a very swift, instinctive dive after it but, instead of clutching it, her fingers banged against the side, giving it an accelerated impulse downwards. In an instant the dish touched the ground and yawned in half a dozen fragments.

N'ga Nenneh stood up, mouth agape, features twisted in horror. *She* herself had done that! Not a sound escaped her. That kind of china had long ago ceased to come on the market. . . . And then, as she turned her head to one side, her eyes focused on Koya's face.

The sides of Koya's mouth were drawn down exactly like her mother Fatmatta's. She was smiling with the kind of satirical enjoyment with which Salome must have regarded John the Baptist's head on the charger. Her face had a look of sophisticated malice that should have been far above her years. But there was the expression undeniably stamped on the young face. As if that was not bad enough, the child giggled and, in the very tones of her mother Fatmatta, piped up:

"N'ga Nenneh—*ain't we careful!*"

Instantly N'ga Nenneh felt as if red-hot oil was blazing all over her brain. She leapt forward like a tigress and brought her sinewy hand with a resounding and satisfying *Thwack* across Koya's shoulders.

For once the sophisticated fledgeling lost her poise, her dignity. Koya, indeed, let out an old-fashioned yell of pain, very proper for a child of her years. And like a child, seeing N'ga Nenneh's hand hovering over her, she broke into a run and fled pell-mell down the yard. But N'ga Nenneh pursued her all over the yard, thwacking her repeatedly, till she ran crying for mercy out of the yard, out of the house and so home to her mother Fatmatta. . . .

All that was a fortnight ago and very properly belonged to the past. Having had time to cool down, N'ga Nenneh had made honourable amends: she had called on N'ga Fatmatta, conquered her pride enough to say how sorry she was she had allowed her temper to get the better of her. The Susus are a very happy people who set great store on good neighbourliness. To heal the breach between the two families, N'ga Nenneh had not come empty-handed; she had excelled herself in the kitchen and sought a way back to N'ga Fatmatta's heart through the unfailing route of the human stomach.

Today, then, Koya was not going to N'ga Nenneh's for lessons. And though she was turned out as colourful as a bird of paradise, she was in fact the dove of peace. Her visit, in short, marked the resumption of social intercourse between the two families. So, with a sigh of relief—for she and N'ga Nenneh had been friends since they were initiated together in the Bundu Society—N'ga Fatmatta put the last touch of antimony powder to Koya's eyelashes. And her last injunction was:

"*Ee nakha nemmou day*, Koya. . . . *Please* don't forget, Koya, if they offer you anything to eat you've just had lunch."

"Yes, N'ga Fatmatta."

Koya walked daintily up the palm-avenued street. A beautiful little town, unspoilt by commerce, the little girl might have been its spirit distilled by sunshine, come to bless the day. She stopped every now and again to exchange greeting with her own or her mother's friends. All the houses were large adobe ones, crowned with grass-thatch or the same golden-honey colour that made Koya look like *their* child, so well did her complexion go with her surroundings.

Just under half a mile from home Koya turned off the street, between two coco-palms, to enter a *kounkoumah* (oblong house) almost exactly like the home she'd come from. She walked smiling into the front veranda. She stopped in the passage between the two raised mounds and, smiling daintily, went down in a curtsy:

"*Bah-bah, ee mah-mah*—Good afternoon, sir."

She was smiling up towards the man on the mound to her right. Bah Saidu was sitting astride a raffia hammock swung from the rafters over the balcony. His eyes were slits, his smile was a slit struggling through the fat that so copiously lined and filled out his moon face.

Thanks to N'ga Nenneh's genius in the kitchen, Bah Saidu was the plumpest, most contented husband in the town.

"How dainty we look, my little Koya!" he said, in a small, sleepy voice. "It's good to see you around again, my child."

When Koya rose to enter the house, she was not quite sure if the master of the house was still smiling or had fallen asleep in his hammock.

Koya sniffed as she went through the main room of the house towards the women's quarters at the back. New rice, cooked as only Susu women know how, courted her nostrils. She stood still a moment, closed her eyes, drew the air deep into her chest. If only N'ga Fatmatta could cook like this!

As she passed through the back door into the rear balcony, N'ga Nenneh, sitting with Bah Saidu's other two wives, was holding a dish over a large beautifully scrubbed and cream-coloured calabash between them. She turned the dish right over so that Koya saw the carefully moulded dome of rice in the calabash disappear in the dreamiest of ground-nut sauce, followed by chunks of chicken legs, beef, liver. All at once the heavenly smell of the sauce took the air.

Again Koya curtsied: "*N'ga-ay we mah-mah.* Good afternoon, Mams. . . ."

"*Koya, Noma dee,* Koya, my ch-child, you're v-v-very w-welcome to our house again."

"Thank you, N'ga Nenneh."

Koya got up again. The women sat at the one mound in this rear veranda. There was no mound to Koya's left and here six little girls were sitting three to a calabash set on the floor between them. They were, indeed, just finishing their meal for N'ga Nenneh, unlike most Susu housewives, had a rule that children must eat before the women of the harem.

"Hello, Koya!" they called to her. "What lovely clothes. . . ."

Koya smiled to them but was more conscious of the contents of the calabash up on the dais on the other side. There were golden chunks of pumpkin in the gourd, among which and the pieces of meat N'ga Nenneh's fingers deftly moved, mixing the sauce into the rice. Koya blinked and swallowed, ashamed that all her salivary glands should be injecting such copious streams into her mouth. . . .

N'ga Nenneh, who treasured children even above the extravagant quota of native women's love of the young, was not unmindful of her visitor. Poor child, she was thinking; she must have had a rotten fortnight at home eating the nasties that Fatmatta maltreated in pots and called food; she must be hungry for good fare. . . .

"K-K-Koya," she called brightly—but just as any other Susu woman would have done in the circumstances—"*Fah n'khe m-m-mondoh*. . . . Come let me give you a fistful of rice."

There's quite an art in making a *mondoh*. N'ga Nenneh's fingers moved daintily, deftly in the mass of rice and she leaned over the mound to hand over a big ball of rice, so that sauce began to crawl down towards her wrist.

Koya stepped forward, cupped her hands. . . . "Thank you, N'ga Nenneh!"

How right N'ga Nenneh was about the rotten fortnight at home with N'ga Fatmatta's cooking! Koya had, in fact, timed her arrival with meal time here and . . . and . . . and . . .

The smell of the wonderful food in her hands nearly brought tears of joy into Koya's eyes. She split the *mondoh* into two, raised one hand towards her mouth. . . . Only then N'ga Fatmatta's last order leapt to her mind: "*If they give you anything to eat, you've just had lunch.*"

Brave, loyal little Koya! Her nose twitched with the urgency of the temptation in her hand. But with a sigh she lowered her hands and murmured, "Thank you, N'ga Nenneh. . . . But . . . but . . . *N'mou say khon*. . . . I do not want this, I've just eaten."

"You impossible child!" N'ga Nenneh cried in fury. "Then why in the n-n-name of Allah d-d-d-did you t-t-take it?"

Her hand ached to give this unnatural child a good smacking. But recalling with shame how she'd had to go on a pilgrimage of apology to Fatmatta, she quickly swallowed her anger and ended: "All right. Give it t-t-to M-M-Maseray. . . ."

The words were hardly out of N'ga Nenneh's mouth before Maseray had leapt off the floor grinning. This was *her* lucky day, though she couldn't imagine what had entered Koya to make her turn down such a *mondoh*. . . . She approached Koya with both hands outstretched.

With a sigh Koya passed the *mondoh* on. At that moment she frankly hated all children with their front teeth out. "Now you've got it," she said with a trace of bitterness, "Maseray, the least you can do is to go and fetch me some water to wash my hands."

Maseray raised her face from her hands. She had so gluttonously buried her mouth into the *mondoh* the rice and sauce made a moustache all round her lips. She grinned impishly at her friend.

"Anything wrong with *your* feet, *Miss* Koya?"

Koya sighed again. Up to a fortnight ago none of the children under N'ga Nenneh's care would have dared to talk to her like that. She sensed she had lost caste through the ignominious way N'ga Nenneh had buffeted and chased her out of her house the last time. She felt intensely resentful, though not quite sure against whom her feelings should be directed. But all at once she was conscious that the women on the mound were watching her. N'ga Nenneh particularly. She quite expected the precocious brat to take the law into her own hands and smack Maseray for her impertinence.

Koya did no such thing. She was betrothed to the Paramount Chief's eldest son and was as conscious of that as she was of the fact that, in the old days, her forefathers had bought and sold Maseray's forebears into slavery. Unfortunately, things had changed and she could not quite put Maseray up for auction. Nor was she going to give N'ga Nenneh more cause to humiliate her. She loved N'ga Nenneh's cuisine as much as she hated her person. So she did what she knew she could do best: she gathered herself as proud as any queen and, with a magnificent and excessively mature shrug of the shoulders, she said sweetly:

"Very well, my dear Maseray. If you won't—you won't!"

And with that Parthian shot she swept magnificently out of the balcony.

Daintily, her hands held away from her sides so she wouldn't soil her clothes, Koya moved down the yard. Never before had she carried herself so much like a mature woman as she did in the sunshine that afternoon. Even N'ga Nenneh said she looked like a queen. And so she walked right down and across the big yard till she disappeared round the side of the kitchen house.

There at last Koya stopped by the large drum of water behind the kitchen. A small gourd was floating on the surface of the water halfway down the drum. Koya lifted her right hand over the edge of the drum. The smell of N'ga Nenneh's heavenly groundnut sauce tickled every nerve in her nose. And promptly Koya's mouth watered in a way that made no concession to either dignity or propriety.

And then.... And then.... Young Koya glanced over one shoulder, then over the other. Except for half a dozen West African chickens—with one sexless and beautiful *bocie* or capon—and three fire finches by the rice mortars down the yard, she was alone in that part of the compound.

Koya raised her right hand to her nose. She drew the air deep into her chest, filled with aroma of the sauce. She tried to imagine how Maseray must have enjoyed the *mondoh* N'ga Fatmatta had obliged her to part with.

She shut her eyes.... And then...

The delicate tip of Koya's tongue peeped from between her lips, darted forward and licked the first grain of rice on her index finger.

Koya opened her eyes in wonder, wonder that any human could cook food so deliciously. She passed her tongue over the roof of her mouth so that every taste-bud, every nerve in her nose should sample the tang and flavour of N'ga Nenneh's genius.

Swiftly her tongue shot in and out of her mouth. First the right hand then the left was licked absolutely clean. Then Koya sighed....

Only then she turned to take water from the drum.

And at that very instant someone coughed.

Koya started guiltily—and turned to see Maseray's gums exposed in a grin stretching from ear to ear.

"And what's amusing you?" Koya asked, with a queenly disdain.

If an African child brimful of mischief and malice can change into a Cheshire cat, Maseray did at that instant. Her throat swelled, her neck shortened on her shoulders, her eyes closed to slits—and laughter burst out of her like a balloon bursting:

"Ha-ha-ha, Miss Koya! But I thought—we all thought ... ha-ha!..."

"Well?" frigidly.

"We all thought," Maseray's voice joined with five others in laughter full of bite and satire, "*N'ga Koya mou say khon*—that *Miss* Koya didn't want any!"

Though they were only grinning at her, Koya felt their malice as intensely as a stag at bay might have felt hounds baying at it. She surveyed these new enemies who were robbing her of her self-esteem. From being a queen in their envy, she'd become a butt of their jest. The corners of her mouth trembled. But she did not cry. She said nothing at all to them. She bent over the drum, picked up the gourd from the water, washed her hands.

Calmly she walked past them, up the yard back to N'ga Nenneh in the house.

But Maseray did not let her leave in peace. She ran ahead to tell the women what they'd caught Koya doing behind the kitchen.

Koya bit her lip and, though her little heart was breaking, she faced the three grinning adult faces in the balcony and curtsied.

"*N'ga Nenneh, ce nou wally*. . . . Thank you, N'ga Nenneh. I'm going home now."

But N'ga Nenneh understood. She loved children too much to have one of them come to her home and return looking so hurt.

"Don't mind them, Koya," she said softly, resting her hand on Koya's head. "Are you sure you won't stay a little longer?"

"No, thank you, N'ga. I want to go now."

She mustered what rag of dignity she had left—in spite of her finery she was feeling utterly naked—and walked out of the house.

The way home was blurred through the tears that swam in front of her eyes. But she was too well-bred to cry in the street.

Back home, an astonished N'ga Fatmatta saw Koya come into the back yard with her features set in a mask of hatred horrible for a child of her age.

"My darling!" the mother cried in anguish. A stab shot painfully through and through her chest as she ran up the yard to Koya. "What have they done to you *again*?"

Koya stood perfectly still. Her mouth tightened and drew down fiendishly at the corners. She was completely spoilt. But that afternoon's experience, even more than the drubbing N'ga Nenneh had given her the fortnight before, had ruined the sacred image of herself her mother's idolatry had helped to create in her mind. As an only child it was, in fact, the beginning of her education. But, as a child, she saw it as the end of the world. The sides of her nose quivered violently. She knotted her fists till the knuckles showed white through the brown skin. Something nasty, sour and intensely bitter felt to be rising inside her chest. Vaguely, instinctively, she knew in a flash the hurt she was feeling stemmed from the woman before her.

"N'ga Fatmatta," she drew in a deep breath and burst out in a passion that made her little body tremble from head to foot, "N'ga Fatmatta—I *hate* you!"

"*Koya!*" the woman looked as shocked as if someone had hit her violently in the pit of the stomach.

"I *hate* you! How I *hate* you, N'ga Fatmatta!"

N'ga Fatmatta grabbed the child to her chest and burst into tears over her:

"Koya! O my little Koya—what have *they* done to you again?"

A Stranger from Lagos

CYPRIAN EKWENSI

She saw the way he looked at her when she was dancing and knew. Only a stranger would look like that at the *Umu-ogbo* dance, and only a man who had fallen would linger on her movements that way. Yet it embarrassed her when, sitting with the elderly woman in the bright hot afternoon she looked up from her sewing and saw him, asking questions. Though she knew he had seen her, he did not once look in her direction. He looked so transparently silly and pitiable.

She wondered what to do. Should she go to his help there—while her mother and her fiancé's mother were present? He seemed to be holding his own, telling fables, something about having missed his way, having recently crossed the Niger. . . . She would go to his aid. Suddenly she caught the hard look on his unsmiling face, a look full of the agony of desire.

Her legs felt too heavy to stir. Too many eyes. In Onitsha Town there were eyes on the walls. In the compound, eyes. In the streets, eyes. Such a small town, and so small-town minded. You went down Market Street, new or old and came back into Market Street, new or old, through a number of parallel feeder streets. Of course, Lilian had lived here since she was born and she knew the way to her lover's house without being seen even by day, and with her mother happily thinking she had gone to market. But once they saw her, once they saw a girl they knew and respected speaking with a glamorous-looking stranger like this one, or in a hotel, or standing in the streets and talking to a *man* in broad daylight, or daring to hold hands or to linger too long with a handshake, the eyes would roll and the tongues would wag and the girl's best course of action would be to leave the town or immediately be branded.

By the time Lilian looked up from her machine, he was gone. Her mother was coming back to the veranda.

"What did he say he wanted?"

"Do I know?" Her mother shrugged and made a face. "These young men from Lagos, who understand the language they speak?"

Lilian knew he had come for her but his courage had failed him. "Did he say his name, or where he lives?"

"He called a name. He is not of a family I know."

Unlike her mother, Lilian cared little for "families she knew". She judged young men by what her instincts told her, and this time, they told her she had made a conquest, full of strange enchantment. She put the scissors through the wax print and shaped it into a skirt that ended well above her knees. Her mother's eyes followed her with resentment. She called such tight clothes "mad people's clothes".

On her way down Market Street, Lilian wiggled in the new dress. Her hair had been newly done, and the loop ear-rings were large enough to play hula-hoop with. Someone stopped just behind her. She looked round. Eyes. From the windows of the hotels, bookshops, sign painters, mechanics' workshops. Eyes focused inquiringly on her and the stranger with such intentness that she felt like something projected on the big cinema screen in Market Street for all Onitsha to view. This was sensation.

He was tall and good-looking and did not show any embarrassment at being made the spectacle of Market Street. Of course, he did not know the town. He would scandalize her and leave her to it. That was the way of strangers. They left you to the gossips.

"I saw you in the compound—is that where you live?"

"Yes. Please, I am in a hurry. Who are you?"

"A stranger from Lagos. If you had time, I would tell you about my mission."

"Now?" She wrinkled her nose.

"I only stopped because I saw you. It is some days now since I came to your compound. I have wanted to see you."

"What for?" She asked unnecessarily, but he did not answer.

"You're from Lagos?" Lilian said.

"Yes."

The eyes from the hotels, bookshops, mechanical workshops, danced. A woman passer-by stopped and greeted Lilian by name. Lilian seemed to remember the face, and yet she could not place it. Her mind was focused on the stranger. "How is your baby?" asked the passer-by. "How is your mother?" Lilian mumbled something....

"You're from Lagos," Lilian said. "Here in Onitsha we do not stop and talk in the streets. It is not considered respectable. It is not done by decent girls of family. . . . Too many eyes. . . . Wait till evening. . . ."

"Till evening, then!"

Lilian walked away. She was conscious that he was watching her. She walked down the road and beyond the roundabout into the market stalls where they sell fish, and down the steps to the Niger. She hoped none of her mother's friends had seen her.

When she got home her mother's coldness was immediately apparent.

"Lilian, they said you were talking with a man in the street and he was holding your waist in the street!"

"Mama, that is impossible."

"A strange man, they said. Wearing Western Nigeria dress—*agbada* and so on. A man who lived many years in the West."

"Mama, he is a man of Nigeria. He only asked me the way to the post office. Mama, don't you believe the wicked gossip."

"But you must respect yourself. You don't want to do anything that would scandalize your father's name. He is a pensioner and worked hard for his good name. You parted from your first husband. Now you have a fiancé. You are staying with me and your father. You want for nothing. Hold this your fiancé well and give him no cause to brand you."

Lilian flashed angry eyes. "Yes, Ma." She bit her lips to hold back the tears.

In the evening they sat in the compound and watched the moonlight. The beams played on the banana fronds, on the pan roofs, on the mud walls. It created shadows welcomed by lovers. Whenever a car passed a fog of dust rose and obscured the street. It was a side street and cars did not pass often.

Lilian's eyes never left the entrance to the compound. On her way back from the market she had seen her fiancé. He had been her fiancé for three years. She bore him a son, and they quarrelled and she went to live in Lagos, leaving the boy with her mother. She did not like Lagos and came back. On her return she saw how glamorous she had become and promised to make good. He bought wine and brought it to her mother saying he still wanted her. She did not much care either way. He was a trader, and his ideas about love tallied more with her mother's than her own.

All she was praying for was that the stranger from Lagos should come quickly and leave before her fiancé arrived. Instinct warned her that her fiancé might decide to come, though this was not his night. Why had she not given the stranger a definite time? But in Onitsha love knows no definite time. Evening begins with the moonlight and ends when sleep comes.

She heard a sound outside. Her mother's voice. It was warm. She guessed it was her fiancé. He came in. She looked into his face, hard, possessive, confident. Every gesture of his showed that he owned her. Yet he had not completed the formalities. He had been at it all of three years. No one would say he was not a successful merchant.

He sat down and ordered six bottles of stout. She sat with him. She could not drink much this evening. She was sure that before the six bottles were empty something would happen. Her eyes never left the gate.

He talked. She listened. She heard a sound. It was her friend, Alice. Oh, if only they would both go out. But Alice had come, not to go out but to spend the evening, ironing clothes, plaiting her hair. She sat with them now and shared their drink. Lilian to distract herself talked loudly and laughed. But it was she who heard the new sound. The stranger was here.

To her surprise her fiancé stood up and greeted him familiarly.

"You are Mr. Okonma from Lagos. I have heard of you."

"How are you?"

"Have a drink?"

"No, thanks."

"I don't know you as a teetotaller," her fiancé said. He laughed, and began to explain how he met Mr. Okonma once when he went to buy things in Lagos. He lived in the same street, and . . .

"I don't touch alcohol, Mr.——"

"Anya is the name."

"I don't touch alcohol, Mr. Anya. You must be mistaken." He sat down, gloomily, and for a moment no one said anything.

"What may be your mission in Onitsha?"

Lilian did not like the way her fiancé was pursuing the stranger. She got up, talked to her friend. As they left, she had half her ear tuned to the conversation of the two men. To her it was conducted in an offended and offensive tone. She felt sorry and isolated, though she could not be sure whether or not the two men were getting at each other.

She and Alice retired and were absorbed with their hair-plaiting when the stranger left. She went back to her fiancé's table. He was sitting alone with empty bottles before him.

"I heard about him," he said in a high voice. "That's why I came here this night. Isn't he one of your lovers from Lagos? When they come to Onitsha the first thing they do is to look for you."

"I don't even know him."

He laughed harshly but said no more. She saw his intense anger and jealousy mounting. He did not linger any more but put on his hat and left. Lilian, puzzled, went back to Alice and resumed her plaiting.

"I have done no wrong. But I must be made to suffer all the same. Now we have quarrelled for a man I don't even know. It's like this, every day. Now he will go and mope and I will not see him for days. . ."

Alice said: "Too many eyes in this town. They see, they don't understand and they talk. . . . He should trust you more. After all, you're no kid. The other day, I was talking to a man . . ."

But Lilian was not listening. She was thinking of the stranger from Lagos and wishing she had been braver.

Coffee for the Road

ALEX LA GUMA

They were past the maize-lands and driving through the wide, low, semi-desert country that sprawled away on all sides in reddish brown flats and depressions. The land, going south, was scattered with scrub and thorn bushes, like a vast unswept carpet. Far to the right, the metal vanes of a windmill pump turned wearily in the faint morning breeze, as if it had just been wakened to set reluctantly about its duty of sucking water from the miserly earth. The car hurtled along the asphalt road, its tyres roaring along the black surface.

"I want another sandwich, please," Zaida said. She huddled in the blanketed space among the suitcases in the back. She was six years old and weary from the long, speeding journey, and her initial interest in the landscape had evaporated, so that now she sagged tiredly in the padded space, ignoring the parched gullies and stunted trees that whisked past.

"There's some in the tin. You can help yourself, can't you?" the woman at the wheel said, without taking her eyes off the road. "Do you want to eat some more, too, Ray?"

"Not hungry any more," the boy beside her replied. He was gazing out at the barbed-wire fence that streamed back outside the turned-up window.

"How far's it to Cape Town, Mummy?" Zaida asked, munching a sandwich.

"We'll be there tomorrow afternoon," the woman said.

"Will Papa be waiting?"

"Of course."

"There's some sheep," the boy, Ray, said. A scattering of farm buildings went by, drab, domino-shaped structures along a brown slope.

The mother had been driving all night and she was fatigued, her eyes red, with the feeling of sand under the lids, irritating the eyeballs. They had stopped for a short while along the road, the night before; parked in a gap off the road outside a small town. There had been nowhere to put up for the night: the hotels were for Whites only. In fact, only Whites lived in these towns and everybody else, except for the servants, lived in tumbledown mud houses in the locations beyond. Besides, they did not know anybody in this part of the country.

Dawn had brought depression, gloom, ill-temper, which she tried to control in the presence of the children. After having parked on that stretch of road until after midnight, she had started out again and driven, the children asleep, through the rest of the night.

Now she had a bad headache, too, and when Zaida said, "Can I have a meatball, Mummy?" she snapped irritably: "Oh, dash it all! It's there, eat it, can't you?"

The landscape ripped by, like a film being run backwards, red-brown, yellow-red, pink-red, all studded with sparse bushes and broken boulders. To the east a huge outcrop of rock strata rose abruptly from the arid earth, like a titanic wedge of purple-and-lavender-layered cake topped with chocolate-coloured boulders. The car passed over a stretch of gravel road and the red dust boiled behind it like a flame-shot smoke-screen. A bird, its long, ribbon-like tail streaming behind it, skimmed the brush beyond the edge of the road, flitting along as fast as the car.

"Look at that funny bird, Mummy," the boy, Ray, cried, and pressed his face to the dust-filmed glass.

The mother ignored him, trying to relax behind the wheel, her feet moving unconsciously, but skilfully, on the pedals in the floor. She thought that it would have been better to have taken a train, but Billy had written that he'd need the car because he had a lot of contacts to visit. She hoped the business would be better in the Cape. Her head ached, and she drove automatically. She was determined to finish the journey as quickly as possible.

Ray said, "I want some coffee." And he reached for the thermos flask on the rack under the dashboard. Ray could take care of himself, he did not need to have little things done for him.

"Give me some, too," Zaida called from the back, among the suitcases.

"Don't be greedy," Ray said to her. "Eating, eating, eating."

"I'm not greedy. I want a drink of coffee."

"You had coffee this morning."

"I want some more."

"Greedy. Greedy."

"Children," the mother said wearily, "children, stop that arguing."

"He started first," Zaida said.

"Stop it. Stop it," the mother told her.

Ray was unscrewing the cap of the thermos. When it was off he drew the cork and looked in. "Man, there isn't any," he said. "There isn't any more coffee."

"Well, that's just too bad," the mother said.

"I want a drink," Zaida cried. "I'm thirsty, I want some coffee."

The mother said wearily: "Oh, all right. But you've got to wait. We'll get some somewhere up the road. But wait, will you?"

The sun was a coppery smear in the flat blue sky, and the countryside, scorched yellow and brown, like an immense slice of toast, quivered and danced in the haze. The woman drove on, tiredly, her whole mind rattling like a stale nut. Behind the sun-glasses her eyes were red-rimmed and there was a stretched look about the dark, handsome, Indian face. Her whole system felt taut and stretched like the wires of a harp, but too tight so that a touch might snap any one of them.

The miles purred and growled and hummed past: flat country and dust-coloured *koppies*, the baked clay *dongas* and low ridges of hills. A shepherd's hut, lonely as a lost soul, crouched against the shale-covered side of a flat hill; now and then a car passed theirs, headed in the opposite direction, going north, crashing by in a shrill whine of slip-stream. The glare of the sun quivered and quaked as if the air was boiling.

"I want some coffee," Zaida repeated petulantly. "We didn't have no coffee."

"We'll buy some coffee," her mother told her. "We'll buy some for the road as soon as we get to a café. Stop it, now. Eat another sandwich."

"Don't want sandwich. Want coffee."

A group of crumbling huts, like scattered, broken cubes, passed them in a hollow near the road and a band of naked, dusty brown children broke from the cover of a sheep-pen, dashing to the side of the road, cheering and waving at the car. Ray waved back, laughing, and then they were out of sight. The wind-scoured metal pylon of a water-pump drew up and then disappeared too. Three black men trudged in single file along the roadside, looking ahead into some unknown future, wrapped in tattered, dusty blankets, oblivious of the heat, their heads shaded by the ruins of felt hats. They did not waver as the car spun past them but walked with fixed purpose.

The car slowed for a steel-slung bridge and they rumbled over the dry, rock-strewn bed of a stream. A few sheep, their fleeces black with dust, sniffed among the boulders, watched over by a man like a scarecrow.

At a distance, they passed the coloured location and then the African location, hovels of clay and clapboard strewn like discoloured dice along a brown slope, with tiny people and ant-like dogs moving among them. On another slope the name of the town was spelled out in whitewashed boulders.

The car passed the sheds of a railway siding, with the sheep milling in corrals, then lurched over the crossing and bounced back on to the roadway. A Coloured man went by on a bicycle, and they drove slowly past the nondescript brown front of the Railway Hotel, a line of stores, and beyond a burnt hedge a group of white men with red, sunskinned, wind-honed faces sat drinking at tables in front of another hotel with an imitation Dutch-colonial façade. There was other traffic parked along the dusty, gravel street of the little town: powdered cars and battered pick-up trucks, a wagon in front of a feed store. An old Coloured man swept the pavement in front of a shop, his reed broom making a hissing sound, like gas escaping in spurts.

Two white youths, pink-faced and yellow-haired, dressed in khaki shirts and shorts, stared at the car, their eyes suddenly hostile at the sight of a dark woman driving its shiny newness, metal fittings factory-smooth under the film of road dust. The car spun a little cloud behind it as it crept along the red-gravel street.

"What's the name of this place, Mummy?" the boy, Ray, asked.

"I don't know," the mother replied, tired, but glad to be able to slow down. "Just some place in the Karroo."

"What's the man doing?" Zaida asked, peering out through the window.

"Where?" Ray asked, looking about. "What man?"

"He's gone now," the little girl said. "You didn't look quickly." Then, "Will we get some coffee now?"

"I think so," the mother said. "You two behave yourselves and there'll be coffee. Don't you want a cool drink?"

"No," the boy said. "You just get thirsty again, afterwards."

"I want a lot of coffee with lots of sugar," Zaida said.

"All right," the mother said. "Now stop talking such a lot."

Up ahead, at the end of a vacant lot, stood a café. Tubular steel chairs and tables stood on the pavement outside, in front of its shaded windows. Its front was decorated with old Coca Cola signs and painted menus. A striped awning shaded the tables. In the wall facing the vacant space was a foot-square hole where non-Whites were served, and a group of ragged Coloured and African people stood in the dust and tried to peer into it, their heads together, waiting with forced patience.

The mother drove the car up and brought it to a stop in front of the café. Inside a radio was playing and the slats of the venetian blinds in the windows were clean and dustless.

"Give me the flask," the mother said, and took the thermos bottle from the boy. She unlatched the door. "Now, you children, just sit quiet. I won't be long."

She opened the door and slid out and, standing for a moment on the pavement, felt the exquisite relief of loosened muscles. She stretched herself, enjoying the almost sensual pleasure of her straightened body. But her head still ached badly and that spoiled the momentary delight which she felt. With the feeling gone, her brain was tired again and the body once more a tight-wound spring. She straightened the creases out of the smart tan suit she was wearing but left the jacket unbuttoned. Then, carrying the thermos flask, she crossed the sidewalk, moving between the plastic-and-steel furniture into the café.

Inside, the café was cool and lined with glass cases displaying cans and packages like specimens in some futuristic museum. From somewhere at the back of the place came the smell and sound of potatoes being fried. An electric fan buzzed on a shelf and two gleaming urns, one of tea and the other of coffee, steamed against the back wall.

The only other customer was a small white boy with tow-coloured hair, a face like a near-ripe apple and a running nose. He wore a washed-out print shirt and khaki shorts, and his dusty bare feet were yellow-white and horny with cracked callouses. His pink, sticky mouth explored the surface of a lollipop while he scanned the covers of a row of outdated magazines in a wire rack.

Behind the glass counter and a trio of soda fountains a broad, heavy woman in a green smock thumbed through a little stack of accounts, ignoring the group of dark faces pressing around the square hole in the side wall. She had a round-shouldered, thick body and reddish-complexioned face that looked as if it had been sand-blasted into its component parts: hard plains of cheeks and knobbly cheek-bones and a bony ridge of nose that separated twin pools of dull grey; and the mouth a bitter gash, cold and malevolent as a lizard's, a dry, chapped and serrated pink crack.

She looked up and started to say something, then saw the colour of the other woman and, for a moment, the grey pools of the eyes threatened to spill over as she gaped. The thin pink youth writhed like a worm as she sought for words.

"Can you fill this flask with coffee for me, please?" the mother asked.

The crack opened and a screech came from it, harsh as the sound of metal rubbed against stone. "Coffee? My Lord Jesus Christ!" the voice screeched. "A bedamned *coolie* girl in here!" The eyes started in horror at the brown, tired, handsome Indian face with its smart sunglasses, and the city cut of the tan suit. "Coolies, Kaffirs and Hottentots outside," she screamed. "Don't you bloody well know? And you talk *English*, too, hey!"

The mother stared at her, startled, and then somewhere inside her something went off, snapped like a tight-wound spring suddenly loose, jangling shrilly into action, and she cried out with disgust as her arm came up and the thermos flask hurtled at the white woman.

"Bloody white trash!" she cried. "Coolie yourself!"

The flask spun through the air and, before the woman behind the counter could ward it off, it struck her forehead above an eyebrow, bounced away, tinkling as the thin glass inside the metal cover shattered. The woman behind the counter screeched and clapped a hand to the bleeding gash over her eye, staggering back. The little boy dropped his lollipop with a yelp and dashed out. The dark faces at the square hatch gasped. The dark woman turned and stalked from the café in a rage.

She crossed the sidewalk, her brown face taut with anger and opened the door of her car furiously. The group of non-Whites from the hole in the wall around the side of the building came to the edge of the vacant lot and stared at her as she slammed the door of the car and started the motor.

She drove savagely away from the place, her hands gripping the wheel tightly, so that the knuckles showed yellow through the brown skin. Then she recovered herself and relaxed wearily, slowing down, feeling tired again, through her anger. She took her time out of town while the children gazed, sensing that something was wrong.

Then the boy, Ray, asked, "Isn't there any coffee, Mummy? And where's the flask?"

"No, there isn't any coffee," the mother replied. "We'll have to do without coffee, I'm afraid."

"I wanted coffee," the little girl, Zaida, complained.

"You be good," the mother said. "Mummy's tired. And please stop chattering."

"Did you lose the flask?" Ray asked.

"Keep quiet, keep quiet," the woman told him, and they lapsed into silence.

They drove past the edge of the town, past a dusty service station with its red pumps standing like sentinels before it. Past a man carrying a huge bundle of firewood on his head, and past the last buildings of the little town: a huddle of whitewashed cabins with chickens scrabbling in the dooryard, a sagging shearing-shed with a pile of dirty bales of wool inside, and a man hanging over a fence, watching them go by.

The road speared once more into the yellow-red-brown countryside and the last green trees dwindled away. The sun danced and jiggled like a midday ghost across the expressionless earth, and the tyres of the car rumbled faintly on the black asphalt. There was some traffic ahead of them but the woman did not bother to try to overtake.

The boy broke the silence in the car by saying, "Will Papa take us for drives?"

"He will, I know," Zaida said. "I like this car better than Uncle Ike's."

"Well, *he* gave us lots of rides," Ray replied. "There goes one of those funny birds again."

"Mummy, will we get some coffee later on?" Zaida asked.

"Maybe, dear. We'll see," the mother said.

The dry and dusty landscape continued to flee past the window on either side of the car. Up ahead the sparse traffic on the road was slowing down and the mother eased her foot on the accelerator.

"Look at that hill," the boy, Ray, cried. "It looks like a face."

"Is it a real face?" Zaida asked, peering out.

"Don't be silly," Ray answered. "How can it be a real face? It just *looks* like a face."

The car slowed down and the mother, thrusting her head through her window, peering forward past the car in front and saw the roadblock beyond it.

A small riot-van, a Land Rover, its windows and spotlight screened with thick wire mesh, had been pulled up half-way across the road, and a dusty automobile parked opposite to it, forming a barrier with just a car-wide space between them. A policeman in khaki shirt, trousers and flat cap leaned against the front fender of the automobile and held a Sten-gun across his thighs. Another man in khaki sat at the wheel of the car, and a third policeman stood by the gap, directing the traffic through after examining the drivers.

The car ahead slowed down as it came up to the gap, the driver pulled up and the policeman looked at him, stepped back and waved him on. The car went through, revved and rolled away.

The policeman turned towards the next car, holding up a hand, and the mother driving the car felt the sudden pounding of her heart. She braked and waited, watching the khaki-clad figure strolling the short distance towards her.

He had a young face, with the usual red-burned complexion of the land, under the shiny leather bill of the cap. He was smiling thinly but the smile did not reach his eyes which bore the hard quality of chips of granite. He wore a holstered pistol at his waist and, coming up, he turned towards the others and called, "This looks like the one."

The man with the Sten-gun straightened but did not come forward. His companion inside the car just looked across at the woman.

The policeman in the road said, still smiling slightly: "Ah, we have been waiting for you. You didn't think they'd phone ahead, hey?"

The children in the car sat dead still, staring, their eyes troubled. The mother said, looking out: "What's it all about?"

"Never mind what's it all about," the policeman said to her. "*You* know what it's all about." He looked her over and nodded. "*Ja*, darkie girl with brown suit and sun-glasses. You're under arrest."

"What's it all about?" the woman asked again. Her voice was not anxious, but she was worried about the children.

"Never mind. You'll find out," the policeman told her coldly. "One of those agitators making trouble here. Awright, listen." He peered at her with flint-hard eyes. "You turn the car around and don't try no funny business, hey? Our car will be in front and the van behind, so watch out." His voice was cold and threatening.

"Where are you taking us? I've got to get my children to Cape Town."

"I don't care about that," he said. "You make trouble here then you got to pay for it." He looked back at the police car and waved a hand. The driver of the police car started it up and backed and then turned into the road.

"You follow that motor car," the policeman said. "We're going back that way."

The woman said nothing but started her own car, manœuvring it until they were behind the police car.

"Now don't you try any funny tricks," the policeman said again. She stared at him and her eyes were also cold now. He went back to the riot-truck and climbed in. The car in front of her put on speed and she swung behind it, with the truck following.

"Where are we going, Mummy?" asked Zaida.

"You be quiet and behave yourselves," the mother said, driving after the police car.

The country-side, red-brown and dusty, moved past them: the landscapes they had passed earlier now slipping the other way. The flat blue sky danced and wavered and the parched, scrub-strewn scenery stretched away around them in the yellow glare of the sun.

"I wish we had some coffee," the little girl, Zaida, said.

Machado

ALFRED HUTCHINSON

Machado, Machado. The word cracked like a fire in the steadily falling drizzle. It caught me and impelled me onward; caught the others, too, so that they broke into a shuffle with the luggage on their heads. Then I stopped, breaking free from the ubiquitous, anxious magic. I stood in the rain—my paper bags sodden. The old man shuffled on with Mweli dragging himself behind to the cavernous iron structure that was the waiting-room.

I was free. I was wet. I went to find the cloakroom and thereafter to look for Nyasa House. The magic that I had fought and conquered was in the soaking streets, leaping with the droplets on the puddles. I had heard the word somewhere, I thought.

I stopped a tall barefooted African and asked him for Nyasa House.

"You want Machado?"

"No. Nyasa House."

I saw the old man plodding and muttering to himself. He came to me with vague eyes.

"Come," said our self-appointed guide. "Machado Store . . . and then Machado. . . ."

I barked at him. I didn't want any of his Machados—I wanted Nyasa House. He ignored me and strode forward, skirting the puddles of water. He was pressing forward and the old man had difficulty keeping up with us. I stopped and the tall man stopped too.

"Look, I'm going to find Nyasa House. . . . Here's a shilling." He moved on, dragging the old man with him.

Someone pointed out Nyasa House at the foot of a hill, three-quarters of a mile away. I thanked him and set off towards it. The tyres of cars sang and an occasional police car slid ghost-like up or down the street. Cyclists swept round the corner like an anxious line of army ants. This was Salisbury, I kept thinking, reminding myself, as if I did not know.

"Is Mr. Chungwa in?" I asked.

"No, he hasn't come yet. Probably the rain. Any message?"

"No. I'll wait."

I descended the steps. Things were not right. A police car stopped opposite where I stood and I walked on. I tried to picture how Chungwa would look in case he passed by. At the end of about half an hour I returned to the building. Chungwa had arrived.

"I am Alfred, George Hutchinson's brother," I said to the short untidy man with protruding teeth.

Something collapsed inside me. I felt with a conviction that he could not help me. We shook hands and I babbled my business to him. I was on my way to Nyasaland and wanted a permit to travel through Portuguese territory.

"Machado? That's at the Machado office. These people are going that way now."

Outside Nyasa House I ran into the old man again. He was with a group of other Nyasas and one of them had a guard's cap on his head. We swung back to the town in the steadily falling rain.

Suddenly I had lost my city poise. We trotted across the streets, narrowly missing being hit by cars. We stood huddled and fearful at street corners. The silent panic infected me. The man with the guard's cap led the way, lifting and sniffing like a suspicious buck testing the wind. We swung from street to street and doubled on our tracks. We were lost. I was annoyed but helpless.

Machado Store . . . Machado Store. The words passed from lip to lip as we swung and twisted, beating robots; bringing smiles to the passers-by.

I confronted the leader.

"Ask man. Ask someone. What do you want?"

"Machado Store . . . Our things are there. . . ."

"You bought things and now you don't know where the store is. . . ."

The man sniffed and snorted. He set off dragging us along. I asked someone for the Machado Store. We struck out in that direction. I asked another. And we struck out in the opposite direction. We stood wavering at street corners. We were lost and our leader was magnificent, heroic almost in our lostness.

We staggered up a flight of stairs past the first floor and stood outside the open door of an office. An African couple sat inside—waiting. Two African clerks made entries. I moved forward. Yes, this was the Machado office. A line formed behind me. I didn't care that this was not the store.

The clerk said something unintelligible in Portuguese. I took a shot in the dark. I gave him my name. He wrote it on a form and banged it with a rubber stamp. I handed him a half-crown. "Next," he said. I should have got a sixpence back in change. But it did not matter.

Alone, my city poise came back to me. Motor cars, robots—the whole paraphernalia of a city, held no terrors for me. I had lost my bearings but there was no cause for alarm. Two schoolboys walked with me towards Nyasa House where Chungwa had told me to meet him at twelve o'clock.

"Ready," Chungwa said, locking his office. "Lots of work."

I had expressed a desire to meet Nyirenda about whom George had spoken in the warmest terms. Cyclists swept past us towards the location. We walked on, hoping to find a taxi, and presently one came. We piled into it heading for Highfield.

Nyirenda had moved and the new occupants did not know where he had gone. But Chungwa thought he would find the new home. We walked through the streets of Highfield which was just another Meadowlands, with neat, hive-like, tedious little houses. . . .

"George's elder brother. He looks younger." The smiling pretty woman, Mrs. Nyirenda, led us to a bare room containing a table and two chairs. "Our things are at the storage. This perpetual shifting. . . ."

Blackmore Nyirenda had not returned from work. He had been returning late during the past few days and spoke of straightening the firm's accounts. Would I wait? Yes, the Umtali train would only be leaving at 8.30 p.m. How was George? Did he know they were married? Au, George's brother! She disappeared into the kitchen to prepare some lunch.

Machado, Chungwa explained, had been a Portuguese consul who had issued permits to Nyasa returning home to enable them to pass through Portuguese territory. Machado was now the name of the permit. And the Machado Store? The consul ran a store and the Amajoyini were induced to touch the store before going to the office. After buying something from the store, the permit was sort of assured.

We had lunch and set out to find a telephone. The full name of the township was Highfield Village Settlement and it was seven miles from town. The trouble, Chungwa explained, was transport. Buses were few and the fares high. Except for Alexandra Township I had not seen so many bicycles before.

When we eventually found a telephone. Chungwa did not know Nyirenda's number. We returned to the house to wait.

Blackmore Nyirenda stepped into the house as night fell over Highfield. He was a tall and handsome young man.

"George's brother's here," I heard his wife saying.

"But I heard you were in the Treason Trial."

"And still am, as a matter of fact."

"You're spending a few days with us?"

"I wish I could, but you understand—I must keep moving."

He was glad to meet me and so was I to meet him. We warmed to each other like old friends. He did not know what to do for me. He ordered beer from a nearby shebeen, and more came. How was George? Fine, very much alive. We mellowed. Chungwa became light-headed and laughed. And we all laughed with him.

Nyirenda radiated warmth. He was solid without being stodgy. He held the post of accountant with a big Salisbury firm and was doing further studies. He gave me an address in Ghana. When he looked at his watch it was time to leave for the station. He packed some beers in my paper bag and pressed me to accept one pound pocket money.

The dilapidated Morris banged to the station. At every bump it threatened to fly to pieces. Chungwa laughed. I laughed. I still had to collect my things from the cloakroom and buy my ticket. But there was no urgency.

The train is about to pull off and Chungwa is at the window. "It sounds like a story from a book. . . . Escape and all that. . . ." And I admit that perhaps it does sound like one. A man comes into the compartment. This is the Umtali train? No. It's the Bulawayo train and we had better hurry. Hell, man, I say laughing. I nearly woke up in Bulawayo. Lucky that chap came in. But this one is the Umtali train. There can be no doubt about it.

The gong sounds. It's like a story from a book, Chungwa is saying, as he clasps my hand and walks along the slowly moving train. He will send a telegram to two chaps to meet me at Blantyre—my "cousins".

I look about the compartment and promise myself a good night's sleep. Panic seizes me. Supposing I had returned to Bulawayo, supposing that chap had not come into the compartment. I have deserted the old man and Mweli who are travelling in a fourth-class compartment, packed and sweating.

When I awoke the following morning the train had gone dead. There was no sign on it. Then someone came in carrying a broom. The train had been in Umtali a long time and was getting ready for the return journey. I opened the last bottle of beer and gave the cleaner a drink.

I am back with the old man and Mweli again. About five hundred of us are sitting in the waiting-room. Some are sitting on railway sleepers, others on rails and a few are in the waiting-room, a huge filthy shed. It is the old scene. The scene that I know so well: the eternal luggage in front, the people standing, talking, eating. Children have joined us and their mothers are feeding them. I spot some of my friends who got me lost in Salisbury and cannot help laughing at the man in the guard's cap.

A group of W.N.L.A. stalwarts rise and there is a murmur of admiration and whispers of Mzilikazi. They form into an Indian file. We rise, too, and join the file as it stumbles past. The twisting burdened line is looped into sections. Forward. We jump down from the platform and on to the rails and struggle into sickly reddish brown carriages. I look for the old man and Mweli but they are nowhere to be seen. I realize now what the old man and Mweli have come to mean to me, after the long journey that has brought us so far.

We are jammed tight in the compartment. The whole train is a monstrosity: brown, filthy, wooden bunks and drinking water in the latrines. Gone is the short-lived comfort of last night. From Umtali to Blantyre the third class and fourth class are one.

We dip to the east. The hills are covered in dense bush and I rest my head on the brown steel table and think. I have travelled west to get to the east. Must I zigzag across Africa to reach Ghana? Weariness is taking hold of me. I am tired of being pushed about: tired of the filth, the constant lining up, tired of not being able to protest in any way. And I tell myself that since I have joined the bedraggled trail I must be truly one of it, live it. There must be no complaining, no protest. I must submit and take whatever comes.

I think I see things now. I think I see something which I did not see before. In Johannesburg I had known a disturbing sympathy for these people as they trotted like frightened animals with bundles on their heads across the streets, or stood trembling at a street corner waiting for the W.N.L.A. escort to take them across. Then I was an outsider. Now I am one of them.

We are dipping to the east, to the coast. Beira is some two hundred miles away.

Perhaps I should have joined in the assault of the W.N.L.A. *matshingilane* (police-boy) that time in Johannesburg outside the Metro Cinema and have struck a blow for these people and myself. Instead I had stood and watched, giving the assailants only my moral support. Why hadn't I got angry like the so-called tsotsis who had punched and kicked the police-boy and trampled on his W.N.L.A. cap? For surely the policeman had been wrong to hit the poor bewildered chap who had narrowly missed being hit by the car. "This is your brother," the tsotsis had said in English for the benefit of the Europeans, as they punched and kicked the police-boy—a middle-aged man.

Now we are at Machipanda in Portuguese territory. It is in the cup of the mountains, mountains whose tops are in the clouds. Homesteads peep through the bush and African kraals are grey spots in the shades of green. The village is below the station whose platform has borders of flaming flowers.

An Indian is sitting on a box on the platform. In front of him are two four-gallon tins, a stack of enamel plates and two large baskets, one containing bananas. African boys are shouting the wares.

We get off the train and stumble across the rails to the platform. What is it again? What is it? Our things are to be searched. But why?

Nobody knows. We form a double line on the platform, but are driven away down a slope off the platform. There are about five hundred of us: men, women and children—but mostly men. We form two rows facing each other. Red-fezzed, barefooted African policemen walk up and down the lines. And a Portuguese in short sleeves and grey flannels surveys us from the top of an earthwork and faces the magnificent mountain to the south. He is stocky, with a bull neck and a shrunken mouth as if parched by cruelty. The flag of Portugal flies from the top of the station building.

We spread our things for inspection on the damp brown soil. Hazel's poor bag . . . if it could have known that one day it would travel like this. . . . The red-fezzed policemen dig into cases and fling things about and pass on. And those who have been searched begin to pack, to stuff things back into the cases. One with more temerity than the rest of us asks a policeman what he is looking for. And the policeman replies that we know.

My policeman is old and perfunctory. He takes one dig into the bag and passes on. And while stuffing things back into the bag I ask Mweli and the old man: Will it happen again? They don't know—perhaps it will; perhaps it won't.

"S'bali, when I get home," says Mweli, "I'll tell them that the way to Nyasaland is hard. . . ." And he looks sorrowfully at his crushed, expensive green hat.

The Portuguese on the earthworks barks an order in a surprisingly thin voice. We lift our things on to our heads and stumble back to the train and I make sure not to lose my friends again. Mweli is having difficulty with his case, and I take it and give him my things to carry.

"S'bali, this illness has finished me."

The heat drives us out of the compartments into the corridors and those who have found a space at the windows hang limply over. Others walk along the rails near the train and some others have vanished, probably to the village. Men in vests show the bulges of rock muscles gained in the months underground. Nobody knows when the train will leave and nobody believes the Indian who says that it will only be leaving in the late afternoon. The latrines at the end of the corridors begin to stink and big, bright green flies buzz noisily.

Through the window, a white building shows its head with BAR written in bold black letters on its forehead.

The Indian is perched on his box under the windows of the train. In front of him are his two tins of soup and tea, and his baskets of rice and bananas. Tea is being sold at twopence a mug, but I pay a tickey. It is too hot for an argument or for bargaining. I take a sip and throw the tea on to the rails, hoping that he will see me. It tastes like no tea I have drunk. I buy a plate of rice and soup for two shillings but cannot swallow the mush.

A change was coming over the old man. I saw it coming and dreaded it. A seed of confidence was germinating, had taken root in fact. His nips of snuff from the Royal Baking Powder tin were marked with confidence and his silences were charged with self-importance. But as the old man's confidence increased, so did Mweli become more critical of him. "Kehla (old man) is funny," Mweli would say, not caring whether the old man heard him or not.

The old man was giving me a preview of Nyasaland: "You'll see, S'bali, you'll see Nyasaland. . . . We are British . . . British. . . . Not this Portuguese. . . ." The old man flung a deprecating arm over the entire territory. "We are British, British. . . ."

"Ag, you and your British, British!" said Mweli scornfully. "Do you hear Kehla, S'bali? Now he's talking like a real Nyasa. . . . A real Brak Scosh. . . . Did you ever see people so black and yet they call themselves Scotsmen!" The old man was looking out of the window through his wire spectacles. "S'bali, you never saw anything more stupid than a Nyasa. . . . All we know is to chase after women. Did you ever hear a Nyasa tell a woman: Thatha Zonke, shiya lopasi kuphela. . . . Take everything, leave only the pass. . . ." Mweli sniffed. "British! British!"

"You'll see for yourself, S'bali," said the old man, returning from surveying the country-side. "The trains are driven by us Blacks . . . yes, you and me. . . . There isn't all the nonsense about passes . . . no tsotsis . . . you can get drunk, S'bali, and sleep in the road and no one will trouble you. . . . Yes, we buy European liquor from the stores. . . . People rule in Nyasaland. . . ."

"If Nyasaland is so wonderful, ask him what he wanted in South

Africa all these years, S'bali, ask him. S'bali, there are no greater fools than we Nyasas. . . . There are only two things we know: chase after women and buy swanky clothes. . . . Blacker than pitch and still call themselves Scotsmen. . . . British! British!"

The price of rice and soup had fallen. Boys walked up and down the corridors carrying plates and shouting: "Ninepence rice! Ninepence rice!" The sun was dipping to the west. The heat was terrific. Clouds were piling over the mountains. The lavatory stank. The flies buzzed, noisier than before.

"Look at them, S'bali. Look what I have been telling you." I followed Mweli's gaze in the direction of the town.

Some of our chaps were returning to the train. They were hot. They were drunk. They swayed and stumbled over the rails, their hob-nailed boots crunching the cobbles. One or two collared bottles. Another broke into a futile song while yet another twanged a no-tune on a home-made guitar. The leader wore his wire spectacles on his squashed mean hat.

There was a look of triumph in Mweli's sick eyes. But the old man was again looking out of the window. "The biggest fools on earth," said Mweli finally and conclusively.

The train shunted and banged into trucks. We rocked; we laughed. The old man broke ecstatic Xhosa. . . . "Tshini Mfondini. (Gee, fellow!)." He let out feeble shouts of "Nyasaland! Nyasaland!" Mweli looked at him pityingly and shook his head.

Night. A lovely night in some Portuguese village. Night and Thonga girls with breasts as hard as unripe mangoes. The moon has shot the clouds into heavenly milk and the trees stand dreaming. Crickets have taken possession of the night; crickets and strident bull-frogs. A fellow goes plucking a no-tune on the home-made guitar—for the girls with breasts like unripe mangoes. . . .

The compartment is an oven. Mweli isn't feeling too good and is sprawled on the sticky brown bunk. The old man sits ruminating, thinking, perhaps, of the son he will meet after fourteen years. I lie on the top bunk and think . . . think in images of heavenly milk and Thonga girls with mango breasts. . . .

A Man Can Try

ELDRED DUROSIMI JONES

"Well, I think this is very satisfactory"—old Pa Demba, the Paramount Chief of Bomp, looked at D. C. Tullock with genuine admiration. "I think you have been very generous to Marie. I really do not see how anyone could have been fairer than you have been—one hundred pounds a year for Marie and a good secondary school education for the boy." Pa Demba turned to Marie: "You should count yourself lucky to have had D. C. Tullock for your husband. I have seen many girls who have lived with men like the D.C. for many years, only to be abandoned at the end without any provision. According to this paper, you and your child have been well provided for. And now you are free to marry anyone you wish. I am going to sign as a witness. Do you agree to the terms?"

As Marie nodded in dumb agreement the tears which had stood poised on the corners of her eyes rolled down her chubby brown cheeks. Tullock looked away through the open office window, and gazed unseeingly at the town beyond. The figure of Marie sitting there stroking the hair of her son Tambah who stood between her knees, was to him a silent indictment. She sat scarcely moving except for her hands which moved so slowly and tenderly along the boy's head that she looked perfectly still. She was like a statue of maternity—mother and child. Tullock thought, she and I have shared in the miracle of creation and here I am about to desert her and the boy. But he persuaded himself that it had to be, although even in the moment of decision he could not avoid condemning himself.

As for Marie, she just sat there stroking her little boy's hair—he had fine silky hair—she was glad that he resembled Tullock in that feature at least. She would always remember him by it. She felt no bitterness at Tullock's departure, only sorrow—intense sorrow. She had known from the first that this moment would come. In their type of relationship, parting was as inevitable as death; but like death, when it actually came, it was still something of a shock. She had served her turn with Tullock. They had been happy within the limits of their relationship for eight years. All the women had called her Marie Tullock, although there was no legal bond between them. Now, Tullock was leaving the service to join his father's law firm—the richer for his experience in Africa. Of course he could not take Marie with him. So he had devised this settlement.

In spite of his generosity by prevailing standards, Tullock felt rather cheap in his own eyes. For unlike some others in his position, he had the uncomfortable habit of judging everyone by a single standard. He could not have disentangled himself from a girl of his own race so easily. He knew this, and the very fact that he could shake off Marie without any complications with a gratuity of his own naming, made him ill at ease with himself.

He, too, had been happy with Marie, at least, quite content with her. She was pretty, cooked well, was affectionate but unobtrusive. True she couldn't read Shakespeare—couldn't read anything at all in fact. The world situation left her completely unmoved, for she knew nothing about what happened outside the town of Bomp where she had lived all her life. In fact to quote Prothero—Old Prothero, the father of the provincial administration—"a barbarian, a pretty barbarian, but a barbarian like the rest of them". It was he who had helped Tullock solve his little problem, although he did not see what the fuss was all about. He saw no problem. He had laughed at Tullock's solemnity. "Look, my boy!" he had said, with his hand on Tullock's shoulder, "I've had a woman—and children—in every district I've worked in. The only rules are—never get your heart involved and never move with a woman from one district to another; creates no end of trouble. After each station, I just paid them off; no problem at all. Glad of the money they were, too. They were soon snapped up by the native burghers of the district. Don't let this worry you, Boy. Pay Marie off. She'll forget you soon enough. And as for you, once on the boat you'll soon forget about her."

Tullock had secretly wondered how one who was so meticulous over the jot and tittle of colonial regulations could be so casual over matters of the heart. But he checked his flow of self-righteousness. Who was he to judge anyway. He was no better than Prothero—in fact he was worse. For while Prothero had never thought his relationship with African women came within his ordinary moral code, he knew that what he was doing was wrong. He had, however, taken Prothero's advice and had arranged a settlement for Marie. He had taken infinite trouble to make it legal—an inadequate sop to his conscience—but he thought it was the least he could do. So here they were signing the agreement.

Pa Demba signed his name, rose and took his leave, still commending Tullock's generosity. The three who were left sat on in silence. There seemed to be nothing to say. Tullock was overcome with shame, Marie with grief. Tambah was just bewildered. He knew his mother's tears were caused by Tullock but he did not know how.

"Well, Marie, this is good-bye."

Marie's eyes welled, her bosom heaved, but she uttered not a sound. She had dreaded this moment almost as soon as she realized how much she liked the feel of Tullock's hair; how longingly she listened for the honk of his horn as he swerved madly into the compound from the office. In her moments of greatest happiness with him she had always felt the foretaste of this parting in her mouth. Now it was here.

"I have got the court messengers to take your things to your uncle's house. Good-bye, Marie; you know I have to go, don't you?"

Marie nodded and tried to smile. She turned suddenly to the door, grasped Tambah's hand and hurried away. Tullock watched her disappear down the drive without once turning to look back. He knew that a part of his heart had gone with her.

Trevor Tullock's decision to return home was not as sudden as it seemed—the reason had been on his mind for quite some time. He had been engaged for three years, to the daughter of his father's oldest friend—a London stockbroker. Only the omnivorousness of the human mind could have accommodated two such different women as Marie and Denise, even at different times. Marie, African, illiterate, soft and melting, was entirely devoted to Tullock—she lived only for him. Denise was English, sophisticated, highly educated and a very forward member of the central office of her political party. She was intensely alert and held strong convictions on almost every subject, particularly the rights of women. She had made it quite clear that she had no intention of leaving her life in England and burying herself in the wilds of Africa. She was too engrossed in what was going on in England. In her own country she was part of the scene. She was always addressing women's gatherings, organizing demonstrations, canvassing on behalf of the party from door to door, and this sort of work she could not bear to leave. So Trevor had to make up his mind to return home if he wanted to marry her. He had put it off long enough already and had just been helped to make up his mind by a long pleading letter from home. "What would people think?" his mother had pleaded. . . . So Trevor had decided that he could decently put it off no longer.

In the whirl of official farewells and the thousand and one things he had to do to catch the boat, Trevor Tullock had had little time to think of his future life. He had taken it all for granted. On the boat, however, he could not stop himself from thinking. But it was the image of Marie that kept coming to his mind, pushing out that of Denise—Marie sitting with Tambah between her knees. He did not think very much about the boy and even this worried him, for after all he was his own flesh and blood. He tried to shut off thoughts of Marie, but he found it difficult. He tried because he thought it was his duty. But he could not. He tried to drown his thoughts in drink, but that only made him morbid. He began to look forward to his arrival in England—England with its distractions and Denise!

Denise! This intrusion of Denise into his thoughts startled him. Now that he started thinking about her, doubts about their relationship came rushing into his mind. Doubts of the most fundamental kind. Did he really want to marry Denise? He brushed the question aside. It did not matter. He had to. So the boat bore him speedily along to a fate from which his mind equally speedily shrank.

At Liverpool, Trevor leaned over the rails and peered into the Severn mist, trying to discern the faces of the visitors on the balcony. There was his mother and yes—beside her was Denise.

His mother waved enthusiastically and Denise put up her right hand in a jerky, almost official act of welcome. Her trim tweeded business-like figure, through sheer force of contrast, brought back the image of the brown, loose-robed, welcoming frame of Marie. His life with her had been relaxed and easy. His home life in Africa had been so dramatically different from his office life. He had never had to argue with Marie. He was always sure of her willing obedience. Denise, on the other hand, had a quicksilver mind. Life with her was a constant mental tug-of-war. That was in fact the very quality in their relationship which had so exhilarated him during their undergraduate days. Now, the thought of a lifetime with her gave him a chilly feeling. The change from one woman to the other was like the physical change he had just made—exchanging the warmth and relaxation of Africa for the chill, bracing air of England. That economical wave of Denise's, symbolic of her detachment and her control over herself, made Trevor realize with horrid clarity that while he had changed, she had not. How had he changed? He tried to think. He had not lost his love for books; he still read them though, now, with a less belligerent attitude towards their authors than before. No doubt Denise, with whom he had cut many an author to pieces, would say that he was less acutely critical; but he still enjoyed reading—probably even more than before. What else? He certainly drank more, and more often than before. His drinking action was now a hearty swallow compared with the old sip and savour of those rather pretentious wine-tasting parties. He was now more concerned with the contents of the bottle than with the suggestions on the label. No doubt Denise would say his palate had coarsened. The more he thought, the more Trevor saw that life with Denise would now have to be one long never-ending effort to live up to a life he no longer believed in . . . "till death us do part".

He braced himself, picked up his bags, and strode down the gangway. "A man can try," he muttered to himself, already aiming a peck at Denise's proffered cheek.

I Can Face You

ELLIS KOMEY

You can see as you enter the "Black Sun" club in Africa that there is segregation. Not colour segregation or tribal. Not even class segregation but segregation nevertheless. And you don't need anybody to point it out to you. It is all there in the hall, grouped in three corners. In one corner, in their three-piece Savile Rows and bowler hats, are the Limeys. In another corner, with their tight pants and two patch back pockets and T-shirts, are the Yankees. In the third corner, often wearing fur caps and leather jackets, are the Reds. Each group is employed in outwitting, outdoing, outmanœuvring and outbluffing the others. The only thing they have in common is that they are all humans and of the same colour—more or less. That is about as far as their similarity goes, apart from the fact that each group, at the bottom of it all, is aiming at the same end. Even their language differs, though by instinct they should be speaking the same language. The Limeys speak English with what is supposed to be an Oxford accent; the Yankees speak English with a distorted blend which they insist on calling American; and the Reds, when it suits them or they want to be co-operative, speak English with the Moscow radio accent. But to make their personality felt, they often substitute a Russian word here and there for an English word in everyday use. For instance, while a Limey will say, "Not at all, old boy," and a Yankee will say, "Nothing doing, buddy," the Red will vomit out, "*Niet.*"

It is all very confusing how these three opposing groups came to meet at the "Black Sun" in the first place. Usually they can't stand being in the same place at the same time. But here, here they are still striving to outbid each other over which of their groups is best equipped to entertain this or that virgin girl. Not that there are lots of virgin girls in the "Black Sun" these days. On the contrary, there has not been a girl in the club for some time now. But they still come to avoid being outmanœuvred behind their backs and also to avoid being branded as cowards. So they come every night, waiting for the time when they will have to put their capabilities to the test.

It was the Limeys who first found the club. They patronized it proudly because, being aloof and conservative, they wanted to be left alone where they could chatter over their own days in London. And the "Black Sun" is in a suitably remote spot. But then a few months after they started going there, word went round why the Limeys were not being seen these days in the centre of other activities and the Yankees began to say that the Limeys were a dead lot anyway and they would kill the place. So the Yankees went in to give the place some life and so save it from dying because, they claimed, they were progressive and young in heart and mind. And of course the Reds got to hear about it and got vexed, protesting that it wasn't the Yankees who were progressive but they themselves. After all, they claimed, they were the first to send a sputnik into orbit while Davy Crockett was still looking for his rocket. If there was any saving to be done about the "Black Sun" they were better equipped to do it. So they went in, too, and the owner is now thinking of closing the place down because, he says, they just stand there as if waiting for something to blow up and telling him how he should run the place but not buying anything. And the very fact that they are there keeps away people who might otherwise patronize the place.

And that night the owner of the club is complaining to the three groups and pleading with them to leave him in peace when she walks in. None of them see her come in, they only smell her entrance. She smells fresh and when they all turn to look, she is standing in the centre of the floor. She is beautiful in a mysterious way. She is rich without giving the impression of knowing how rich she is and her appearance of innocence baffles them all. For a moment nobody moves. As if struck by lightning they stick firm where they stand. She looks tall and large and satisfied, yet there are traces of sadness in her eyes. The Yankees whistle and the Russians murmur something. But it is the Limeys who see the sadness in her eyes. One moves slowly forward and stretches out his hand.

"My dear," he says, "come and join our Commonwealth and soon, very soon, we will make you our queen."

When the Red sees him getting close to the lady, he moves confidently towards her. The Yankee, seeing the Red ready to interrupt, shoots forward, passing the Red and, with open arms, pushes the Limey aside.

"Say, honey," he says, "don't listen to that Limey."

"But I don't want to be a queen," the lady tells the Limey.

"That's right, baby," the Yankee says, "tell him, and don't listen to any of his Commonwealth talk, honey. Them Commonwealths are dying anyhow. Now you hitch up with me, honey, and I'll give you a Cadillac for Christmas, a sable for New Year and perhaps a trip into space and all the trimmings that go with press-button living. Now what d'ya say, honey?"

"My dear chap," the Limey says, "the gracious lady may not want all that and, besides, you are interfering in my territory. I saw her first."

"But I don't want a Cadillac for Christmas, a sable for New Year or a trip into space and all the trimmings that go with press-button living. All I want is. . . ."

"Bah," says the Red, who is now quite close to the lady and the other two. Don't listen to their capitalistic and imperialistic double-talk. *Niet!* It's all lies, *bourgeois* lies. What you want is socialism and I am the only one who can offer that to you with no strings attached. And when you feel free I can send you to the moon. I have already been and I know it's nice there, away from all these imperialists. I am the only friend you have got. If I had not been around they would have sucked you bone dry. . . ."

"You leave her alone," cries the Yankee, "and keep out of this if you know what's good for you. . . ."

"Is that a threat?" demands the Red.

"Take it any way you like, Red," replies the Yankee.

"Withdraw that threat," says the Red, "and apologize."

"I'll do no such thing."

"If you don't," says the Red, "I must warn you that one of these days I will shatter your headquarters to smithereens. And I have the capabilities to do it, too."

"You just try it once, just once," says the Yankee, "and see whose headquarters are blown to kingdom come. I have capabilities more powerful than yours, I can assure you."

"*Niet*," says the Red.

"Gentlemen," interrupts the Limey, "you must be calm. The situation can be approached calmly and it can only be solved democratically. In the first place, I am the one who spoke to the gracious lady first but, as we cannot all be with the same lady, the only solution is to allow the lady to choose for herself which one of us she would like to be with."

"That's right, Mac," agrees the Yankee.

"*Da*," says the Red.

"Furthermore, seeing that I was the first to speak to her, I feel it is my duty to guide her as to her choice. So if you two gentlemen . . ."

"*Niet!*" says the Red. "Colonialist double-talk."

"You keep out of this, Red," says the Yankee. "You go ahead, Mac. And don't forget that you have more in common with me than with the Red."

"As I was saying before I was interrupted," the Limey says. "If you two gentlemen will leave alone with the lady I am sure I can bring her to some agreeable solution."

"*Niet!*" says the Red. "I am staying to stop you from spreading false propaganda about me."

"Well," says the Yankee, "in that case, I'm staying too, if only to stop the Red from interfering and to protect the lady from his evil intentions."

The quarrel starts again with the Red, at the top of his voice, accusing the Yankee of imperialism and the Yankee accusing the Red of slavery and dictatorship. The virgin lady watches them, perplexed. All she had wanted was to be directed on her way to "Peaceville". The proprietor renews his pleading with the three groups that their presence in his club is not helping him at all and that they must leave him in peace. But they do not pay any attention to him or to his plea; for they believe their presence there is for the good of the place. Then, suddenly, they stop arguing and withdraw to their segregated corners. The virgin lady has already receded unobserved into the darkness to find her own way.

The Second Coming

JAMES MATTHEWS

Around him, on the slopes of the hill, sheep grazed. At their edge, a huge, long-haired dog stood on guard, red tongue hanging out and sides heaving. He stretched out a hand for the pig's bladder, filled with water, at his side and a tremor ran the length of his body. His hand stiffened and he slid from the flat stone on which he was seated. With eyes dilated, he lay staring at the sky.

Clouds took the shape of a man shrouded in a robe, head bare and a long beard which came to the waist. A voice boomed louder than thunder and yet the sound did not shatter his ear-drums.

"Jan! You are the chosen one!" Three times it was repeated then the clouds broke apart and resumed their white nothingness.

A wet warmness brought him to consciousness. The dog towered above him, whining distractedly, its tongue caressing his cheeks.

He dug his fingers in the dog's coat and pulled himself to a seated position. In front of him the sheep grazed calmly. Only the dog had sensed that some unaccountable thing had taken place. He fondled the dog behind its ears.

"Dankie, Held," he said, his controlled voice and soothing fingers reassuring the dog that everything was as it should be.

An adventurous sheep attracted the dog's attention as it hopped stiff-legged away. With a mock display of anger Held snapped at its heels to send it scampering back to the safety of the flock.

He was filled with the wonder of it. To him all things were simple. It was either black or white. If there were any shades in between, it escaped his simplicity.

A voice had spoken to him. It was no mortal voice but as to whether it could have been the voice of God he could not tell. The message was not clear but he did not doubt it. He was the chosen one. Chosen for what? He did not possess the answer. It was enough that it was said that he was the chosen one.

All through the afternoon his mind dwelt upon it and when the stretching shadows marked its lateness, he reluctantly got up and, with the aid of the dog, moved the sheep to the sheltered section of the hill where the camp was.

Darkness came with the suddenness of the country-side. One instant it was still light, then all objects lost their familiar shape and only his trained eye could make out their position.

A dassie was impaled on a length of wire and broiled in the open fire. At his feet the dog lay drooling, anticipating the pleasure of crunching dassie bones. The dassie sufficed both their needs and a mug of hot coffee, black, was drunk by him to end the meal. The dog jumped up and investigated the security of the flock enclosed by the rough *doring-bos* corral.

With one last look at the heavens, he wrapped himself in his blankets and was soon asleep.

Early the next day they were on the move to fresh pastures. Each day the sheep grazed on a different section of the hill. Several times, during the passing of the day, he looked at the sky and was disappointed when no voice boomed.

A cloud of dust on the trail below told of one of the farmer's rare visits. Five minutes later, the farmer dismounted from the back of the prancing horse. Tossing the reins to him, the farmer moved to the shade. After tying the bridle to a bush, he advanced hat in hand.

"More, Baas Dirk."

The farmer acknowledged the greeting with a grunt and a nod of the head. They walked towards the sheep, Jan a few paces behind. The farmer picked up a lamb and weighed it, put it on the ground, cornered a ewe, sank his hands into its wool and smiled, satisfied.

"Any losses from jackals?"

"Nee, Baas. One lamb broke its leg and I had to kill it."

"You sure you didn't break the leg so that you could eat it?"

"A good shepherd does not harm his flock."

The sincerity of the words appeased the farmer.

Without further speech, the farmer turned upon his heel and walked towards the tethered horse. Placing a leg into the stirrup, he anticipated the prancing to follow and when the horse reared he came down heavily on its back and tugged sharply at the reins so that the bit pressed into the soft velvet lining its mouth. The horse submitted and the farmer, pleased, inched it forward until it was almost on top of the shepherd. From his height he spoke.

"Saturday night Ampies will be at the camp with your supplies. Two months from now you bring all the sheep down to the farm for shearing and God help you if there is a loss of lambs."

Wheeling the horse, he sent it spurting with a slash of his riding crop and the shepherd was left coughing from the dust thrown into his face by the horse's hooves.

Twice, before the arrival of Ampies, the voice spoke to him and each time his body stiffened and he fell to the ground with eyes wildly staring, unseeing. Nothing was added to the message. He was still the chosen one. That was all. The dog had become accustomed to his sudden collapses and no longer stood whining at his side.

Saturday night brought Ampies with the supplies and news of the farm: "Baas Dirk sent you food. He also said for you to remember his warning about the lambs at shearing time."

Short and slight of build, Ampies's features showed his mixed blood. The nose flat, nostrils round caverns; the eyes, slits. His complexion was a muddy, yellowish brown and his head covered with tight, crinkly curls. His age could have been anything between twenty-five and fifty years.

He dropped to his knees and slid the heavy rucksack off his shoulders. Loosening the straps he burrowed beneath the parcels of foodstuffs and withdrew a bottle of brackish farm wine.

"This is for me," he said, "it's all the food I want."

While Jan busied himself with transferring the supplies to the shed where he slept during bad weather, Ampies made himself comfortable in front of the fire. He raised the bottle to his mouth and the gurk-gurk of the flowing liquor told of his deep swallow. Rubbing his lips with the palm of his hand, he gave a contented sigh and wriggled his buttocks deeper into the soft soil.

Taking two blankets from the bed in the corner, Jan strode to the doorway of the shed.

"Are you going to sleep inside?"

"No. I'll sleep outside with you. On the farm, like a prisoner, I sleep in my cottage every night, rain or shine. I've almost forgotten how it feels to have the earth beneath me and the stars above."

Walking towards the fire, Jan threw one of the blankets at Ampies who wrapped himself in it, leaving only his hands and the upper portion of his body free.

"You're lucky that it's not every day you're under the heavy fist of Baas Dirk. Every day the fist lands heavier on the necks of us folks. It's work and more work from the moment the sun wakes until it dips from sight behind the kranse and even then if it's still light, Baas Dirk finds more work so that at night your body is so tired that there is no pleasure in joining the others in a last smoke and you turn away from the enjoyment of your woman's body."

He gave a deep sigh and peered at Jan for signs of sympathy.

"It is heavy, this life of ours!" Jan responded, and Ampies repeated, "Yes! It is heavy, this life of ours!"

Another deep swallow and Ampies continued.

"Saturday nights are no longer nights of joy for us. Baas Dirk has forbidden us to have our pleasures into the late hours of the night and no longer, far in the night, is heard the twang of guitar strings and the young girls no longer entice the men of their choice with the swaying of their hips as they dance to the music. And, once, when Boeta Haas was found drunk on the Sabbath day, Baas Dirk came to the cottage of Aunt Minna where a *bid-uur* was held and stood at the open door. 'Haas has befouled the fair day of the Lord and shall be punished! All of you come outside and bear witness to what befalls those who heed not the words of the Lord and, myself, His servant,' he said; and although we were preparing for prayers we had to follow him like little children and share in the shame of Boeta Haas.

"Boeta Haas was under the tree near the dam, unaware of our presence. Baas Dirk plucked the shirt from Boeta Haas's back and, wielding a heavy switch, hit him all over the body with it, all the time crying in a loud voice that Boeta Haas, in his drunken state, was like the swine, possessed by demons, that had fled into the sea. Baas Dirk was so filled with the spirit that I feared that he might command us to pitch Boeta Haas into the dam.

"When blood flowed from Boeta Haas's back, some of the women wept and Baas Dirk told them to stop their weeping and instead concern themselves with guarding their children from falling into the slothful ways of their elders.

"We carried Boeta Haas home after Baas Dirk left. Every Sunday morning, early, we have to attend service in the big house."

After his long recital Ampies raised the bottle and greedily drained it of its contents.

"Ampies, will you listen to what I have to say?" Jan asked in a low voice. At first hesitant, then more assured, he told of the voice from the heavens.

Ampies looked at him with a doubtful countenance. "Are you sure the lonely days and nights haven't affected your mind?"

"No, Ampies. There is no . . ." he fell backwards, body stiffening.

Ampies threw his blanket from him and jumped across the intervening space. Dropping to his knees beside Jan, he raised his head. Except for the dilated eyes, Jan had the appearance of one in deep slumber or dead.

"Magtig, Jan! What's the matter?" Ampies whimpered. He looked round him as if to draw aid from the surrounding darkness. Near him the dog lay with eyes half-closed, mouth opened in a contented grin. Ampies's fear mounted when Jan failed to respond to his ministrations and, to seek relief for his strained nerves, he screamed a curse at the dog who answered him with a wag of its tail.

A moan from the rigid body assured Ampies that Jan was still with the living.

Jan's open eyes and calm manner angered Ampies and, to hide his fear, he accused Jan of secretly drinking.

"Did you hear it? It was wonderfully clear—like organ music we hear in the church in the dorp."

Ampies shook his head. "I didn't hear anything."

"The voice said, it said that our necks will be pressed deeper into the dirt and the fist of our oppressor will grow heavier but we must not despair. Soon I will know the honour that is to be mine and then our sufferings will be at an end. Tomorrow you must tell the others of what I speak."

Jan rolled himself in his blanket and was soon fast asleep, but to

Ampies sleep did not come so easily and far into the night he pondered over what took place.

Ampies rose before the dawn but Jan was already busy at the fire and handed him a mug of coffee. The hot coffee banished the chill of the morning air and Ampies gratefully swallowed it.

"I have to go now so that I'll be in time for my morning service or else Baas Dirk's heavy hand will find my neck."

Jan watched Ampies trudge down the hill.

With the aid of Held, he shepherded his flock to their pasture.

At the farm the service had just begun.

Dirk van Zyl stood at the head of the room, one hand resting on the table and the other clasping a heavy Bible. Facing him was his family. His wife, two sons and their wives with children, and three daughters. Behind them, an open space. At the back of the room and lining the passage, were the farm workers. Ampies took his place amongst them.

The sermon was a long one and white and black writhed under it as the self-appointed preacher and guardian of morals taxed them on their duty to a God whom he presented as a stern and just one, and one who would punish the transgressors with brimstone, fire and damnation. The sermon ended with a warning to the labourers to yield their will to him, Baas Dirk, their master by divine right.

At the *bid-uur*, later, Ampies repeated the incident at the camp in the hills and, with the exception of Aunt Minna and two women, all were sceptical of his report. Their recollection of Jan consisted of a quiet boy who grew up apart from the other children and whose parents were for ever complaining that he seemed to be living in a dream world. He preferred the solitude of the hills to the babble of humans and, when he obtained his manhood, while those of his age courted and mated, he further cut himself off by taking the job of shepherd and had since rarely been seen on the farm. To their knowledge he had yet to lie with a woman. This observation, in their eyes, marked him as being queer. Ampies persisted that his story was true and Aunt Minna argued that all they said only clinched the matter. To whom else, but the pure in heart, would a voice from the heavens speak.

Their minds could still not associate the silent Jan of their memories with the figure, painted by Ampies's story, who would bring their sufferings to an end. They decided that three men, accompanied by Ampies, should visit Jan at his camp in the hills.

Nightfall, when the farm was preparing for sleep, four figures slipped from the quarters of the workers and silently made their way past the outbuildings. A barking dog was hushed and, when a light shone from a window in the big house and a curtain was raised, they flattened themselves into the shadows.

When some distance from the farm they quickened their pace. They had to be back well before sunrise, before the others departed for the fields. There was no time for resting and the nine miles were covered in one stretch.

With sweat-stained bodies and tired limbs they approached the camp.

Ampies apprehensively called to Jan as a snarling Held confronted them. A whistle from Jan brought the dog slinking back to the still-smouldering fire and they came forward.

Dried wood was thrown on to the fire and was soon ablaze. They squatted round it.

"They would not believe me when I told them of what you said."

Jan looked at them. "It is true. Every word of it. I would not lie."

They recalled Aunt Minna's words. Only to the pure in heart would a voice from the heavens make itself heard. Jan was known never to have uttered an untruth.

"When will there be an end to our sufferings?" . . . "What is going to happen?" . . . "What is this great honour you are to receive?"

Jan shook his head at their outcry. "It has not yet been made known to me. When it is time, I shall know."

When they left the camp, although still in the dark as to what the voice could have meant, they no longer doubted and said they would visit Jan again and hoped that when they should come, he could reveal how the end of their sufferings would come about.

The following day, as they worked in the fields, word spread as to the authenticity of Jan's message and they stood in groups, heads together, and when they broke apart they tackled their work with renewed vigour.

The barking of the farm dogs nightly grew more frequent and the number of visitors to the camp in the hills increased and, after each visit, their excitement spread as, according to Jan, the day of their release crept nearer.

The farmer observed their restlessness and took to watching them secretly, growing disturbed at the number of times during the day they came together and stood whispering, and at the unaccounted-for light of joy on their faces after each whispering.

Ampies grew in importance in the eyes of the rest. He assumed the position of disciple and through him was relayed all the news. As he approached the farm he could hardly restrain himself. He was to tell them that at last they were to know when their sufferings would end. When Jan had told him of the plans of the Voice, he could have swooned with the joy of it all and was all for rushing down to the farm and shouting the glad tidings at the top of his voice. Jan had cautioned him and told him that he was to tell everyone to come to the camp the following evening and he would tell them himself. He was dejected when Jan made him promise not to tell more than the message from Jan.

A figure detached itself from the shadows and touched him on the shoulder as he passed the outbuildings. He turned and almost fell on his knees from shock.

Dirk van Zyl, with a sjambok trailing in his right hand, stood before him.

"Well, Ampies. And where do you come from?" The voice held a quiet menace which could be felt.

"Nowhere, Baas. I couldn't sleep any longer and went for a walk."

"And last night? And the night before, and the many nights before that when you and the others left the farm and only returned before the sun arose? Couldn't you sleep then? And couldn't all the others also sleep?" The voice rose. "Now tell me where you were, Ampies."

"Nowhere, Baas. I couldn't sleep."

"Get in there." The sjambok pointed to a barn.

Closing the barn door, the farmer drove Ampies into a corner and struck him across the shoulders with the sjambok. After four strokes the farmer stopped.

"Will you tell me now, Ampies?"

Ampies shook his head and was knocked down by a blow in his face. Blood streamed from his nostrils and the sjambok bounced off his body. When the farmer paused for breath, Ampies whimpered that soon all his sufferings would be a thing of the past. The farmer stooped and grabbed hold of his coat collar, shaking him like an empty sack. "What was that?"

"Ja, Baas Dirk," he said defiantly. "Soon all our sufferings will be at an end and the heavy yoke smashed from our necks and Jan leads us away from your bondage." His eyes lit up as he continued. "The voice from the heavens told him that he is the one to lead us away from the land of our suffering and whoever raised his hand against Jan shall be destroyed."

The farmer was speechless against such a sacrilegious declaration. When he regained his voice, he hoarsely screamed: "Get out of here!"

Ampies told the crowd of anxious workers to prepare themselves, that at nightfall he would lead them with their families and possessions to the camp in the hills from where the track to freedom would start. They had nothing to fear from Baas Dirk.

Dirk van Zyl watched them from the window of his bedroom as they made their way to the fields. The blood rushed to his head, preventing clear thinking. On his sons' return from the fields for their midday meal, he ranted at them.

"There is a pestilence on our lands which must be done away with to the death. The volk has the audacity to believe that the voice of God has made itself heard to Jan, the shepherd." He paused for an instant to wipe away the froth forming at the sides of his mouth. "To Jan, the shepherd, the hotnot, and not to me, His dutiful servant. Do they think that God, if He would consent to speak to us, would use a hotnot as His mouthpiece? I forgave them when they drank and when they whored, but this, this I cannot. On your knees, my Sons."

Hand aloft, he faced his kneeling sons.

"O Lord, hear the prayer of your vassal. Grant me the power to strike the fear of wrath into the hearts of these misguided fools. Let me be the instrument destroying those who lend their ears to blasphemous tales. Let my hand be the one which strikes down this hotnot who. . . ."

Overcome with the fervour of his prayers, his body shook with sobs. His sons left him to his weeping and joined the cowering women in the kitchen.

The workers were a silent lot as they waited for the day's ending. Inside the big house Dirk van Zyl kept to his room and spent his time in weeping and praying. When darkness fell, he was calmed and stood watching the line of laden workers pass through the farm gate on their way to the camp in the hills. Ampies, slightly drunk, in the lead, a bottle swinging from one hand. During supper not a word was spoken and, when the meal ended, he made a sign to his sons and they strode from the kitchen. In the barn they saddled their horses and rode out in a canter, sjamboks dangling from their saddle-horns. Once clear of the farm they slowed down to a walk. Now that events were moving, Dirk van Zyl felt no urge to rush.

In the hills, the camp site was filled to overflowing; they sat in a semicircle, all eyes on Jan. The light from the fire played on his features; his smooth, beardless face, and eyes filled with love. When he spoke, his voice was gentle and carried to all of them.

"No more shall we suffer. The days of suffering are done with. It has been made known to me, the honour that is mine. I am to lead you on a trek to freedom. Away from the heavy hand of Baas Dirk.

"No longer shall we be used like the animals they own, fit only for work. For no man should own another and make of him a. . . ."

His words were cut off by the clatter of hoof-beats and the crowd scrambled to their feet and scattered as the three riders rode into their midst.

A string of unintelligible words poured from the mouth of Dirk van Zyl as he slashed with his sjambok at the heads of those around him. He drove his horse at Jan and sent him spinning to the ground. The horse reared and repeatedly he brought its front hooves smashing on to the prostrate shepherd, whose attempts to crawl to safety were soon stopped and who lay helpless under the flaying hooves.

His sons rounded up those of the workers who had not fled.

Jumping from his horse, Dirk van Zyl ordered his sons to pick up Jan and bind him to a *doring-bos*. They tied his hands with leather thongs so that he hung between two trees, the thorns pressing into his arms, his feet hanging free off the ground.

A fanatical gleam in his eyes, the farmer addressed his workers. "Now you will see what the Lord has commanded me to do." Then he strode towards the hanging Jan. "Hotnot! You dare presume that

God would converse with you!" Each word was punctuated with a blow from the sjambok, wringing an answering moan from the crushed body of Jan.

Ampies moved forward but was stopped by a sjambok slash across the face and those who had to watch Jan's beating gave themselves over to loud wailing.

Dirk van Zyl continued beating until his arm tired and no sound came from the mouth of Jan, then he and his sons drove Ampies and the others back to the farm like so many sheep.

Jan raised his head once and moaned for water. His moan went unanswered. Then his head sank on to his breast and his body swayed as the wind sported with it. The dog returned to the camp and sat on its haunches beneath the swaying Jan, pointing its mouth to the sky, and howled its sorrow to the night.

Sketches of South African Life

CASEY MOTSISI

I. IF BUGS WERE MEN

It was the year 1758. Two bugs were sitting and chatting in a nook of the wall in the House of Discussion. One bug yawned and confessed it was feeling sleepy. But it dared not sleep. It always enjoyed listening.

A leading official had just remarked that half the members of the Opposition were asses, whereupon someone asked him to withdraw by saying that half the members of the Opposition were *not* asses, whereupon he was roundly congratulated for being the first person to withdraw a remark instead of stamping out of the house like a bull.

"Do you believe in evolution?" the yawning bug asked its friend.

"Yes. Why do you ask?"

The first bug scratched and said: "Well, I was just thinking. Last night I bugged that chap who calls himself President. His blood is flowing in my veins, so I'm his blood relation in a way. Maybe some centuries to come I might evolve into a human being, and who knows I might be elected President too!"

"What will you do when you're a President?"

"I will make laws. Humane and human laws. Nothing but laws."

"That means you will forget your bug brothers, even me?"

"Nix, Chum. I will appoint a Minister of Squalor, whose sole business would be to see to it that every human being stays dirty. I will ban all disinfectants; encourage bug immigration; and tighten up on emigration. Anybody who disagrees with me, even on such a small matter as weather, will be named a bugomist and banished to a concentration camp for an indefinite period. By bugs, I'll make such laws bugs will build me a monument after I'm dead, for being the one bug who fought relentlessly to uphold Bug supremacy."

"You wouldn't escape criticism from other democratic countries if you carried on like that."

"Woe unto those who dared point a finger at me! I would of necessity have to be tough. After all, my problems would be unique. What with a President who was once a bug."

But the other bug was bored with all this kind of rambling. It stifled a yawn and said: "Stop talking like a human being and let's sleep. Wake me up at midnight."

The two bugs fell asleep immediately and dreamed of human beings.

2. ON THE BEAT

The other day the phone rings and a voice I can't recognize says to me how about having a little "do" somewhere in Western after five pee-em. It is only when this voice tells me the address where the booze session will take place that I get to know who is on the other side of the line. It's Kid Jailhouse Blues.

Kid Jailhouse Blues explains that he's throwing this little "do" to celebrate his recent release from the jug. I go to this place after five pee-em, and I find Kid Jailhouse Blues with a dozen other guys in this room. I settle down and lick my lips in anticipation for the hooch which I reckon will flow like malten lava.

But it turns out that Kid Jailhouse Blues has invited more people than he can get happy and high. Whoever heard of Veterans of the Bottle getting happy and high, all twelve of them, on a poor nip? Which is what Kid Jailhouse Blues pulls out and announces like follows: "Gents, this is all I could organize."

Well, Kid Jailhouse Blues comes with twelve glasses and a teaspoon which he uses as a measure to pour droplets of mahog[1] into the glasses. We all lick at the droplets in the huge glasses and sing, "For he's a jolly good fellow", although I wish he drops dead.

After the licking and singing we settle down on some benches,

[1] Mahog=mahogany brandy (from the colour).

whereupon Kid Jailhouse Blues starts playing us some real cool jazz. Anyway, the music is good, and I'm just beginning to forget that I was wanting for Kid Jailhouse Blues to drop dead, when he comes to me and whispers something which nearly makes me wish I had a jawbone of an ass and do a Samson on him.

What he whispers into my ears is that—can't I loan him a fiver so's he can go and buy some hooch for the boys. He explains that he had the boodle that same morning when he went to town to gweva some bottles for the party, but that when he tried to get the boodle from his hip-pocket, it wasn't there.

That kind of jazz coming from an accomplished pickpocket like Kid Jailhouse Blues is not easy to swallow. I can smell that he's just up to one of his confidence tricks again. And what he says after I tell him I have no mazuma, proves that I am right.

He says loudly to me: "Hao! But you *Drum* chaps got paid today." When he says this, everybody's head in the room jerks in my direction and I am just in time to see one of the boys nudge at the guy sitting next to him. These two guys stand up and walk out.

Everything begins to dawn on me. I was invited here by Kid Jailhouse Blues just so his pals can roll me and unload me of all my hard-earned boodle. I'm sure those two blokes who walked out are waiting for me at some dark corner just ready to pounce when I go out.

I'm just wondering what I'm going to do when who should walk in but Kid Hotwater Bottle carrying his inevitable hot-water bottle! He goes about with this thing on account he carries his hooch in it. He is no end pleased to see me and he offers me the hot-water bottle and tells me to take swig. I take my swig and then stash all my boodle into it while nobody is looking and give it back to him.

He puts the hot-water bottle back into a leather case such as photographers use for their cameras and walks out. I say so long and follow him. Suddenly some guys attack me and go through my pockets. They find only tuppence and I hear one of them curse that Kid Jailhouse Blues sent them on a false alarm.

I go to Kid Hotwater Bottle's place, explain everything, and after some struggle manage to retrieve my booze-bathed boodle out of his hot-water bottle. . . .

Casey Motsisi

3. EDITORS

The Editor gives me an ultimatum. He says to me I've got to choose between boozing and working.

Now you will agree that this is no easy proposition by any means seeing as boozing and working are bedfellows. Look at it this way: I like to get boozed up and I hate to work. But to get boozed up you must have the necessary boodle to buy the booze. And to have the boodle you have to work to earn it.

All the same, I decide to lay off the booze for a day and see how things will work out. That's why I'm sitting in this fly-ful Hotela Bantu sipping some soda water and thinking what a terrible thing life can be when you're not supposed to pep it up with hooch.

But I just have to lay off the stuff on account my Editor makes boozing a very expensive hobby for me by threatening all over the place that he will knock off five quid from my monthly allowance—which is what he calls my salary—if I come into the office smelling like an old empty vat of hooch.

I'm still racking my brainpan on the major problem of how the world can rid itself of editors and still run smoothly when who should walk into this fly-ful Hotela Bantu but this character called Kid Nice.

Now the gang calls this character Kid Nice on account each time he wants to get drunk he says, "I wanna get nice, man, nice." Kid Nice spots me the same time as I spot him and he walks over to where I'm sitting and sipping soda water. He takes the bottle from me and downs what's left of the soda water, whereupon he makes such a face you'd think he had swallowed caustic soda. After regaining his normal features, he says he thought I was sipping gin.

Before I can tell Kid Nice why for I'm committing the unpardonable sin drinking soda water while vines still grow, he says to me we should go and get nice seeing as his ship is in. Now Kid Nice is one tough character who never takes no for an answer.

Jobs and fivers are tight these days, but I reckon I might as well go with Kid Nice on account a set of false teeth cost many times more than a fiver and I'll definitely need a set if I refuse to go with Kid Nice on account he'll ram my God-given set down my throat.

That is why, in spite of my editor's ultimatum, I find myself sitting in Aunt Peggy's joint and listening to Kid Nice ordering a straight of mahog, which is the sweetest music my soda-water-sodden soul ever hears in many hours.

By the time the straight is polished off I'm feeling so at peace with the world and instead of going down to the courts to cover the case the Editor assigns me to, I zigzag right down to Marshall Square Police Station, singing: "I wish I were a brewer's son-in-law," which song I make up myself.

Now the reason I'm going to Marshall Square is to beg these cops to arrest me on account the charge for "dronkennoise" is just a quid—which is four quid less the price my editor wants me to pay for being just human. But these cops refuse to arrest me on account of this Better Deal affair, which says they shouldn't arrest God's children for petty offences. I get a brainwave and tell them they should arrest me for not having squared up with my poll tax and they reckon that's no petty offence and throw me in.

And what do you know? The Editor hears about it the following morning and he nearly breaks his neck running down to pay the necessary before the law ships me down to some farm or other.

Just goes to show the wonderful miracles a little booze can work....

Grieg on a Stolen Piano

EZEKIEL MPHAHLELE

Those were the days of terror when, at the age of fifteen, he ran away from home and made his way towards Pietersburg town. Driven by hunger and loneliness and fear he took up employment on an Afrikaner's farm at ten shillings a month plus salted mealie-meal porridge and an occasional piece of meat. There were the long scorching hours when a posse of horsemen looked for him and three other labourers while they were trying to escape. The next morning at dawn the white men caught up with them.

Those were the savage days when the whole white family came and sat on the stoep to watch, for their own amusement, African labourers put under the whip. Whack! Whack! Whack! And while the leather whip was still in the air for the fourth stroke on the buttocks, he yelled *Ma-oeeee!* As the arm came down, he flew up from the crude bench he was lying on, and, in a manner that he could never explain afterwards, hooked the white foreman's arm with his two, so that for a few seconds he dangled a few feet from the ground. Amid peals of laughter from the small pavilion, the foreman shook him off as a man does a disgusting insect that creeps on his arm.

Those were the days when, in a solo flight again towards Pietersburg, terror clawed at his heart as he travelled through thick bush. He remembered the stories he had so often listened to at the communal fireplace; tales of huge snakes that chased a man on the ground or leapt from tree to tree; tales of the giant snake that came to the river at night to drink, breaking trees in its path, and before which helpless people lay flat on their stomachs wherever they might be at the time; none dared to move as the snake mercifully lifted its body above them, bent over, drank water and then, mercifully again, turned over backwards, belly facing up, rolling away from the people; stories that explained many mysteries, like the reason why the owl and the bat moved in the dark. Always the theme was that of man, helpless as he himself was in the bush or on a tree or in a rock cave on a hill, who was unable to ward off danger, to escape a terrible power that was everywhere around him. Something seemed to be stalking him all the time, waiting for the proper moment to pounce upon him.

But he walked on, begged and stole food and lifts on lorries, until he reached Thswane—Pretoria.

There was the brief time in "the kitchens", as houses of white people are called where one does domestic work, as if the white suburbs were simply a collection of kitchens. There were the brutal Sundays when he joined the Pietersburg youth, then working in the kitchens, on their wild march to the open ground just outside Bantule location for a sport of bare fisticuffs. They marched in white shorts on broad slabs of feet in tennis shoes and vaseline-smeared legs; now crouching, now straightening up, now wielding their fists wrapped in white handkerchiefs. One handkerchief dangled out of a trouser pocket, just for show. The brutal fisticuffs: mouths flushed with blood; then the white mounted police who herded them back to the kitchens; the stampede of horses' hooves as the police chased after them, for fun. . . .

Those were the days when chance lifted him like a crane out of the kitchens and out of the boxing arena, and deposited him in Silvertown location. This was when his aunt, having been alerted by her brother, had tracked him down.

There was regular schooling again. At twenty he began teacher-training at Kilnerton Institution nearby. There were the teaching days, during which he studied privately for a junior secondary school certificate.

Those were the days, when, as the first black man in the province to write an examination for, he timidly entered a government office for the first paper. The whites stared at him until he had disappeared into the room where he would write in isolation. And those were the days when a black man had to take off his hat as soon as he saw a white man approach; when the black man had to keep clear of street pavements.

Then the return home—the first time in seven years—as a hero, a teacher. The parents bubbled over with pride. Then the feast. . . .

It was one of those hot sub-tropical nights when Pretoria seems to lie in its valley, battered to insensibility by the day's heat; the night when a great friend of his was tarred and feathered by white students of the local university at Church Square: Mr. Lambeth, a British musician who had come to teach at Kilnerton and there discovered this black young man's musical talent. He had given his time free to teach him piano. Many were the afternoons, the nights, the week-ends that followed of intensive, untiring work at the instrument. What else had Mr. Lambeth done wrong? he asked himself several times after the incident. The Englishman had many friends among African teachers whom he visited in their locations: he adjudicated at their music competitions.

This black young man was my uncle. He is actually a cousin of my late father's. So, according to custom, my father had referred to him as "my brother". As my father had no blood brothers, I was glad to avail myself of an uncle. When my father died, he charged my uncle with the responsibility of "helping me to become a man". It meant that I had someone nearby who would give me advice on a number of things concerned with the problem of growing up. My mother had died shortly after. Uncle has seven children, all but one of whom are earning their living independently. The last-born is still in school.

Uncle is black as a train engine; so black that his face often gives the illusion of being bluish. His gums are a deep red which blazes forth when he smiles, overwhelming the dull rusty colour of his teeth. He is tall and walks upright. His head is always close-shaven, because, at sixty, he thinks he is prematurely greying, although his hair began to show grey at thirty. He keeps his head completely bald because he does not want a single grey hair to show.

His blackness has often led him into big-big trouble with the whites, as he often tells us.

"*Hei! Jy!*"

Uncle walks straight on, pretending not to see the bunch of them leaning against a fence. He is with a friend, a classmate.

"*Hei! Jy! die pikswart een, die bobbejaan!*"—the pitch-black one, the baboon.

One of them comes towards the two and pushes his way between them, standing in front. They stop dead.

A juvenile guffaw behind sends a shiver through Uncle. He breaks through his timidity and lunges at the white boy. He pommels him. In Pietersburg boxing style he sends the body down with a knee that gets him on a strategic place in the jaw. The others are soon upon them. The Africans take to their heels. . . .

A new white clerk is busy arranging postal orders and recording them. The queue stretches out, out of the post office building. The people are making a number of clicking noises to indicate their impatience. They crane their necks or step out of the queue in order to see what is happening at the counter.

Uncle is at the head of the queue.

"Excuse me," he ventures, "playtime will soon be over and my class will be waiting for me, can you serve us, please?"

The clerk raises his head.

"Look here," he says aggressively, "I'm not only here to serve Kaffirs, I'm here to work!"

Uncle looks at him steadily. The clerk goes back to his postal orders. After about fifteen minutes he leaves them. He goes to a cupboard and all the eyes in the queue follow each movement of his. When he comes back to the counter, he looks at the man at the head of the queue, who in turn fixes his stare on him. The white man seems to recoil at the sight of Uncle's face. Then, as if to fall back on the last mode of defence, he shouts, "What are you? What are you?—just a black Kaffir, a Kaffir monkey, black as tar. Now any more from you and I'll bloody well refuse to serve the whole bloody lot of you. Teacher—teacher, teacher *to hell*!"

Irritation and impatience can be heard to hiss and sigh down the queue.

Uncle realizes he's being driven into a corner and wonders if he can contain the situation. Something tells him it is beyond him. The supervisor of posts comes in just then, evidently called in by his junior's shout.

"*Ja?*" he asks. "*Wat is dit?*"

"Your clerk has been insulting me—calling me a Kaffir monkey."

The clerk opens his mouth to speak, but his superior leads him round a cubicle. After a few moments the clerk comes back, ready to serve but sulky and mute.

Uncle says that throughout, the white clerk seemed to feel insulted at the sudden confrontation of such articulate human blackness as thrust itself through the wire mesh of the counter.

This time, Uncle had the satisfaction of causing the removal of the white clerk after a colleague, who had been an eye-witness of the incident in the post office, had obtained support from fellow-teachers at Silverton to petition a higher postal authority against the clerk.

"Can you see that happening today?" he asked. "No, man, I'd have been fired at once on a mere allegation out of the clerk's important mouth."

Years later, Uncle was promoted to the post of junior inspector of African schools (the white man being always senior). He went to live in the western Transvaal. This is where his wife died while giving birth. He really hit the bottom of depression after this. The affection he had for his wife found a perverse expression in drink and he took to his music with a deeper and savage passion which, as he puts it, was a kind of hot fomentation to help burst the boil of grief inside him. He kept his children with him, though. Each one had the opportunity to go to an institution of higher education. Here he was lucky. For although all of them were mediocre, they used what they had profitably and efficiently. One did a degree in science; another played the saxophone in a band; another was a teacher and "pop singer"; another became a librarian for an institute of research into race relations; one daughter went in for nursing, and a son and a daughter were still in secondary school.

There were nights of sheer terror when their father failed to return home, and they knew he must be in some drinking orgy somewhere. Then they got to know that he was doing illicit diamond-buying. As he visited schools in his circuit, he sold or bought small stones. But he was always skating near the edge. Once he had the bitter experience of discovering that he had bought a few fakes for £50 from an African agent.

Then there was the day he says he'll never forget as long as he lives. The C.I.D. after crossing his path several times and picking up and losing trails, finally came to the converging point—Uncle. They found him in a train from Johannesburg to Kimberley. They took him to the luggage van and questioned him. Nothing was found on him and he wouldn't talk. When eventually they realized they might have a corpse on their hands, they put him out on a station platform, battered, bleeding and dazed. His suitcase was thrown in his direction.

Uncle was transferred to Johannesburg, but not without incident. A white educational officer wanted him to carry his typewriter—a heavy table model—to his car outside. Uncle told him he wouldn't. He had before refused to wash the official's car when asked to do so. As the educational authorities had a high opinion of his work, after serving several years in the department, they engineered a transfer for him. If you ask him how he managed to keep his post, he will tell you, "I made more or less sure I don't slip up that side, and besides whites don't like a correct black man, because they are so corrupt themselves."

Each time after some verbal tiff with a white man, Uncle says he felt his extra blackness must have been regarded as an insult by those who found themselves working in the shadow it seemed to cast around him.

His arrival in Johannesburg was like surfacing. He went slow on his drinks, and even became a lay preacher in the Methodist church at Orlando. But he started to go to the races and threw himself into this kind of gambling with such passion that he resigned as preacher.

"I can't keep up the lies," he said. "There are people who can mix religion with gambling and the other things, but I can't. And gamble I must. As Christ never explained what a black man should do in order to earn a decent living in this country, we can only follow our instincts. And if I cannot understand the connection, it is not right for me to stand in the pulpit and pretend to know the answers."

The "other things" were illicit diamond dealing and trading as a travelling salesman, buying and selling soft goods, mostly stolen by some African gang or other that operated in the city. There were also workers who systematically stole articles from their employers' shops and sold them to suburban domestic servants and location customers. While he was visiting schools, he would call this man and that man round the corner or into some private room to do business.

Uncle married again. He was now living with three of his children, two of whom were still in secondary school. A cloud descended upon his life again. His wife was an unpleasant, sour woman. But Uncle woke up to it too late. She sat on the stoep like a dumpling and said little beyond smiling briefly a word of greeting and giving concise answers to questions. The children could not quarrel with her, because she said little that could offend anyone. But her ant-heap appearance was most irritating, because she invited no one's co-operation and gave none beyond fulfilling the routine duties of a wife. She did not seem to like mothering anyone.

Once she succeeded, perhaps in all innocence, in raising a furore in the house.

"You must find out more about the choir practice your daughter keeps going to every week," she said to Uncle in the presence of the other children. They had stopped calling her "Ma" because she insisted on referring to them as "your daughter" or "your son" when she talked to their father about them.

"It's a choir practice," Uncle said brusquely.

"*Wai-i-i!* I know much about choir practices, me. A man's daughter can go to them without stopping and one-two-three the next time you look at her she has a big choir practice in her stomach."

The girl ran into her bedroom, crying. Soon tongues were let loose upon her. But she continued to sit like an ant-heap, her large body seeming to spread wider and wider like an overgrown pumpkin. Her attitude seemed to suggest much Uncle would have liked to know. What *was* she hiding?

"What do you do with such a woman?" Uncle sighed when he told me about the incident.

He was prepared to go through with the "companionship", to live with her to the end of his days. "I promised I'd do so in church," he remarked. "And I was in my full senses, no one forced me into the thing."

Another time he threatened, "One day I'll get so angry, Neph', I'll send her away to her people. And at her station I'll put her on a wheelbarrow like a sack of mealies and wheel her right into her people's house if I've to bind her with a rope."

I knew he was never going to do it.

Uncle could only take dramatic decisions which were not going to leave him any need to exercise responsibility either to revoke them or fall back on them. He made decisions as a man makes a gamble: once made, you won or lost, and the matter rested there. It was the same with his second marriage, I think. He met the woman during a church conference, when he was by chance accommodated in her house in Randfontein together with two other delegates, according to the arrangements of the local branch. His wife had been dead twelve years. He had decided that his children were big enough not to look so helpless if a second marriage soured the home atmosphere by any chance. His personal Christian belief would not permit him to get out of a marriage contract. This was the kind of responsibility he would want to avoid. If there was a likely chance that he might have to decide to revoke a step later, he did not take it.

There was in Uncle a synthesis of the traditional and the westernized African. At various periods in his life he felt that ill luck was stalking him, because misfortune seemed to pour down on him in torrents, particularly in money matters, family relations, and relations with white educational authorities. At times like these, Uncle went and bought a goat, slaughtered it, and called relations to come and eat the meat and mealie-meal porridge with their bare hands, sitting on the floor. He then buried the bones in the yard. At such times his mind searched the mystery of fate, groping in some imagined world where the spirits of his ancestors and that of his dead wife must be living, for a point of contact, for a line of communion.

After the feast, he felt peace settle inside him and fill his whole being until it seemed to ooze from the pores of his body as the tensions in him thawed. . . . Then he would face the world with renewed courage or with the reinforced secure knowledge that he was at peace with his relations, without whom he considered he would be a nonentity, a withered twig that has broken off from its tree.

Twice, when I was ill, Uncle called in an African medical doctor. But when my migraine began and often seemed to hurl me into the den of a savage beast, he called in an African herbalist and witch-doctor. The man said he could divine from his bones that I had once —it didn't matter when or where—inhaled fumes that had been meant to drive me insane, prepared by an enemy. So he in turn burned a few sticks of a herb and made me inhale the smoke. It shot up my nasal cavity, hit the back of my skull, seeming to scrape or burn its path from the forehead to the nape of my neck. Each time, after repeated refusals to be seen by a witch-doctor my resistance broke down. I felt temporary relief each time.

So he was going to keep his wife, rain or shine. When her behaviour or her sullenness depressed him, he went back to his whisky. Then he played excerpts from Grieg's piano concerto or a Chopin nocturne, or his own arrangement of Mohapeloa's *Chuchumakhala* (the train) or *Leba* (the dove) and others, vocalizing passages the while with his deep voice. He loved to evoke from his instrument the sound of the train's siren *Oi—oi-i-i* while he puffed *chu-chu, chu-chu.*

"If she knew this piano was lifted out of a shop," he thought often, this dumpling would just let off steam about the fact, simply to annoy me, to make me feel I'm a failure because she knows I'm not a failure and she wants to eat me up and swallow me up raw the way she did her first husband."

He had lately disposed of his twenty-year-old piano.

The keyboard felt the impact of these passionate moments and resounded plaintively and savagely. Self-pity, defiance, despite, endurance, all these and others, played musical chairs in his being.

"Look, Neph'," Uncle said one day when he was his cheerful, exuberant self again, "look, here's an advertisement of an African beauty contest in *Afric.*"

"Oh, there is such a rash of beauty contests these days we're all sick of them. It's the racket in every big town these days. Haven't they learned that a woman is as beautiful as your eyes make her?"

"You're just too educated, that's all. You know nothing, my boy, wait till I tell you."

"Is it a new money-catching thing again? Don't tell me you're going to run a gambling game around the winning number."

Uncle and beauty queens simply did not dovetail in my mind. What was behind that volume of blackness that frightened so many whites? I was curious to know.

"Better than that, Neph'. If you want to co-operate."

"In what?"

"Now look at the prizes: £500, £250, £150 and consolation prizes. One of these can be ours."

"But this is a beauty contest, not a muscle show."

"Don't be so stupid. Now, here. I know a lovely girl we can enter for this contest."

I felt my curiosity petering out.

"I go and fetch the girl—she's a friend's daughter living in the western Transvaal, in a village. Just the right kind of body, face, but she needs to be brought up to market standard. The contest is nine months away still, and we've time."

"But——"

"Now listen. You put in £25, me the same. We can then keep the girl in my house—no, your aunt will curdle again—now let me think —yes, in my friend Tau's house: his wife has a beautiful heart. The money will go to feeding her and paying for her lessons at Joe's gym. Your job will be to take her out, teach her how to smile when she's introduced; how to sit—not like a brooding hen; how to stand in public—not like an Afrikaner cow. You've got to cultivate in her a sense of public attention. Leave the body work to Joe. If she wins, we give her £100, and split £400."

Joe was one of these people who know just when to come in for profit. He set up his gym in a hired hall with the express aim of putting candidates through "body work".

For my part, I simply did not like the idea at all. Beauty on a platform; beauty advertised, beauty mixed up with money; that is how the thing seemed to me, a person with the simple tastes of a lawyer's clerk. To what extent Uncle had assimilated these jazzy urban habits, I couldn't tell.

"Thought about it yet, Neph'? We can't wait too long, you know."

"Yes, Unc', but I just don't see the point of it. Why don't we leave beauty queens to the—er—experts?" I actually meant something much lower than experts. "Like Joe, for instance."

"Joe's just a spiv," Uncle replied. "He just loves to rub shoulders with top dogs, that's all. We are investing."

"But I've only £30 in the post office savings; if I take out £25 I shall be almost completely out."

"A black man never starves if he lives among his people, unless there is famine. If the worst came to the worst, you would have to be content with simply having food, a roof over your head, and clothing."

"That's rural thinking. The extra things a man wants in the city I can't afford."

"Two hundred pounds can give you the extras."

I paused to think.

"No, Unc', gambling is for the rich, for those who can afford to lose, not for people like us."

"You think I'm rich? Don't be silly, you mean to say all those hunchbacked, dried-up, yellow-coloured whites you see at the races and betting booths are rich?"

I relented after a good deal of badgering. Who knows, I thought, we may just win. What couldn't I do with £200 if it came to me!

What a girl!

Her face was well shaped all right: every organ on it was in place, although she had a dry mouth and an unpleasant complexion. She could not have been well fed in the western Transvaal. Her bones stuck out at the elbows, and her buttocks needed pumping a good deal.

"What is your name?" I asked her.

"Tryphina." I almost giggled, thinking: what names some people have!

"That name won't do, Unc'," I said to him at the house, affecting a tough showmanship. "I can't imagine the name coming out of the mouth of the M.C. when he calls it out."

"Call her 'Try' or 'Phina' or 'Tryph'," he said indifferently.

"No, they sound like syllables in a kindergarten reading class. Just as bad as 'Jemina' or 'Judida' or 'Hermina' or 'Stephina'."

"Let's use her Sesotho name, she should have one I'm sure.

"Torofina," she said.

"No, not the school name spoken in Sesotho, I mean your real Sotho name. You see, in things like a beauty competition, people like an easy name that is smooth on the tongue (I meant *sweet to the ear*). They may even fail you for having a difficult name."

Didn't I loathe *Afric's* cheap, slick, noisy journalism!

"Oh, Kefahliloe," she said sweetly, which means "something has got into my eye". "That is what they call me at home."

"Nice," I commented, meaning nothing of the sort. "But you don't have a shorter Sesotho name?"

"No." She was still all innocence and patience.

"Well—er—maybe you can—er—think of an English name. Just for the contest, you see, and for the newspapers and magazines. Your picture is going to appear in all the papers. We'll call you Kefahliloe—a person's name is her name, and there's nothing wrong in it. Do not hurry, you can tell us the name you've chosen later. Is it all right?" She nodded. Things never seemed all wrong with her. Sometimes there was something pathetic about her pliability, sometimes irritating.

The next day she gave it us, with a take-it-over-leave-it tone: Mary-Jane.

The first three months showed a slight improvement. Her weight was going up, her paleness was disappearing, the lips moistening and softening, her small eyes taking on a new liveliness and self-confidence. Joe was doing the body work efficiently. I felt then, and Uncle agreed, like one who had known it all along, that there was something latent in the girl which we were going to draw out in the next few months.

She had finished her primary schooling and done part of secondary school, so she was all right on that side.

I took her to the bioscope on certain Saturdays, especially musicals, which appealed to her more than straight drama or bang-bang movies. I took her to Dorkay House in Eloff Street where African musicians go each Saturday afternoon for jazz improvisations. There we found other boys and girls listening eagerly, ripples of excitement visibly travelling through the audience as now again they whistled and clapped hands. The girls were the type called in township slang "rubber-necks", the ostentatiously jazz type. We found the same type at parties.

Mary-Jane was drinking it all in, I noticed.

I invited her to my room to listen to my collection of jazz records. She took in small doses at a time, and seemed to digest it and her bodily movements were taking on a city rhythm.

Uncle and I shared entertainment expenses equally. We went for cheap but good entertainment.

After six months, Uncle and I knew we were going to deliver a presentable article of good healthy flesh, comportment, and luscious charm. Charm? Strange. Through all this I did not notice the transformation that was taking place in this direction. She was close on twenty-one, and at the end of the next six months, I was struck by the charm that was creeping out of her, seeming to wait for a time, not far off, when it would burst into blossom. She was filling up, but her weight was in no danger of overshooting the mark. Her tongue was loosening up.

I was becoming aware of myself. I felt a twinge of guilt at treating her like an article that should be ready against a deadline. Before I could realize fully what was happening, the storm had set in.

The thing was too delicate; I would have to go about it carefully. Particularly so because I had sensed that she was innocent and untutored in a rustic manner about things like love. And one didn't want the bird to take fright because one had dived into the bush instead of carefully burrowing in. Besides, I am a timid fellow, not unlike my uncle in other things.

Uncle had expensive photographs taken of Mary-Jane for the press. Publicity blazed across the African newspapers, and the air was thick with talk about *Afric's* beauty contest at which Miss Johannesburg would be selected; who was going to be the £500 consignment of beauty dynamite? the journal screamed. . . .

I heard a snatch of conversation in the train one morning amid the continuous din of talking voices, peals of laughter and door-slamming.

"Hey, man, see dat girl's picture in *Afric*?"

"Which?"

"De one called Mary-Jen—er—Tumelo?"

"Ja-man, Jesus, she's reely top, eh!"

"God, de body, hmm, de curves, de waist, dis t'ings!" (Indicating the area of the breasts.)

"Ach, man, dat's number one true's God jealous down."

I warmed up towards the boys and wished they could continue.

"I've seen the three judges," Uncle said.

"The judges? But *Afric* hasn't published the names!"

"They don't *do* such things, you backward boy."

"How did you know them?"

"I've my contacts."

"But we don't do such things, Uncle!" I gasped.

"What things?"

"Talking to judges about a competition in which you have vested interests."

"Don't talk so pompously. You're talking English. Let's talk Sesotho. Now all I did is I took photographs of Mary-Jane to each one at his house, paid me respects with a bottle of whisky and asked them if they didn't think she's a beautiful girl. What's wrong with just talking?"

"What did they think?"

"What are you talking, Neph'! Each one almost jumped out of his pants with excitement."

I wanted badly to laugh, but wanted also to show him that I disapproved.

"I didn't suggest anything to them. I just said she is my niece and I was proud to see her entering the contest. They swore they hadn't seen such beauty so well photographed among all the pictures they had seen in the papers. We're near the winning-post, Neph', I can see the other side of September the fifteenth already—it's bright. Those judges caught my hint."

I continued to sit with my eyes fixed on the floor, wondering whether I should feel happy or alarmed.

"By the way, Neph', do you realize you have got yourself a wife, home-grown and fresh? Anything going on between you two?"

"What do you mean?" I asked, without wanting an answer. His eyes told me he wasn't impressed by my affectation. He waited for me to crawl out of it.

"I haven't thought of it," I lied. After a pause, "Was this also on your mind when you thought of her as a beauty queen, Uncle?"

"Yes, Neph'. I got to liking her very much while I visited her people during my inspection trips. It was sad to think that such a bright pretty girl would merely become another villager's wife and join the rest who are scratching the soil like chickens for what food there still remains in those desolate places. Her father and me are like twin brothers, we were at school together."

"But the contest? Surely you could obtain a husband for her without it? And you're not so sure she'll win, either."

He was silent.

"Nor are we sure she'll like me for a husband."

"Her father knows my plans. He has told her since she came here."

"But the contest, why that?"

Silence.

"It's too difficult to explain. All I ask you is to trust me enough to know that I'm not simply playing a game with Mary-Jane for my own amusement."

During the next few days vanity blew me up. I abstracted the whole sequence of events from their setting and the characters who acted them out. Gradually I built up a picture of myself as someone who needs to be independent and around whom a hedge was being set up, a victim of a plot. I regarded myself as a sophisticate who couldn't willingly let others choose a sweetheart or wife for me. But in fact I sensed that the real reason for my resentment was that I was actually in love with Mary-Jane but could not face the prospect of living with someone I had presumed to raise to a level of sophistication for reasons of money. I had often been moved by films in which the hero eventually married the less-privileged, artless and modest girl rather than the articulate, urbanized girl who goes out to get her man. Now I had the opportunity of doing the same thing, and I couldn't. In either case, I realize now, one saw a different version of male vanity at work.

Another disturbing element was my uncle's motive for doing what he did by throwing Mary-Jane into a beauty contest when he could arrive at his other objective without going into all the trouble. Although he declined to say it, I think it was his gambling urge that pushed him to it. I wondered what Mary-Jane herself thought about all this; the manner in which she was simply brought to the city and put through a machine to prepare her for a beauty competition, probably without her opinion being asked. Did she perhaps take it that this was how townspeople did things, or one of the things country people were bound to do when they came to the city? I still wonder.

Mary-Jane had to enter the competition in spite of our vanities. She looked forward to it with zest and a certain vivacity which one would not have guessed she was capable of about nine months before. Yes, she was charming, too. How I wished I had found her like this or it had arrived as if through someone else's efforts and planning!

Uncle himself infected me with his high spirits. We decided to have an Indian dinner at the Crescent, after the event.

That night came.

The lights went on full beam, washing out every bit of shade from every corner of the hall. The Jazz Dazzlers struck up "September in the Rain". Masses of faces in the packed hall looked up towards the rostrum. The music stopped. The M.C.'s voice cut through the noise in the hall and the people held their breaths, unfinished words and sentences trailing off in a sigh.

It came to me with a metallic mockery—the announcement that *Afric* had decided that this was going to be a you-pick-the-winner show. The queen and the other two prize-winners would be chosen by popular vote. There was hilarious applause and whistling from the crowd of what must have been about two thousand people. The M.C. explained that as the people filed out of the hall after the contest, each person would, in the presence of supervisors at the door, drop two tickets each into a box fixed at every one of the four exits. One ticket would bear the numbers of the winners of the three prizes in evening dress, and the other card numbers of the winners in beach attire. The categories were indicated on the cards. These and pencils were distributed while the band played.

I looked at Uncle next to me. He kept saying, "Stupid! Hoodlums! Cheats! Burn the bloody *Afric*! Nothing ever goes right in things organized by the Press. You take my word for it, Neph'. Ah!"

"Anything happens in beauty competitions," I said, for lack of a stronger remark to match my sagging mood.

"Anyway, Neph'," Uncle said, his face cheering up, "two thousand people looking with two eyes each must be better than three men looking with two eyes each, with the possibility of a squint in one of them."

This really tickled me, in spite of myself. It gave me hope: who could be sure that all three judges knew a lovely bust from the back of a bus or a bag of mealies? We could at least enjoy our Indian dinner and leave the rest in the hands of fate.

What use would it be to describe Mary-Jane's superb performance?

We had two couples—friends—with us at dinner. Mary-Jane was most relaxed. Her ingenuous abandon and air of self-assurance went to my head. The dinner proved worth waiting for. That went to my stomach and made me feel what a glorious thing it is to have a healthy receptacle for such exquisite food.

During our twelve-mile trip by car to Orlando, I felt the warm plush body of Mary-Jane press against me slightly, and I was glad to have things in contact like that. She, in turn, seemed to respond to something of what was radiating from me.

"Are you worried about the results?" I ventured to ask, merely for the sake of saying something to relieve the drowsy full-bellied silence in the car.

"No," she replied warmly. "Not a bit. But I'm glad it's all over."

We lost.

Mary-Jane wasn't in the least worried. Uncle regarded it simply as a match that was lost and couldn't be replayed. For my part, I suspected that I had often heard a faint whisper within me telling me that I should be better off if we lost. So I did not know what I ought to feel.

On a Sunday I went to Uncle's house for a casual visit. I found his wife in one of her sour moods. She greeted me with the impatience of one who waves off a fly that hovers over the face and hinders conversation. She was actually talking alone, in a querulous mood. Her right elbow was resting on her huge breast and in the cup of the left hand, the right hand stroking her cheek and nose.

I passed hastily on to the room where Uncle played and sang an excerpt from Grieg's piano concerto. He saw me as I went to seat myself but continued to play. At the end of a passage he said, casually, "She is gone," and continued playing. I shrugged my shoulders, thinking, "That's beyond me."

"She left me a note," he said. "Did you receive one?"

His eyes told me that he had just visited his whisky cupboard. I realized that he wasn't talking about his wife.

"Who? Are you talking about Mary-Jane?"

He nodded. "Who do you think I mean—Vasco da Gama's daughter-in-law?" Then he shouted, "*Ja*. Gone with Joe!"

He went back to some *crescendo* passages of Grieg, picking them up and dropping them in turn. Then he suddenly stopped and came to sit by me.

"How's everybody in the house?" I asked.

"Still well. Except your aunt. That stupid native boy who sold me this piano comes here and finds your aunt and tells her this is a stolen piano. Just showing off, the clever fool. *Setlatla sa mafelelo*—fool of the last order. His mother never taught him not to confide everything in woman. Kind of lesson you suck from your brother's breast. The native! Now your aunt thinks all the house money goes out for the piano. Nothing can convince her that I'm paying £30 only, and in bits, too. So you see she's staging one of her boycotts."

Uncle did not even pretend to lower his voice. Has it gone this far —no bother about what she thinks? I asked myself. No, he did care. He was too sensitive not to care. Always, when he told me about her, he spoke with a sense of hurt. Not such as a henpecked husband displays. Uncle had tremendous inner resources and plenty of diversions and could not buckle up under his wife's policy of non-collaboration, the way a henpecked man would do. This "speaking up" was just a bit of defiance.

"She worries about a stolen piano." Uncle continued, lying back on the divan, his eyes looking at the ceiling, his thumb playing up and down under his braces. "She forgets she sleeps between stolen sheets; every bit of cutlery that goes into her mouth was stolen by the boys from whom I bought it; her blouses are stolen goods, her stockings." And then, looking at me he said, "Don't we steal from each other, lie to each other every day and know it, us and the whites?"

I said, "*Ja*," and looked at my tie and shoes. But I considered this superfluous explanation.

"You know, Neph'," he continued in rambling fashion, "a few days ago I had a sickening experience involving a school I've been inspecting. A colleague of mine—let's call him J.M.—has been visiting the school for oral tests. At no time when his white superior calls him or asks him a question does J.M. fail to say "Yes, baas,' or 'No, baas,' or 'I'll get it for you, baas.' Now, during lunch break, some of the staff say to him in the staff-room they feel disgraced when a black man like him says, 'baas, baas' to the white man. They say they hope he'll stop it—just a nice brotherly talk, you see. Guess what J.M. goes and does? He goes and tells his white superior that the staff members of such-and-such a school don't want him to call him 'baas'! Guess what the white man does? He comes and complains to me about the bad conduct of those teachers. Now I ask you; what chance do you or I stand against idiots like these two who have so much power? We don't all have the liver to join the Congress Movement. So we keep stealing from the white man and lying to him and he does the same. This way we can still feel some pride."

As I rose to go, I said, "So Mary-Jane's gone off with Joe, eh!" as though her image had not been hovering over me all the time since Uncle had announced her "flight".

"Yes, because I've a stupid timid nephew. Are you going to wait till horns grow on your head before you marry?"

I laughed.

"Any country girl who starts off with Joe has made a real start in town-living, Neph'."

As I went out, the woman in the lounge was saying: "Kiriki, Kiriki —who do they say he is?—Kiriki with the stolen piano. Me, I cannot eat Kiriki, I want money for food. He can take that Kirikinyana and Mohapeloanyana of his, put them in the lavatory bucket."

By saying "He can take . . ." she clearly wanted me to listen. The use of the diminutive form for the names of the musicians was meant for his ears.

"What do you do with your aunt, Neph', if she does not understand Grieg and cannot like Mohapeloa?"

If you had pricked me with a pin as I was going out, I should have punctured, letting out a loud bawl of laughter which I could hardly keep back in my stomach.

A Meeting in the Dark

JAMES NGUGI

He stood at the door of the hut and saw his old, frail but energetic father coming along the village street, with a rather dirty bag made out of a strong calico swinging by his side. His father always carried this bag. John knew what it contained: a Bible, a hymn-book and probably a notebook and a pen. His father was a preacher. He wondered if it had been he who had stopped his mother from telling him stories when he became a man of God. His mother had stopped telling him stories long ago. She would say to him, "Now, don't ask for any more stories. Your father may come." So he feared his father. John went in and warned his mother of his father's coming. Then his father entered. John stood aside, then walked towards the door. He lingered there doubtfully, then he went out.

"John, hei, John!"

"Baba!"

"Come back."

He stood doubtfully in front of his father. His heart beat faster and an agitated voice within him seemed to ask: Does he know?

"Sit down. Where are you going?"

"For a walk, Father," he answered evasively.

"To the village?"

"Well—yes—no. I mean nowhere in particular." John saw his father look at him hard, seeming to read his face. John sighed, a very slow sigh. He did not like the way his father eyed him. He always looked at him as though John was a sinner, one who had to be watched all the time. "I am," his heart told him. John guiltily refused to meet the old man's gaze and looked past him and appealingly to his mother who was quietly peeling potatoes. But she seemed oblivious of everything around her.

"Why do you look away? What have you done?"

John shrank within himself with fear. But his face remained expressionless. He could hear the loud beats of his heart. It was like an engine pumping water. He felt no doubt his father knew all about it. He thought: "Why does he torture me? Why does he not at once say he knows?" Then another voice told him: "No, he doesn't know, otherwise he would have already jumped at you." A consolation. He faced his thoughtful father with courage.

"When is the journey?"

Again John thought, why does he ask? I have told him many times.

"Next week, Tuesday," he said.

"Right. Tomorrow we go to the shops, hear?"

"Yes, Father."

"Then be prepared."

"Yes, Father."

"You can go."

"Thank you, Father." He began to move.

"John!"

"Yes?" John's heart almost stopped beating.

"You seem to be in a hurry. I don't want to hear of you loitering in the village. I know young men, going to show off just because you are going away? I don't want to hear of trouble in the village."

Much relieved, he went out. He could guess what his father meant by not wanting trouble in the village.

"Why do you persecute the boy so much?" Susan spoke for the first time. Apparently she had carefully listened to the whole drama without a word. Now was her time to speak. She looked at her tough old preacher who had been a companion for life. She had married him a long time ago. She could not tell the number of years. They had been happy. Then the man became a convert. And everything in the home put on a religious tone. He even made her stop telling stories to the child. "Tell him of Jesus. Jesus died for you. Jesus died for the child. He must know the Lord." She, too, had been converted. But she was never blind to the moral torture he inflicted on the boy (that was how she always referred to John), so that the boy had grown up mortally afraid of his father. She always wondered if it was love for the son. Or could it be a resentment because, well, they two had "sinned" before marriage? John had been the result of that sin. But that had not been John's fault. It was the boy who ought to complain. She often wondered if the boy had . . . but no. The boy had been very small when they left Fort Hall. She looked at her husband. He remained mute though his left hand did, rather irritably, feel about his face.

"It is as if he was not your son. Or do you. . . ."

"Hm, Sister." The voice was pleading. She was seeking a quarrel but he did not feel equal to one. Really, women could never understand. Women were women, whether saved or not. Their son had to be protected against all evil influences. He must be made to grow in the footsteps of the Lord. He looked at her, frowning a little. She had made him sin but that had been a long time ago. And he had been saved. John must not follow the same road.

"You ought to tell us to leave. You know I can go away. Go back to Fort Hall. And then everybody. . . ."

"Look, Sister." He hastily interrupted. He always called her sister. Sister-in-the-Lord, in full. But he sometimes wondered if she had been truly saved. In his heart he prayed: Lord, be with our sister Susan. Aloud, he continued, "You know I want the boy to grow in the Lord."

"But you torture him so! You make him fear you!"

"Why! He should not fear me. I have really nothing against him."

"It is you. You. You have always been cruel to him. . . ." She stood up. The peelings dropped from her frock and fell in a heap on the floor. "Stanley!"

"Sister." He was startled by the vehemence in her voice. He had never seen her like this. Lord, take the devil out of her. Save her this minute. She did not say what she wanted to say. Stanley looked away from her. It was a surprise, but it seemed he feared his wife. If you had told the people in the village about this, they would not have believed you. He took his Bible and began to read. On Sunday he would preach to a congregation of brethren and sisters.

Susan, a rather tall, thin woman, who had once been beautiful, sat down again and went on with her work. She did not know what was troubling her son. Was it the coming journey? Still, she feared for him.

Outside, John was strolling aimlessly along the path that led from his home. He stood near the wattle tree which was a little way from his father's house and surveyed the whole village. They lay before his eyes, crammed, rows and rows of mud and grass huts, ending in sharply defined sticks that pointed to heaven. Smoke was coming out of various huts. It was an indication that many women had already come from the Shambas. Night would soon fall. To the west, the sun —that lone day-time traveller—was hurrying home behind the misty hills. Again, John looked at the crammed rows and rows of huts that formed Makeno Village, one of the new mushroom "towns" that grew up all over the country during the Mau Mau war. It looked so ugly. A pain rose in his heart and he felt like crying—I hate you, I hate you! You trapped me alive. Away from you, it would never have happened. He did not shout. He just watched.

A woman was coming towards where he stood. A path into the village was just near there. She was carrying a big load of Kuni which bent her into an Akamba-bow shape. She greeted him. "Is it well with you, Njooni (John)?"

"It is well with me, Mother." There was no trace of bitterness in his voice. John was by nature polite. Everyone knew of this. He was quite unlike the other proud, educated sons of the tribe—sons who came back from the other side of the waters with white or Negro wives who spoke English. And they behaved just like Europeans! John was a favourite, a model of humility and moral perfection. Everyone knew that though a clergyman's son, John would never betray the tribe. They still talked of the tribe and its ways.

"When are you going to—to——"

"Makerere?"

"Makelele." She laughed. The way she pronounced the name was funny. And the way she laughed, too. She enjoyed it. But John felt hurt. So everyone knew of this.

"Next week."

"I wish you well."

"Thank you, Mother."

She said quietly, as if trying to pronounce it better, "Makelele." She laughed at herself again but she was tired. The load was heavy.

"Stay well, Son."

"Go well and in peace, Mother."

And the woman who all the time had stood, moved on, panting like a donkey, but she was obviously pleased with John's kindness.

John remained long, looking at her. What made such a woman live on day to day, working hard, yet happy? Had she much faith in life? Or was her faith in the tribe? She and her kind, who had never been touched by ways of the white man, looked as though they had something to cling to. As he watched her disappear, he felt proud that they should think well of him. He felt proud that he had a place in their esteem. And then came the pang. *Father will know. They will know.* He did not know what he feared most; the action of his father would take when he knew, or the loss of the little faith the simple villagers had placed in him, when they knew. He feared to lose all.

He went down to the small local teashop. He met many people who all wished him well at the college. All of them knew that the priest's son had finished all the white man's learning in Kenya. He would now go to Uganda. They had read all this in the *Baraza*, a Swahili weekly paper. John did not stay long at the shop. The sun had already gone to rest and now darkness was coming. The evening meal was ready. His tough father was still at the table reading his Bible. He did not look up when John entered. Strange silence settled in the hut.

"You look unhappy." His mother first broke the silence.

John laughed. It was a nervous little laugh. "No, Mother," he hastily replied, nervously looking at his father. He secretly hoped that Wamuhu had not blubbed.

"Then I am glad."

She did not know. He ate his dinner and went out to his hut. A man's hut. Every young man had his own hut. John was never allowed to bring any girl visitor in there. Stanley did not want "trouble". Even to be seen standing with one was a crime. His father could easily thrash him. He feared his father, though sometimes he wondered why he feared him. He ought to have rebelled like all the other young educated men. He lit the lantern. He took it in his hand. The yellow light flickered dangerously and then went out. He knew his hands were shaking. He lit it again and hurriedly took his big coat and a huge *Kofia* which were lying on the unmade bed. He left the lantern burning, so that his father would see it and think him in. John bit his lower lip spitefully. He hated himself for being so girlish. It was unnatural for a boy of his age.

Like a shadow, he stealthily crossed the courtyard and went on to the village street.

He met young men and women lining the streets. They were laughing, talking, whispering. They were obviously enjoying themselves. John thought, they are more free than I am. He envied their exuberance. They clearly stood outside or above the strict morality that the educated ones had to be judged by. Would he have gladly changed places with them? He wondered. At last, he came to the hut. It stood at the very heart of the village. How well he knew it—to his sorrow. He wondered what he should do! Wait for her outside? What if her mother came out instead? He decided to enter.

"Hodi!"

"Enter. We are in."

John pulled down his hat before he entered. Indeed they were all there—all except she whom he wanted. The fire in the hearth was dying. Only a small flame from a lighted lantern vaguely illuminated the whole hut. The flame and the giant shadow created on the wall seemed to be mocking him. He prayed that Wamuhu's parents would not recognize him. He tried to be "thin", and to disguise his voice as he greeted them. They recognized him and made themselves busy on his account. To be visited by such an educated one who knew all about the white man's world and knowledge and who would now go to another land beyond, was not such a frequent occurrence that it could be taken lightly. Who knew but he might be interested in their daughter? Stranger things had happened. After all, learning was not the only thing. Though Wamuhu had no learning, yet charms she had and she could be trusted to captivate any young man's heart with her looks and smiles.

"You will sit down. Take that stool."

"No!" He noticed with bitterness that he did not call her "mother".

"Where is Wamuhu?"

The mother threw a triumphant glance at her husband. They exchanged a knowing look. John bit his lips again and felt like bolting. He controlled himself with difficulty.

"She has gone out to get some tea leaves. Please sit down. She will cook you some tea when she comes."

"I am afraid . . ." he muttered some inaudible words and went out. He almost collided with Wamuhu.

In the hut: "Didn't I tell you? Trust a woman's eye!"

"You don't know these young men."

"But you see John is different. Everyone speaks well of him and he is a clergyman's son."

"Y-e-e-s! A clergyman's son? You forget your daughter is circumcised." The old man was remembering his own day. He had found for himself a good virtuous woman, initiated in all the tribe's ways. And she had known no other man. He had married her. They were happy. Other men of his *Rika* had done the same. All their girls had been virgins, it being a taboo to touch a girl in that way, even if you slept in the same bed, as indeed so many young men and girls did. Then the white men had come, preaching a strange religion, strange ways, which all men followed. The tribe's code of behaviour was broken. The new faith could not keep the tribe together. How could it? The men who followed the new faith would not let the girls be circumcised. And they would not let their sons marry circumcised girls. Puu! Look at what was happening. Their young men went away to the land of the white men. What did they bring? White women. Black women who spoke English. Aaa—bad. And the young men who were left just did not mind. They made unmarried girls their wives and then left them with fatherless children.

"What does it matter?" his wife was replying. "Is Wamuhu not as good as the best of them? Anyway, John is different."

"Different! Different! Puu! They are all alike. Those coated with the white clay of the white man's ways are the worst. They have nothing inside. Nothing—nothing here." He took a piece of wood and nervously poked the dying fire. A strange numbness came over him. He trembled. And he feared; he feared for the tribe. For now he saw it was not only the educated men who were coated with strange ways, but the whole tribe. The old man trembled and cried inside, mourning for a tribe that had crumbled. The tribe had nowhere to go to. And it could not be what it was before. He stopped poking and looked hard at the ground.

"I wonder why he came. I wonder." Then he looked at his wife and said, "Have you seen strange behaviour with your daughter?"

His wife did not answer. She was preoccupied with her own great hopes. . . .

John and Wamuhu walked on in silence. The intricate streets and turns were well known to them both. Wamuhu walked with quick light steps; John knew she was in a happy mood. His steps were heavy and he avoided people, even though it was dark. But why should he feel ashamed? The girl was beautiful, probably the most beautiful girl in the whole of Limuru. Yet he feared being seen with her. It was all wrong. He knew that he could have loved her; even then he wondered if he did not love her. Perhaps it was hard to tell but, had he been one of the young men he had met, he would not have hesitated in his answer.

Outside the village he stopped. She, too, stopped. Neither had spoken a word all through. Perhaps the silence spoke louder than words. Each was only too conscious of the other.

"Do they know?" Silence. Wamuhu was probably considering the question. "Don't keep me waiting. Please answer me," he implored. He felt weary, very weary, like an old man who had suddenly reached his journey's end.

"No. You told me to give you one more week. A week is over today."

"Yes. That's why I came!" John whispered hoarsely.

Wamuhu did not speak. John looked at her. Darkness was now between them. He was not really seeing her; before him was the image of his father—haughtily religious and dominating. Again he thought: I, John, a priest's son, respected by all and going to college, will fall, fall to the ground. He did not want to contemplate the fall.

"It was your fault." He found himself accusing her. In his heart he knew he was lying.

"Why do you keep on telling me that? Don't you want to marry me?"

John sighed. He did not know what to do. He remembered a story his mother used to tell him. *Once upon a time there was a young girl . . . she had no home to go to and she could not go forward to the beautiful land and see all the good things because the Irimu was on the way. . . .*

"When will you tell them?"

"Tonight."

He felt desperate. Next week he would go to the college. If he could persuade her to wait, he might be able to get away and come back when the storm and consternation had abated. But then the government might withdraw his bursary. He was frightened and there was a sad note of appeal as he turned to her and said, "Look, Wamuhu, how long have you been pre—I mean, like this?"

"I have told you over and over again, I have been pregnant for three months and mother is being suspicious. Only yesterday she said I breathed like a woman with a child."

"Do you think you could wait for three weeks more?"

She laughed. Ah! the little witch! She knew his trick. Her laughter always aroused many emotions in him.

"All right," he said. "Give me just tomorrow. I'll think up something. Tomorrow I'll let you know all."

"I agree. Tomorrow. I cannot wait any more unless you mean to marry me."

Why not marry her? She is beautiful! Why not marry her? Do I love her or don't I?

She left. John felt as if she was deliberately blackmailing him. His knees were weak and lost strength. He could not move but sank on the ground in a heap. Sweat poured profusely down his cheek, as if he had been running hard under a strong sun. But this was cold sweat. He lay on the grass; he did not want to think. Oh, no! He could not possibly face his father. Or his mother. Or Reverend Carstone who had had such faith in him. John realized that, though he was educated, he was not more secure than anybody else. He was no better than Wamuhu. *Then why don't you marry her?* He did not know. John had grown up under a Calvinistic father and learnt under a Calvinistic headmaster—a missionary! John tried to pray. But to whom was he praying? To Carstone's God? It sounded false. It was as if he was blaspheming. Could he pray to the God of the tribe? His sense of guilt crushed him.

He woke up. Where was he? Then he understood. Wamuhu had left him. She had given him one day. He stood up; he felt good. Weakly, he began to walk back home. It was lucky that darkness blanketed the whole earth and him in it. From the various huts, he could hear laughter, heated talks or quarrels. Little fires could be seen flickeringly red through the open doors. Village stars, John thought. He raised up his eyes. The heavenly stars, cold and distant, looked down on him impersonally. Here and there, groups of boys and girls could be heard laughing and shouting. For them life seemed to go on as usual. John consoled himself by thinking that they, too, would come to face their day of trial.

John was shaky. Why! Why! Why could he not defy all expectations, all prospects of a future, and marry the girl? No. No. It was impossible. She was circumcised and he knew that his father and the church would never consent to such a marriage. She had no learning—or rather she had not gone beyond standard four. Marrying her would probably ruin his chances of ever going to a university. . . .

He tried to move briskly. His strength had returned. His imagination and thought took flight. He was trying to explain his action before an accusing world—he had done so many times before, ever since he knew of this. He still wondered what he could have done. The girl had attracted him. She was graceful and her smile had been very bewitching. There was none who could equal her and no girl in the village had any pretence to any higher standard of education. Women's education was very low. Perhaps that was why so many Africans went "away" and came back married. He too wished he had gone with the others, especially in the last giant student airlift to America. If only Wamuhu had learning . . . and she was uncircumcised . . . then he might probably rebel. . . .

The light still shone in his mother's hut. John wondered if he should go in for the night prayers. But he thought against it; he might not be strong enough to face his parents. In his hut the light had gone out. He hoped his father had not noticed it. . . .

John woke up early. He was frightened. He was normally not superstitious, but still he did not like the dreams of the night. He dreamt of circumcision; he had just been initiated in the tribal manner. Somebody—he could not tell his face, came and led him because he took pity on him. They went, went into a strange land. Somehow, he found himself alone. The somebody had vanished. A ghost came. He recognized it as the ghost of the home he had left. It pulled him back; then another ghost came. It was the ghost of the land he had come to. It pulled him from the front. The two contested. Then came other ghosts from all sides and pulled him from all sides so that his body began to fall into pieces. And the ghosts were unsubstantial. He could not cling to any. Only they were pulling him and he was becoming nothing, nothing . . . he was now standing a distance away. It had not been him. But he was looking at the girl, the girl in the story. She had nowhere to go. He thought he would go to help her; he would show her the way. But as he went to her, he lost his way . . . he was all alone . . . something destructive was coming towards him, coming, coming. . . . He woke up. He was sweating all over.

Dreams about circumcision were no good. They portended death. He dismissed the dream with a laugh. He opened the window only to find the whole country clouded in mist. It was perfect July weather in Limuru. The hills, ridges, valleys and plains that surrounded the village were lost in the mist. It looked such a strange place. But there was almost a magic fascination in it. Limuru was a land of contrasts and evoked differing emotions at different times. Once John would be fascinated and would yearn to touch the land, embrace it or just be on the grass. At another time he would feel repelled by the dust, the strong sun and the pot-holed roads. If only his struggle were just against the dust, the mist, the sun and the rain, he might feel content. Content to live here. At least he thought he would never like to die and be buried anywhere else but at Limuru. But there was the human element whose vices and betrayal of other men were embodied in the new ugly villages. The last night's incident rushed into his mind like a flood, making him weak again. He came out of his blankets and went out. Today he would go to the shops. He was uneasy. An odd feeling was coming to him—in fact had been coming—that his relationship with his father was perhaps unnatural. But he dismissed the thought. Tonight would be the day of reckoning. He shuddered to think of it. It was unfortunate that this scar had come into his life at this time when he was going to Makerere and it would have brought him closer to his father.

They went to the shops. All day long, John remained quiet as they moved from shop to shop buying things from the lanky but wistful Indian traders. And all day long, John wondered why he feared his father so much. He had grown up fearing him, trembling whenever he spoke or gave commands. John was not alone in this.

Stanley was feared by all.

He preached with great vigour, defying the very gates of hell. Even during the Emergency, he had gone on preaching, scolding, judging and condemning. All those who were not saved were destined for hell. Above all, Stanley was known for his great and strict moral observances—a bit too strict, rather pharisaical in nature. None noticed this; certainly not the sheep he shepherded. If an elder broke any of the rules, he was liable to be expelled, or excommunicated. Young men and women, seen standing together "in a manner prejudicial to church and God's morality" (they were one anyway) were liable to be excommunicated. And so, many young men tried to serve two masters by seeing their girls at night and going to church by day. The alternative was to give up church-going altogether. . . .

Stanley took a fatherly attitude to all the people in the village. You must be strict with what is yours. And because of all this he wanted his house to be a good example of this to all. That is why he wanted his son to grow upright. But motives behind many human actions may be mixed. He could never forget that he had also fallen before his marriage. Stanley was also a product of the disintegration of the tribe due to the new influences.

The shopping did not take long. His father strictly observed the silences between them and neither by word nor by hint did he refer to last night. They reached home and John was thinking that all was well when his father called him.

"John."

"Yes, Father."

"Why did you not come for prayers last night?"

"I forgot . . ."

"Where were you?"

Why do you ask me? What right have you to know where I was? One day I am going to revolt against you. But, immediately, John knew that this act of rebellion was something beyond him—unless something happened to push him into it. It needed someone with something he lacked.

"I—I—I mean, I was . . ."

"You should not sleep so early before prayers. Remember to turn up tonight."

"I will."

Something in the boy's voice made the father look up. John went away relieved. All was still well.

Evening came. John dressed like the night before and walked with faltering steps towards the fatal place. The night of reckoning had come. And he had not thought of anything. After this night all would know. Even Reverend Carstone would hear of it. He remembered Reverend Carstone and the last words of blessing he had spoken to him. No! he did not want to remember. It was no good remembering these things; and yet the words came. They were clearly written in the air, or in the darkness of his mind. "You are going into the world. The world is waiting even like a hungry lion, to swallow you, to devour you. Therefore, beware of the world. Jesus said, Hold fast unto . . ." John felt a pain—a pain that wriggled through his flesh as he remembered these words. He contemplated the coming fall. Yes! He, John, would fall from the Gates of Heaven down through the open waiting Gates of Hell. Ah! He could see it all, and all that people would say. All would shun his company, all would give him oblique looks that told so much. The trouble with John was that his imagination magnified the fall from the heights of "goodness" out of all proportion. And fear of people and consequences ranked high in the things that made him contemplate the fall with so much horror.

John devised all sorts of punishment for himself. And when it came to thinking of a way out, only fantastic and impossible ways of escape came into his head. He could not simply make up his mind. And because he could not, and because he feared Father and people and did not know his true attitude to the girl, he came to the agreed spot having nothing to tell her. Whatever he did looked fatal to him. Then suddenly he said:

"Look, Wamuhu. Let me give you money. You might then say that someone else was responsible. Lots of girls have done this. Then that man may marry you. For me, it is impossible. You know that."

"No. I cannot do that. How can you, you . . ."

"I will give you two hundred shillings."

"No!"

"Three hundred."

"No!" She was almost crying. It pained her to see him so.

"Four hundred, five hundred, six hundred." John had begun calmly but now his voice was running high. He was excited. He was becoming more desperate. Did he know what he was talking about? He spoke quickly, breathlessly, as if he was in a hurry. The figure was rapidly rising—nine thousand, ten thousand, twenty thousand. . . . He is mad. He is foaming. He is quickly moving towards the girl in the dark. He has lain his hands on her shoulders and is madly imploring her in a hoarse voice. Deep inside him, something horrid that assumes the threatening anger of his father and the village, seems to be pushing him. He is violently shaking Wamuhu, while his mind tells him that he is patting her gently. Yes, he is out of his mind. The figure has now reached fifty thousand shillings and is increasing. Wamuhu is afraid. She extricates herself from him, the mad, educated son of a religious clergyman, and runs. He runs after her and holds her, calling her by all sorts of endearing words. But he is shaking her, shake, shake, her, her—he tries to hug her by the neck, presses. . . . She lets out one horrible scream and then falls on the ground. And so all of a sudden, the struggle is over, the figures stop, and John stands there trembling like the leaf of a tree on a windy day.

Soon everyone will know that he has created and then killed.

The Judge's Son

ABIOSEH NICOL

"I love you, Mummy," he shouted across the small valley.

"Love you, mummy . . ." the echo came back.

He sat down and leant back against the tree. He shared the solitude with his reflected voice, his double-barrelled gun and Toby the dog, now whining with excitement. The dog wagged its stump of a tail furiously, its mongrel eyes lit up. But it was a good hunter. The boy continued, sitting back and thinking, his close-cropped head bowed and his dark young African face serious with sadness. The late tropical afternoon remained silent among the hills.

It was about three years ago one night that there had been much passing to and fro and he had lain awake listening in his little room at their home—a large house of brick and wood with surrounding verandas and gabled roof, built in the Portuguese colonial style much favoured in the British West African coastal cities. He was eleven then. He had been packed off to relations next morning. When he came back he understood his mother had gone away indefinitely and had left behind a small tiny brown baby—his sister—who whimpered, fed from a bottle, then slept, in that order. His paternal aunt stayed on with them. A thin, long-faced, pious African woman in her fifties, always dressed severely in black, but kindly in speech.

Amadu, the head servant, had told him secretly that his mother had died giving birth to the new baby girl. Amadu in those days was his special friend and had often allowed him to help with cleaning the silver on Saturday afternoons or putting a shine on his father's shoes every morning. When he was younger Amadu would hoist him high in the kitchen so that he could touch the zinc roof. He liked that. One day Amadu had said that the small master had grown too heavy, and that was that.

In those last few weeks before his mother went away, he remembered how she would puff as she slowly climbed the stairs and how enormously swollen she seemed all round. She spoke to him often alone in his small room about his father. "Your papa works too hard with all his meetings and court cases and committees and commissions. The government are bound to make him a knight one day; only then will he be happy, if at all." He seldom saw his father, a brisk grave man, completely westernized, tall, black, smelling always of shoe-leather and cigar-smoke. He feared him and admired him. His father was a High Court judge, the only African one. He never spoke of his work at home. Except once when he had fined instead of imprisoning a drunken white soldier who in rage and disappointment had set fire to a local brothel. Then he had sent him out of the room on some pretext or other and had told his mother in shocked tones (he had listened at the keyhole) that the government should not allow such people from Britain to come to the colonies.

That was about the time his father had bought him an air-gun in spite of the repeated protests of his mother who hated noise. He had gone out into the yard and put an empty petrol can against the wall and walked back a long way. Amadu and the other servants had come out to watch. He aimed at the can and fired. He hit some masonry off the wall. One of the underservants, the cook's assistant who had a turn of humour, jumped into the air and held his buttock, arching his bottom in mock pain. The others had laughed. He had not liked that. He aimed again, fired and missed. Amadu, who loved him, did not laugh like the others, but scolded them in their language which the boy did not understand. He came forward, took the gun from the boy's hands and showed him how to hold and aim. Amadu had been in the 1914 war fighting against the Germans in the Cameroons. The boy took the gun, aimed it and fired, hitting the can with a loud bang. The servants cheered and then went quietly away. Amadu stood by for a few seconds looking on, then went off bristling with pride for his young master. He hit the can several times until his mother came out and told him to stop as she had a headache. Later he had tried empty wine bottles and could shatter them wherever he wanted—at the neck or at the waist. He soon grew tired of shooting immobile things. One day, when his cousin visited them in the country to play, he boasted he could hit anything. His cousin laughed, so he went and brought out his gun. He loaded it against his knee and then looked round. There was a lizard against a tree, but he decided that was too small. A speckled hen passed a few yards off, strutting and clucking. He shot it and it subsided noisily squawking and flapping, still alive. His mother had come out and called for Amadu to come and put the chicken out of its misery. That evening his father had called him up when he came back home from the courts and had given him a beating. Later he had told him that only the low-born killed for pleasure or out of vanity. Kill for food, kill dangerous things, kill for King and country. Sometimes one killed for love, his father had added, not meaning him however to hear. But that was about a year before his mother died. He remembered even further back than that. When Toby was a small helpless pup with round appealing eyes flapping one ear down and the other up like the rakish Victorian hat his slightly mad grandmother still wore. His mother had always picked Toby up and carried the dog about with her and he had been slightly jealous. But Toby had solved the problem by attaching himself to him and following him about everywhere. Toby had been the gift of his father who had said that to control a dog well was the best way of learning how to control men.

Then also long ago, once when he had gone to the crowded village market with his mother and Amadu. His mother wore native dress so that the vendors would not overcharge her, and they had left the car some way off for the same reason. Amadu carried him on his shoulders with his legs astride the servant's neck. It was in the morning before it became really hot. The women sat with easy grace on low stools by their stalls heaped high with goods. They wore simple dyed cloth and gay head scarves. The children played about in the dust. Foodstuffs of all descriptions were laid out for purchase. Dried fish, salted fish and raw fish; okras, sorrel leaves, and red chillies mixed with green ones; manioc, sweet potatoes, bananas and plantains; rice, ground-nuts and millet seed heaped up in small pyramids with a tin cup as measure at the apex; red palm oil, ground-nut oil and coconut oil placed in empty gin bottles and stoppered with a bit of rag or crumpled paper. Amadu had put him down for a few minutes and he had somehow got lost. He remembered the confused cold fear which had caught hold of him and how he had run here and there calling out their names and stumbling and crying. Someone had trampled on him and he had been borne along with the crowd without his feet touching the ground. He had struck out wildly and blindly, perspiring, panicky, until a woman had seen him and pulled him out, holding him up and comforting him, before going out to find his distraught and worried mother who was so relieved that she forgot to scold him or Amadu. He had never been taken to market again.

He missed his mother very much, even now three years after her death. He often thought she might turn up suddenly one day apologizing for being a little late; and everything would be as it had been; their talks together, her understanding, her comforting and even her scolding. He knew his father missed her too, because he never cared much to see the little baby whom they both blamed for their loss. His aunt moved with the baby to the farthermost room from where his room and his father's were, and looked after her with the help of a nurse. The baby was left alone often and got used to amusing herself cooing and kicking in her raffia cot on the veranda.

Soon after this he himself started wanting to be alone. His father was away all day and after his aunt had given the orders for the day to the servants she went indoors or went visiting friends. He went to school by bus and on coming back in the afternoon amused himself somehow. He took to roaming the fields with Toby shooting birds or reading books on self-improvement and physical fitness. He used to play with the servants, but soon gave that up. Now he tried to model himself on his father in every way. He copied the way his father walked with easy strides. The way his father rested his elbow on his desk and then rested his head on his wrist. He worked hard at his books and found that knowledge gave him fairly easy mastery over others. Toby slept with him now at the foot of his little bed in the way he had gathered from a picture in one of his father's books that English noblemen were buried fully dressed with their hounds. Sometimes at night he would dream of his mother and wake up, the atmosphere of his room filled with the odour of the perfume she wore when alive, and he would sniff hopefully until he was fully awake when he would remember with a pang of disappointment that it was only the perfume clinging to her little Bible which had always been in her handbag, but which his aunt had now placed under his pillow. Toby would growl too before settling down again.

His aunt who had been widowed early, had concealed religious mania, and her room was filled with pamphlets and books on the Second Coming, some of which he had borrowed to look at. He liked the pictures of Christ holding a sword with an army of angels behind Him storming the gates of Hell. He wished the heavenly host had been on horseback, but he felt he could understand the technical difficulty of animals getting into Heaven because Aunty had said that animals had no souls. Except Toby, of course, she had added with rare understanding.

One afternoon he had gone out on to the field with the small air-gun. He was tired of the gun and had asked his aunt to ask his father to buy him a bigger gun. She had done so. His father with years of the Government Civil Service behind him had ignored the request, feeling that he would ask again if he really wanted one. But he had been afraid to, again. He carried the small gun lightly and looked for field rats and pigeons. Suddenly a small wild antelope came into view. It was the dwarfed variety and had not seen him. I could have got him if I had had a bigger gun, he thought bitterly. The beast pricked its ears and stood up. He decided to try. Aiming carefully he shot it where the ear joined the side of the head. The animal leapt and fell down stunned. He went nearer, reloaded, and shot the moving head again. He waited until it stopped twitching, then went nearer carefully from the rear, gazing at it. It was pregnant. He kicked its backside. It twitched again. He jumped backwards. Standing at a safe distance, he blazed away at its head again and again, until it bobbed up wearily and lifelessly against the twigs after each hit, and his little bag of pellets was empty. It lay still. He threw a stone at it. It did not move. He went nearer again and kicked it. Nothing happened. He examined it and prodded its side with his foot. He felt somehow he had revenged his mother. He looked at its one eye remaining, the other having been shot away. It had a thin glazed film over it, like the way his father's eyes looked soon after his mother had died. He dragged it home, as it was too heavy and bloody for him to carry. He left it in the middle of their compound and covered its head with green leaves, the way real hunters did. He called out for Amadu in the loud, polite but offhanded way his father used with servants. Amadu came running out of the servants' quarters. Amadu ran because in the past few months he had noticed the growing hardness in the young master's voice, and his unsmiling industry at little tasks and he had understood at once that the young master had now become truly his father's heir, the judge's son, and no longer the servants' pet. Amadu stopped in his tracks when he saw the dead animal. "Did you kill this?" he asked softly. The boy nodded, trying not to look too pleased. Amadu wanted to pick him up and swirl him round with joy; but restrained himself and instead shouted for the others as he danced round the dead antelope with pride. They told his father who was incredulous at first and had asked him if he had really killed it with his small gun. He mistook the question for anger and said hesitantly he had killed it for food as he had heard the price of meat was going up. His father turned away hiding a smile and gave instructions for the venison to be cut up, distributed and some dressed for Sunday. That was on a Friday. On Saturday afternoon, there was no one about and he strolled out to bathe in a little brook down the valley. He returned the back way by a small track past one of the isolated huts of the peasants on his father's estate. As he passed, the only small window of the mud hut was opened and a woman's head appeared; she called out to him and asked him to come and help her. He stood at the door of the hut, a tall slim watchful youth, and she told him to come in. He hesitated as his father had warned him against familiarity with peasants. His father had said that although they all had the same skin colour as the peasants yet he was four generations of Christian civilization away from them. He should be courteous but never familiar. However he went in. He squinted to get his eyes accustomed to the semi-darkness of the one-roomed hut after the bright afternoon. He recognized the woman. One of the three wives of the head gardener. "What's the matter?" he asked harshly because he was nervous. She sat on a low bed. "I have hurt my knee," she said, "please look at it for me." He knelt on the cow-dung floor and looked at it. There seemed nothing wrong with it. "I ate of the beef you killed yesterday," she said, "your father gave a little piece to each of us. You are a man, now, you have killed a four-footed beast." "Thank you," he said, looking up briefly at her. She was smiling down at him. She wore only a long cloth from arm-pit to knee round her body. With an easy gesture she undid it. He saw to his horror that except for the girdle of black and red beads round her bare waist, she had nothing on. He could just see from the light of the window the carved raised intricate tribal scars on her abdomen and great thighs. She pulled him to her and his lips bit her navel and the coarse scars. He pushed with all his might and fell backwards. She fell on him, her breasts momentarily suffocating him. He rolled over fiercely and sprang to his feet and ran down the bush track with panic. He heard her mocking laugh following him down the hot empty afternoon.

He slept badly that night. His aunt had gone out for a meeting that evening and he had to give the servants their wages. He could not look them in the eye but looked over their shoulders as he paid them and they thanked him. "Praise be to Allah," said Amadu to the others aloud in his hearing, "that I have this day eaten meat killed by my young master's hands." "Praise be," the others said. He thanked them briefly and formally and paid them off stiffly. They had not been offended, but in fact their respect for him had grown more by his distant attitude. "Every inch like his father," they had chattered on the way back to their huts, "this one will be great, too." He had been more moved than he had cared to admit, but in bed that night his fear and contempt for the poor and for women had grown and crystallized. The poor, like Amadu and the other servants from up-country, were poor because they were not Christians, because they were shiftless, because they did not work hard like his father or like himself. Women were weak and when not weak, over-religious. He was not sure whether both were not the same thing because the heavenly army should have been but were not on horseback. But of course Christ was. Christ held His flaming sword high and cried "Purity, purity!" and rode on a fast galloping steed. On His flank there galloped too the pregnant antelope with easy speed, its head battered and bleeding. They turned briefly as they sped by and he saw that the face of the steed was that of Amadu and that of the antelope, his mother's. They saw him wrestling with the naked, laughing woman. In all their eyes there was a look of fathomless pity. His father stood by nonchalantly looking away as did Toby. He woke up with a start and clamped his hand to his nostrils to stop the overpowering smell of lavender. He put his other hand under his pillow to find the Bible but it was not there. It had fallen on the floor. His father picked it up as he entered. "Are you all right? I heard you calling out." "Yes, Papa." His father sat by his bedside. "I just wanted to say how proud I am of you and your progress at school and everything. I attended the Rotarians' dinner last night and your headmaster told me what a leader you had become at your age at school." He could just discern his father's stern, dark grey features softened by the early and diffuse dawn. "It is not often white people speak of us the way he spoke of you," his father continued. "Papa, I am sorry I shot the antelope; I did not know it was a female, and . . . and . . ." "Never mind," his father said, "there is a time for everything and I shall teach you about the time to hunt deer and how to do it. I shall let you have one of my own guns." His father remained silent for a while and thought sadly and understandingly of the number of pellets Amadu had told him proudly the cook had to remove from the dead beast. He spoke to the boy again. "I am sorry I have not seen much of you these last few years, I have been so busy. But I shall retire soon, and we shall have more time together." Then he added on a lighter note, "Amadu and the head gardener were very proud of your shooting, especially the latter. That gardener and his family come from a hunting tribe in the interior where in the old days you had to kill an enemy or something sizeable before you could take a wife. But they have left that behind now. We are all making progress," he finished off gravely, getting up to go. Sunday luncheon had passed off happily. His father was in such a good mood that he called for his daughter who was borne in and placed between them. His father gave him a little wine for the first time. He liked the taste of the game and put a lot of pepper on it and ate it with rice and sweet potatoes. His father mashed up a little bit of game and put it in the baby's mouth, his aunt protesting. The baby chewed it between its red gums and few teeth, smacked its lips, blew bubbles and made satisfied movements with its legs. "God's blessings," his father had said, "you have helped to feed us all this afternoon. I wish your mother were here to see this day." "But she *is* here . . ." his aunt began, leaning forward to join the battle. "Yes, yes," his father agreed hastily.

That afternoon, they had gone out and he had taken his first shot with the twin-barrelled gun. The recoil had knocked him down. He had got up, his shoulder sore, and looked at his father. The father was looking away at the tree some yards away he had asked him to hit. So was Toby. The boy stared at them, his mouth dropping open with fear and wonder. The man and the dog were standing exactly, looking away, as they had done in his nightmare. A fly buzzed into his open mouth. He shut it quickly, dusted himself, and picked up the gun again. This time he balanced his feet well and truly. He fired and splintered a branch, this time remaining on his feet. His father had nodded with pleasure and they had walked back together. His father told him casually that the tree he had hit was exactly the boy's own age as it had been planted over his afterbirth and umbilical cord, as the custom was, on the day he was born.

Amadu had retired and had gone back to his village in the interior to farm by the next year, and his sister toddled about, accepted now by her father and brother. His aunt had become interested in faith-healing. He missed Amadu but was glad he had gone, as he was the only one left among the servants who had known him as a child.

As he had restlessly come up the valley an hour ago a few miles from home, he had recollected the morning. It was the birthday of the ageing bearded King of England and his father had put on extra-formal dress with his long judge's wig, and had gone off to the old eighteenth-century castle by the sea which was the governor's residence. His aunt and himself had not gone but had stood in an upstairs room looking across the country-side and the bay to the towering fort five miles away in the capital city where his father had gone.

At noon the announcement of the royal honours and decorations awarded each year on the king's birthday anniversary started. His aunt and himself had seen the flash of cannon and then heard the boom, which told them the first name had been called out. They knew his father's was second and his aunt's hands had trembled with pride as she waited, her lips moving in prayer and thanksgiving. The second flash and the roar told them it had happened. The servants in the compound cheered and struck up some drumming. His aunt's eyes moistened as she turned away. For long and distinguished service as a judge and public servant, his father had received a knighthood.

Afterwards his father had returned with his friends and colleagues. All the servants had come out in their best clothes and prostrated before the new knight. The boy had stood by the door in the billiard-room helping with the drinks and looking wonderingly out into the hall at the guests, the serious dark-faced urbane men, the high British officials and their wives, a chief from thc interior, a few relations, all surrounding his father whose face shone with satisfaction as he said deprecatingly that the honour belonged to the position, not to him personally. He had felt a sudden and overwhelming urge for his mother, who sometimes made silly mistakes and was not perfect or ambitious. He had slipped out after lunch with his gun and Toby to be alone and had tramped far out to this, his private valley.

There were two steep hills on either side and a low range blocked the end of it. It was partly covered with thick green vegetation near the bottom where a small stream noisily flowed. There was high grass nearer the top. He sat down on a rock against the thick bare roots of a tall tree.

"Come back, Mummy, I love you," he called again. The echoes jumbled but "I love you" came back quite distinctly.

Toby was not used to this and wagged his tail uncertainly, then looked up sharply across to where there were some guinea-fowls in the long grass. "She loved you, too, Toby," he said softly to the dog, who however whined impatiently and lifted its wet hunting nose proudly into the air. The boy lifted the gun and shot one of the ungainly birds. Toby waited quivering for the second shot. But the hunter had put his smoking muzzle down. The dog understood and made off ecstatically into the undergrowth. It soon came back dropping the dead bird before the boy, wagging its tail, and waiting for praise and patting.

Instead of that the boy lifted the gun half-way, aimed at the dog and shot it, blowing out its brains. Then he threw the empty gun down the valley, turned round and began running home, crashing through the thickets, crying, calling out, "Mummy, Mummy, Amadu, Amadu, where are you?"

The Gambler

NKEM NWANKWO

A small group of tired men, most of them carrying football pools coupons, squatted or stood by the steps of a Lagos post office. The postal workers had all gone home for the midday break. It was yet some minutes before they were to resume but the waiting group, smarting from the sun, were restless.

"They no go come," said an old man, getting up from the stone he had made a seat. "They no go come."

"No mine am," said a lanky young man. "I sabe these post office people. They don suffer me three years but they no go suffer me again. My frend don teach me how I go play pools. Yes—no be small small money like that de win. No I go save big money and throw' am in my time." He glanced a challenge at the smilingly sceptic group. His clothes were shabby, his shoes down at heels but eyes were deadly optimistic.

"Yes," shouted the orator. "My frend Bay we de work with me last month no de work with me again. He throw in one hundred pounds, yes one hundred and he win thousands. Now I see am ride fine fine cars and carry fine fine women. You no see am." This last was directed at a shortish, self-effacing clerk standing by. "You no see am." The young orator had a way of converting anybody into an acquaintance with a glance.

"Perhaps," the man addressed said very cautiously, and glanced at the five-shilling note he meant to invest that week.

"Yes," said the orator, "I no go wait for this dam people. I go go for nother place." He smiled a companionable smile all round and straggled off.

As soon as he was gone the post office opened. The sturdy clerk of the five-shilling note dashed to the counter, and getting there first bought his postal order, registered his pools coupon and emerged feeling as he had felt for the past ten years that the world would be kind to him at last.

"One hundred pounds," he said to himself, remembering the fiery orator's words "Impossible". He smiled a smile of diffidence mixed with optimism. Some passers-by noted the smile and thinking it was for them returned it, but Okoli Ede nicknamed "Time up" by his friends of the Government department where he worked, did not notice. His thoughts were engaged in contemplating the vagaries of that new mysterious god football pools. He came to the bus stop and looked a little wistfully at a standing vehicle. He would have liked to go by it, his home was a mile away and the sun eagerly pricked his head, but his salary did not allow for casual expenses. He walked therefore and after sweating at the neck for some time came to his home, a small sooty room in the back yard of a rakish-angled building. The room had a tone of minimum convenience not of comfort. It was furnished with an iron bed, a table and a chair. A corner of it segregated with an old blanket served for kitchen.

Okoli Ede took off his workaday clothes; blue khaki shorts and white shirt, and changed into brown wrapper and singlet. Then he set about boiling water for his garri.

"No, impossible," he murmured to himself. He could not stop the train of thoughts set on by the orator. Mightn't there be something in it though? To gamble on a grand scale? But with one hundred pounds! Fifty perhaps . . .

The pot was aboil. Okoli Ede prepared his lunch, ate, washed up and then came to his table to work on his G.C.E. papers. That was the pervasive aspect of his life. He was always eager to get home to it and his nickname "Time up" commemorated the haste with which he got away from the office at close of day.

But this time Okoli Ede could not concentrate. There was a restlessness inside him; bred of a mental conflict which was growing and spreading. Wasn't life ordinarily tedious. For five years he had been taking the G.C.E. and failing. Will he ever reach where he had all along aimed. A voyage to England. A law degree. Back to Nigeria. A prosperous car, long and American. Women. . . . Politics. More women. Ministerial office. More money than one could have need of . . . or would it not be better to gamble with everything. If one won. . . . In one jump the end achieved £75,000. Okoli Ede got up, excited by the overwhelming figure. He had always loved money. There was a time he lost a shilling, he went without his meal for the whole day to pay for that loss.

A reaction against optimism set in and Okoli Ede with a hiss of disapproval sat down hard and resumed his work. . . . But after some minutes the figure 75,000 persistently danced across his line of vision. He unlocked a drawer set in the table and slipped out a bank account book. He opened it. His assets stood at exactly £100. A coincidence? But it might be an omen. In the newspaper his stars for that week had said: "Do not be afraid to take a chance"; why should his credit stand at exactly the figure the young orator mentioned?

But one might fail even with a hundred pounds. Suppose he failed. He had responsibilities, his father and mother struggling against a perverse land which yearly failed to yield them enough to eat. Memories of that land had haunted him like an evil spectre forcing him to accumulate, to place a barrier between himself and want. Suppose he failed. He threw the accounts book inside the drawer and recommenced work. He must never again think of the mad scheme.

But he did think of it. Deep inside where the mind of men acted without awareness the conflict went on.

"I will not fail." Okoli Ede woke up the next morning with those words on his lips. "I will not fail." His nerves tingled, his body was all warm, his hands clammy with sweat, his throat constricted with excitement. With £100 it is impossible to fail. He jumped up and sought activity, anything that would prevent him from thinking, for to think is to hesitate and tremble. When Okoli Ede went to work that morning he carried with him his bank book; but he still had not the strength to tell himself what he wanted to do with it. Work was slack that day and when the chief clerk, bored with inactivity, left to chat with a pretty girl in the next section, Okoli Ede slipped out. The excitement was still on him. He walked hurriedly, he could not look himself in the face. The bank clerks divined his purpose and treated him with the insouciance reserved for those who withdrew rather than deposited.

That afternoon when he reached home he could not summon up life to boil water for his garri. He lay on his bed face down, exhausted with the strain, his mind torpid, unable to contemplate the terrible deed that would pitch him up or send him right down. Some force, some energy accumulated over the years had smoked off leaving only hope.

His mind was clearing now secking points of contact with solid elements, boyhood memories. He remembered on a certain occasion being tempted to give his school fees to a money doubler. His father's friend had dragged him away by the ears. But this very day he had done it.

He slipped out of his pocket a wad of notes. Thirty pounds. The remains of five years' honey pot. Some instinct had prevented him from throwing in everything, he had remembered that he had to live until the fortune came. . . . He thought of the awed faces of the crowd at the post office when he had asked for a money order for seventy pounds. . . . And so he had fed the god twice in two days.

The morning sun flooded Okoli Ede's room revealing its dingy starkness, but fresh invigorating air came with it and gave out promises of a fuller more adventurous living. Okoli Ede was suddenly filled with a discontent and a shame for his stingy colourless way of living. When the money came—there was no doubt now that it would come —how would it look in that room. But no matter. It was wonderful what fresh paint, colourful curtains and a new carpet could do for a room. . . . A little bouncy, Okoli Ede went out to work. Afterwards he walked into a silver plush store and equipped himself for the role he was to play in a few days' time. Back home he sang and danced as he cleaned out his room. "Not bad," he said at last, stepping back and examining his handiwork; the almanacs covered the putrid parts of the wall and the curtains looked fetching. . . . With a pleasurable feeling of achievement which he had never known in all his thirty years he opened a leather box lying on the bright new carpet. Reverently he examined the contents: a made-to-measure two-piece suit, an up-to-date tie, black shoes, shirt—why not put them on now. Would that be a little pushing. Okoli Ede smiled with a little of his old diffidence. At last he was arrayed and trying to see himself in a small mirror, many things still lacked but some can wait. . . . He went to work the next day smartened, suited and stiff.

"Eh, 'Time up' don rise high," several clerks gathered, eager for banter.

"Na so!"

"Wetin be her name?"

"Why 'eeno tell us make we prepare?"

"I never know say ee has one."

"Whosai plenty-you no sabee them quiet ones. . . . Women die for'am."

"Na waya O!"

The chief clerk looked up sharply and the clerks hustled to their places. That always inflated his dignity a little. He was a tall, thin man with museum-piece spectacles and the yellowing eyes of the drunkard. He peered suspiciously at Okoli Ede and remarked his suit. Then he looked furtively down at his own cigarette-ash-speckled bargain shirt and frowned. He would set down any clerk who got above himself. The office was not the place for show.

A thirst for experience, for pleasurable irresponsibility for secret sensation possessed Okoli Ede. His caution, rooted by upbringing, had not quite died, once or twice it had murmured from the deep recesses but Okoli Ede had pushed it down, after all one had to live, and with the coming fortune he was only living on his expectation. He entered a pub and for the first time in his life stared at the hired women, drank beer and listened to vigorous music—he would have liked to follow up and mingle with the whirling mass on the dance floor in riotous abandon, but timidity restrained him. He gulped more beer, his eyes glassed and his head swam. He rose to go. On his way a girl made eyes at him and his suit; but when he crawled near her she turned from him cold and proper. "Time will come. She will run after me," Okoli Ede consoled himself.

His change from steady modesty to recklessness gave neighbours matter for talk. But Okoli Ede did not heed brows or pointed whispers. He plunged violently into looseness borne on the crest of desire and hope.

The results of the football matches appeared on Sunday. Okoli Ede did not remember to buy the papers for he was suffering from the body's reaction to immoderate pleasure; the bowels moved funnily at painful intervals, the mouth was coated with spider webs, the eyes smarted, the legs were heavy.

The dividends were declared a few days later—£50,000 for top points. The excitement was too much for Okoli Ede. He had to walk the street to cool off. He wasn't afraid but his heart beat very loud.

While waiting, his craving for pleasure increased but there was no money to gratify it. Then one night he hired a girl. He woke very late in the morning and started dressing hastily. The girl woke, too, and when he wanted to pay her he was a shilling short. She made a point of it.

"Come tomorrow," said Okoli Ede roughly. "I no go come no time. You go pay me now." She was a hungry-looking waspish creature used to fights over pennies. Okoli Ede was afraid of her and of what the neighbours might say.

"If you no pay me you no go work," she grasped him. . . . "Or I go take this." She left him and dived for his new coat.

"No! No! Not that. Please make e take that," he gave her a tin of face powder . . . she considered, then threw the coat and powder contemptuously at him and stamped out, she would have preferred a fight—Okoli Ede was very late. The chief clerk, a little triumphant, watched him come in. He had had a difficult morning himself. A quarrel with his wife had left him as empty as a deflated football. The clerks had sensed his need to recover his prestige on somebody and were keeping out of his way.

"Na jus now 'ee de come," asked the chief clerk, darting a baleful glance at the dishevelled Okoli Ede.

"Yes," said the latter sullenly, going to his seat.

"You no hear me!" roared the chief clerk, his rage suddenly touched off. "If you no take time we go sack you . . . yes, sack you one time. . . . You come work when you like, eh. Abi you think you be a director . . . you think say na you alone sabe wear suit?"

This sally was too much for the other clerks. They roared and slapped their thighs and shouted, "Oga ejo—O!"

The plea only swelled the chief clerk and stimulated his tongue. "Look 'am!" he said. The clerks directed their several gazes at Okoli Ede who was standing scowling by his table.

"He no fit fill 'im belle and 'ee de wear suit. . . . No be your name be director or——"

He did not go further. The clerks stifled their mirth and a hiss of amazement escaped them as they saw their chief's face a bewildered world of black-blue and spouts of blood.

Okoli Ede glared murderously for a moment, and assured that the bottle had made its mark, walked out of the office.

"Let them sack me," he shouted as he got home. "They don't know who I am . . . but they will."

He slumped on his wooden chair and put his head in his hands. He sat in that position all day. Evening had set in when he rose, still unsteady with passion. Just at that moment, a blue envelope crept through the aperture below the door.

"Who be that?" Okoli Ede shouted nervously.

"Na me."

"Who be you?"

No answer. Okoli Ede picked up the letter. Foreign postmark. The letter dropped twice from his shaking hands but he hastily picked it up each time. . . . He couldn't open it, for once opened the secret will no longer be a secret. Clutching the letter he lay on his bed and closed his eyes. Then he suddenly jumped up and in one swift movement tore it open and stared at it hard; his mind curiously enfeebled could not grasp the full meaning, but his body divining by reflex knew, and the heart thumped dumbly.

Ten shillings. Okoli Ede murmured at last with a dull voice. . . . Won. . . . Ten shillings. The thought circled on the wave of consciousness. Impossible—impossible, I spent a hundred—he would go and find out. The pools people had representatives somewhere. . . . No, impossible. Ten shillings. It isn't true. But when he reached the streets his purpose started reflecting its futility. His legs didn't seem to belong to him.

Something must be done. . . . One can find a place where money was kept carelessly and steal. . . . He couldn't find another job and his parents and neighbours would have a poor opinion of him if he went home to farm. . . . If only there were no policemen around.

There was a deafening screech near Okoli Ede and suddenly a demoniac taxi careered wildly and halted near the pavement. The driver leapt out and came and towered angrily above him.

"Why 'ee no look wey 'ee de go? . . . You wan die? . . . If you wan die why 'ee no fall into lagoon there."

Okoli Ede didn't answer but walked on with the same mechanical gait.

"Oloriburuku, man of evil omen!" shouted the taxi-driver. "I no go kill you."

He walked back to his car and dashed away. Okoli Ede stood by the lagoon and watched the expanse of water calm and opalescent with the evening coloration. Far out to sea many brightly coloured boats squatted like sated sea-monsters of old. Then a canoe with two pullers came by trailing close to the shore. The fishermen seemed pleased about something. They pulled with vigour lapping the invigorating evening breeze gratefully. . . . Then they broke into a song, anxious to drown their nagging fear of not being able to provide enough garri for their large families.

"They are happy," thought Okoli Ede, watching them until they had formed black specks that merged with the blue misty haze in the distance. Far in the west the sun had broken into little ridges that flamed like blood on fire. A little later the night with its usual formidable suddenness blotted out the day.

Okoli Ede looked around to make sure that no one was near, then sprcad his hands wide and went with the day.

The Rain Came

GRACE A. OGOT

The chief was still far from the gate when his daughter Oganda saw him. She ran to meet him. Breathlessly she asked her father, "What is the news, great Chief? Everyone in the village is anxiously waiting to hear when it will rain." Labong'o held out his hands for his daughter but he did not say a word. Puzzled by her father's cold attitude Oganda ran back to the village to warn the others that the chief was back.

The atmosphere in the village was tense and confused. Everyone moved aimlessly and fussed in the yard without actually doing any work. A young woman whispered to her co-wife, "If they have not solved this rain business today, the chief will crack." They had watched him getting thinner and thinner as the people kept on pestering him. "Our cattle lie dying in the fields," they reported. "Soon it will be our children and then ourselves. Tell us what to do to save our lives, oh great Chief." So the chief had daily pleaded with the Almighty through the ancestors to deliver them from their great distress.

Instead of calling the family together and giving them the news immediately, Labong'o went to his own hut, a sign that he was not to be disturbed. Having replaced the shutter, he sat in the dimly-lit hut to contemplate.

It was no longer a question of being the chief of hunger-stricken people that weighed Labong'o's heart. It was the life of his only daughter that was at stake. At the time when Oganda came to meet him, he saw the glittering chain shining around her waist. The prophecy was complete. "It is Oganda, Oganda, my only daughter, who must die so young." Labong'o burst into tears before finishing the sentence. The chief must not weep. Society had declared him the bravest of men. But Labong'o did not care any more. He assumed the position of a simple father and wept bitterly. He loved his people, the Luo, but what were the Luo for him without Oganda? Her life had brought a new life in Labong'o's world and he ruled better than he could remember. How would the spirit of the village survive his beautiful daughter? "There are so many homes and so many parents who have daughters. Why choose this one? She is all I have." Labong'o spoke as if the ancestors were there in the hut and he could see them face to face. Perhaps they were there, warning him to remember his promise on the day he was enthroned when he said aloud, before the elders, "I will lay down my life, if necessary, and the life of my household, to save this tribe from the hands of the enemy." "Deny! Deny!" he could hear the voice of his forefathers mocking him.

When Labong'o was made chief he was only a young man. Unlike his father he ruled for many years with only one wife. But people mocked him secretly because his only wife did not bear him a daughter. He married a second, a third and a fourth wife. But they all gave birth to male children. When Labong'o married a fifth wife, she bore him a daughter. They called her Oganda, meaning "beans", because her skin was very smooth. Out of Labong'o's twenty children, Oganda was the only girl. Though she was the chief's favourite, her mother's co-wives swallowed their jealous feelings and showered her with love. After all, they said, Oganda was a girl whose days in the royal family were numbered. She would soon marry at a tender age and leave the enviable position to someone else.

Never in his life had he been faced with such an impossible decision. Refusing to yield to the rain-maker's request would mean sacrificing the whole tribe, putting the interests of the individual above those of the society. More than that. It would mean disobeying the ancestors, and most probably wiping the Luo people from the surface of the earth. On the other hand, to let Oganda die as a ransom for the people would permanently cripple Labong'o spiritually. He knew he would never be the same chief again.

The words of Nditi, the medicine-man, still echoed in his ears. "Podho, the ancestor of the Luo, appeared to me in a dream last night and he asked me to speak to the chief and the people," Nditi had said to the gathering of tribesmen. "A young woman who has not known a man must die so that the country may have rain. While Podho was still talking to me, I saw a young woman standing at the lakeside, her hands raised above her head. Her skin was as a tender young deer's. Her tall slender figure stood like a lonely reed at the river bank. Her sleepy eyes wore a sad look like that of a bereaved mother. She wore a gold ring on her left ear and a glittering brass chain around her waist. As I still marvelled at the beauty of this young woman, Podho told me, 'Out of all the women in this land, we have chosen this one. Let her offer herself a sacrifice to the lake monster! And on that day, the rain will come down in torrents. Let everyone stay at home on that day, lest he be carried away by the floods.' "

Outside there was a strange stillness, except for the thirsty birds that sang lazily on the dying trees. The blinding midday heat had forced the people into their huts. Not far away from the chief's hut two guards were snoring away quietly. Labong'o removed his crown and the large eagle-head that hung loosely on his shoulders. He left the hut and, instead of asking Nyabogo the messenger to beat the drum, he went straight and beat it himself. In no time the whole household had assembled under the *siala* tree where he usually addressed them. He told Oganda to wait a while in her grandmother's hut.

When Labong'o stood to address his household his voice was hoarse and tears choked him. He started to speak but words refused to leave his lips. His wives and sons knew there was danger, perhaps their enemies had declared war on them. Labong'o's eyes were red and they could see he had been weeping. At last he told them, "One whom we love and treasure will be taken away from us. Oganda is to die." Labong'o's voice was so faint that he could not hear it himself. But he continued, "The ancestors have chosen her to be offered as a sacrifice to the lake monster in order that we may have rain."

For a moment there was dead silence among the people. They were completely stunned; and as some confused murmur broke out Oganda's mother fainted and was carried off to her own hut. But the other people rejoiced. They danced around singing and chanting, "Oganda is the lucky one to die for the people; if it is to save the people, let Oganda go."

In her grandmother's hut Oganda wondered what the whole family was discussing about her that she could not hear. Her grandmother's hut was well away from the chief's court and much as she strained her ears, she could not hear what they were saying. "It must be marriage," she concluded. It was an accepted custom for the family to discuss their daughter's future marriage behind her back. A faint smile played on Oganda's lips as she thought of the several young men who swallowed saliva at the mere mention of her name.

There was Kech, the son of an elder in a neighbouring clan. Kech was very handsome. He had sweet, meek eyes and roaring laughter. He could make a wonderful father, Oganda thought. But they would not be a good match. Kech was a bit too short to be her husband. It would humiliate her to have to look down at Kech each time she spoke to him. Then she thought of Dimo, the tall young man who had already distinguished himself as a brave warrior and an outstanding wrestler. Dimo loved Oganda, but Oganda thought he would make a cruel husband, always quarrelling and ready to fight. No, she did not like him. Oganda fingered the glittering chain on her waist as she thought of Osinda. A long time ago when she was quite young Osinda had given her that chain and, instead of wearing it around her neck several times, she wore it round her waist where it could permanently stay. She heard her heart pounding so loudly as she thought of him. She whispered, "Let it be you they are discussing, Osinda the lovely one. Come now and take me away. . . ."

The lean figure in the doorway startled Oganda who was rapt in thought about the man she loved. "You have frightened me, Grandma," said Oganda laughing. "Tell me, is it my marriage you were discussing? You can take it from me that I won't marry any of them." A smile played on her lips again. She was coaxing her grandma to tell her quickly, to tell her they were pleased with Osinda.

In the open space outside the excited relatives were dancing and singing. They were coming to the hut now, each carrying a gift to put at Oganda's feet. As their singing got nearer Oganda was able to hear what they were saying: "If it is to save the people, if it is to give us rain, let Oganda go. Let Oganda die for her people and for her ancestors." Was she mad to think that they were singing about her? How could she die? She found the lean figure of her grandmother barring the door.

She could not get out. The look on her grandmother's face warned her that there was danger around the corner. "Mother, it is not marriage then?" Oganda asked urgently. She suddenly felt panicky, like a mouse cornered by a hungry cat. Forgetting that there was only one door in the hut, Oganda fought desperately to find another exit. She must fight for her life. But there was none.

She closed her eyes, leapt like a wild tiger through the door, knocking her grandmother flat to the ground. There outside in mourning garments Labong'o stood motionless, his hands folded at the back. He held his daughter's hand and led her away from the excited crowd to the little red-painted hut where her mother was resting. Here he broke the news officially to his daughter.

For a long time the three souls who loved one another dearly sat in darkness. It was no good speaking. And even if they tried, the words could not have come out. In the past they had been like three cooking-stones, sharing their burdens. Taking Oganda away from them would leave two useless stones which would not hold a cooking-pot.

News that the beautiful daughter of the chief was to be sacrificed to give the people rain spread across the country like wind. And at sunset the chief's village was full of relatives and friends who had come to congratulate Oganda. Many more were on their way, coming, carrying their gifts. They would dance till morning to keep her company. And in the morning they would prepare her a big farewell feast. All these relatives thought it a great honour to be selected by the spirits to die in order that the society might live. "Oganda's name will always remain a living name among us," they boasted.

Of course it was an honour, a great honour, for a woman's daughter to be chosen to die for the country. But what could the mother gain once her only daughter was blown away by the wind? There were so many other women in the land, why choose her daughter, her only child? Had human life any meaning at all?—other women had houses full of children while Oganda's mother had to lose her only child!

In the cloudless sky the moon shone brightly and the numerous stars glittered. The dancers of all age groups assembled to dance before Oganda, who sat close to her mother sobbing quietly. All these years she had been with her people she thought she understood them. But now she discovered that she was a stranger among them. If they really loved her as they had always professed, why were they not sympathetic? Why were they not making any attempt to save her? Did her people really understand what it felt like to die young? Unable to restrain her emotions any longer, she sobbed loudly as her age-group got up to dance. They were young and beautiful and very soon they would marry and have their own children. They would have husbands to love and little huts for themselves. They would have reached maturity. Oganda touched the chain around her waist as she thought of Osinda. She wished Osinda were there too, among her friends. "Perhaps he is ill," she thought gravely. The chain comforted Oganda —she would die with it around her waist and wear it in the underground world.

In the morning a big feast of many different dishes was prepared for Oganda so that she could pick and choose. "People don't eat after death," they said. The food looked delicious but Oganda touched none of it. Let the happy people eat. She contented herself with sips of water from a little calabash.

The time for her departure was drawing near and each minute was precious. It was a day's journey to the lake. She was to walk all night, passing through the great forest. But nothing could touch her, not even the denizens of the forest. She was already anointed with sacred oil. From the time Oganda received the sad news she had expected Osinda to appear any moment. But he was not there. A relative told her that Osinda was away on a private visit. Oganda realized that she would never see her dear one again.

In the afternoon the whole village stood at the gate to say good-bye and to see her for the last time. Her mother wept on her neck for a long time. The great chief in a mourning skin came to the gate barefooted and mingled with the people—a simple father in grief. He took off his wrist bracelet and put it on his daughter's wrist, saying, "You will always live among us. The spirit of our forefathers is with you."

Tongue-tied and unbelieving Oganda stood there before the people. She had nothing to say. She looked at her home once more. She could hear her heart beating so painfully within her. All her childhood plans were coming to an end. She felt like a flower nipped in the bud never to enjoy the morning dew again. She looked at her weeping mother and whispered, "Whenever you want to see me, always look at the sunset. I will be there."

Oganda turned southwards to start her trek to the lake. Her parents, relatives, friends and admirers stood at the gate and watched her go. Her beautiful, slender figure grew smaller and smaller till she mingled with the thin dry trees in the forest.

As Oganda walked the lonely path that wound its way in the wilderness, she sang a song and her own voice kept her company.

> "*The ancestors have said Oganda must die;*
> *The daughter of the chief must be sacrificed.*
> *When the lake monster feeds on my flesh,*
> *The people will have rain;*
> *Yes, the rain will come down in torrents.*
> *The wind will blow, the thunder will roar.*
> *And the floods will wash away the sandy beaches*
> *When the daughter of the chief dies in the lake.*
> *My age-group has consented,*
> *My parents have consented,*
> *So have my friends and relatives;*
> *Let Oganda die to give us rain.*
> *My age-group are young and ripe,*
> *Ripe for womanhood and motherhood;*
> *But Oganda must die young,*
> *Oganda must sleep with the ancestors.*
> *Yes, rain will come down in torrents.*"

The red rays of the setting sun embraced Oganda and she looked like a burning candle in the wilderness.

The people who came to hear her sad song were touched by her beauty. But they all said the same thing: "If it is to save the people, if it is to give us rain, then be not afraid. Your name will for ever live among us."

At midnight Oganda was tired and weary. She could walk no more. She sat under a big tree and, having sipped water from her calabash, she rested her head on the tree trunk and slept.

When she woke up in the morning the sun was high in the sky. After walking for many hours she reached the *tong*, a strip of land that separated the inhabited part of the country from the sacred place—*kar lamo*. No lay man could enter this place and come out alive—only those who had direct contact with the spirits and the Almighty were allowed to enter his holy of holies. But Oganda had to pass through this sacred land on her way to the lake, which she had to reach at sunset.

A large crowd gathered to see her for the last time. Her voice was now hoarse and painful but there was no need to worry any more. Soon she would not have to sing. The crowd looked at Oganda sympathetically, mumbling words she could not hear. But none of them pleaded for her life. As Oganda opened the gate a child, a young child, broke loose from the crowd and ran towards her. The child took a small ear-ring from her sweaty hands and gave it to Oganda, saying, "When you reach the world of the dead, give this ear-ring to my sister. She died last week. She forgot this ring." Oganda, taken aback by this strange request, took the little ring and handed her precious water and food to the child. She did not need them now. Oganda did not know whether to laugh or cry. She had heard mourners sending their love to their sweethearts, long dead, but this idea of sending gifts was new to her.

Oganda held her breath as she crossed the barrier to enter the sacred land. She looked appealingly at the crowd but there was no response. Their minds were too preoccupied with their own survival. Rain was the precious medicine they were longing for and the sooner Oganda could get to her destination the better.

A strange feeling possessed the princess as she picked her way in the sacred land. There were strange noises that often startled her and her first reaction was to take to her heels. But she remembered that she had to fulfil the wish of her people. She was exhausted, but the path was still winding. Then suddenly the path ended on sandy land. The water had retreated miles away from the shore, leaving a wide stretch of sand. Beyond this was the vast expanse of water.

Oganda felt afraid. She wanted to picture the size and shape of the monster, but fear would not let her. The people did not talk about it, nor did the crying children who were silenced at the mention of its name. The sun was still up but it was no longer hot. For a long time Oganda walked ankle-deep in the sand. She was exhausted and longed desperately for her calabash of water. As she moved on she had a strange feeling that something was following her. Was it the monster? Her hair stood erect and a cold paralysing feeling ran along her spine. She looked behind, sideways and in front, but there was nothing except a cloud of dust.

Oganda began to hurry but the feeling did not leave her and her whole body seemed to be bathing in its perspiration.

The sun was going down fast and the lake shore seemed to move along with it.

Oganda started to run. She must be at the lake before sunset. As she ran she heard a noise coming from behind. She looked back sharply and something resembling a moving bush was frantically running after her. It was about to catch up with her.

Oganda ran with all her strength. She was now determined to throw herself into the water even before sunset. She did not look back but the creature was upon her. She made an effort to cry out, as in a nightmare, but she could not hear her own voice. The creature caught up with Oganda. A strong hand grabbed her. But she fell flat on the sand and fainted.

When the lake breeze brought her back to consciousness a man was bending over her. "O . . . !" Oganda opened her mouth to speak, but she had lost her voice. She swallowed a mouthful of water poured into her mouth by the stranger.

"Osinda, Osinda! Please let me die. Let me run, the sun is going down. Let me die. Let them have rain."

Osinda fondled the glittering chain around Oganda's waist and wiped tears from her face. "We must escape quickly to an unknown land," Osinda said urgently. "We must run away from the wrath of the ancestors and the retaliation of the monster."

"But the curse is upon me, Osinda, I am no good for you any more. And moreover the eyes of the ancestors will follow us everywhere and bad luck will befall us. Nor can we escape from the monster."

Oganda broke loose, afraid to escape, but Osinda grabbed her hands again. "Listen to me, Oganda! Listen! Here are two coats!" He then covered the whole of Oganda's body, except her eyes, with a leafy attire made from the twigs of *bwombwe*. "These will protect us from the eyes of the ancestors and the wrath of the monster. Now let us run out of here." He held Oganda's hand and they ran from the sacred land, avoiding the path that Oganda had followed.

The bush was thick and the long grass entangled their feet as they ran. Half-way through the sacred land they stopped and looked back. The sun was almost touching the surface of the water. They were frightened. They continued to run, now faster, to avoid the sinking sun.

"Have faith, Oganda—that thing will not reach us."

When they reached the barrier and looked behind them, trembling, only a tip of the sun could be seen above the water's surface.

"It is gone! It is gone!" Oganda wept, hiding her face in her hands.

"Weep not, the daughter of the chief. Let us run, let us escape."

There was a lightning flash in the distance. They looked up, frightened.

That night it rained in torrents as it had not done for a long, long time.

The Crooks

GABRIEL OKARA

Their hair was all brown with dust. The clothes they had on were dirty and torn. Their barefeet were as dirty and as brown as their hair. The only luggage they had was a bulging haversack. It was neatly buckled down, and one of them carried it on his shoulder as they walked along the bridge towards Idumota. They were two men who had apparently just arrived from the provinces by lorry.

Traders arriving dirty and dusty from head to foot, and carrying haversacks, are a familiar sight in Lagos. But these two had an air about them of being in a strange place. They walked one behind the other as if they were picking their way in the forest. They avoided bodily contact with the people walking briskly to and fro past them, and were startled over and over again by the strident horns of the cars. They gaped at the lagoon and at the stream of cars, motor-cycles and bicycles rushing in both directions across the gigantic bridge.

On the other side, a man was cycling leisurely along on a brand-new bicycle from the Idumota end of the bridge. His shirt and trousers were a dazzling white, and his two-tone black and white shoes were spotless. Tilted over his forehead was a white cork helmet. He put on his brakes as his practised eyes caught the two men on the other side, stopping now and again to allow people to pass, or looking for an opening through the milling throng on the pavement. The man on the bicycle studied them for a few minutes from his side of the bridge and waited for a break in the traffic. His eyes never left them. An old car wheezed past. He looked quickly left and right. Another car was approaching, but he dashed across narrowly missing death. Safe on the other side he cycled up to the two men.

"Hallo," he said, with a broad smile.

The two men were startled and moved on faster. But the cyclist stuck to them.

"I know you for somewhere," he said, smiling. "I tink na Enugu. I get friend dere and you resemble'am."

The man carrying the haversack moved to the railings and his partner, turning to the cyclist, said, "Yes na from Enugu we come. You go for Enugu before?"

"Yes," the cyclist said, "I stay for Enugu long time. Okonkwo be my big friend an' you resembl'am for face. You be him broder?"

"Yes," said the stranger, "one Okonkwo be one farder one moder with me. He be big contractor for Enugu an' we stay for Asata. Na him be your frien'?"

"Ah, na him!" said the cyclist, "we be big frien's. All the lorry wey he get na me arrange for'am. I be agent for lorry. Dis na firs' time you come for Lagos?"

"Yes, dis na firs' time an' na lorry I wan buy sef."

"Ah, you be lucky man!" said the cyclist. "Waiten be your name?"

"Okonkwo."

"An' your friend?"

"Okeke."

"You be lucky, man. Na lorry I go give person for Ebute Metta jus' now. Na God say make you meet me. Wayo plenty for here. They for wayo you an' take your money for nothin'. How many lorry you wan' buy?"

"Na only one," said Okonkwo.

"Na only one you want. I go fit arrange ma quick for you if na today or tomorrow. Only today late small. But tomorrow I go fit getam for you easy. . . . You get place for stay?"

"The person wey I know, I no know the place he stay. But we go look for am," said Okonkwo.

"Make you no worry," said the cyclist, "you stay for my place. Your broder be my big frien' and he go vex when he hear say I see you an' no keep you for my house. Come we go."

At this invitation Okonkwo shook his head and said, "I fear for dis town. They tell me say wayo plenty. I no know you. You say you be my broder frien' but I dey fear."

"You right," said the cyclist, "you right for fear. But your broder an' me be big frien's an even 'e write me letter say him broder dey come. I forget for tell you de firs' time I see you. So make you no fear. Na God make wey I see you."

"I dey fear O," said Okonkwo, "I dey fear but make I tell Okeke firs'."

With this he went over to Okeke and told him. But Okeke replied with a vigorous shake of his head and said loudly that it was all a trick to get their money. But after much persuasion he reluctantly agreed and they went with the cyclist.

It was evening. Okonkwo and Okeke had eaten a well-pounded foofoo and egusi soup specially prepared for them and were sitting close together with the haversack between them in their host's parlour. The latter, who had been out for some little time, had just come in with a party of other people. The new-comers were dressed in heavily embroidered velvet agbadas and slippers.

"Dis na my frien's," their host said, introducing the people to Okonkwo and Okeke. "I tell dem say I get big 'tranger so they come salute you. All be big people. Na we dey sell motor for dis town."

As the men went forward to shake hands with them, Okonkwo and Okeke looked awed and fidgeted. The hand shaking over, their host beckoned one of his friends into his bedroom.

"You see how them be?" he said, after shutting the door. "They be moo-moo and they get plenty money for bag. Now listen, as I say before we go play big. We go make them win hundred 'redboys'. When you wan' kill big fish you use big hook and big bait. So you know waiten you go do. Tomorrow we go rich." Then he opened a small wooden box and bringing out three cards, said, "Dis na the cards," as he handed them over to his partner who took them and put them in his pocket. Then the two men went back into the parlour to join the others. Soon drinks were produced from their bag-like pockets and as they drank and boasted of their riches the cards were brought out. They invited Okonkwo and Okeke to play, but they refused as they didn't know how.

"Very easy," said the man with the cards. "When I cutam putam for ground you pick dis one," showing them an ace of spades as he continued, "you pick dis one you win, you pick another I win, easy you see."

Still Okonkwo and Okeke were reluctant, but they soon seemed to be impressed by the easy way some of the people won money and joined the game.

"Na one one poun'," said the man with the cards. "Put your money for ground. You take dis you win, you take dis you lose." Okonkwo and Okeke watched carefully as the man cut the cards and put them face downwards on the floor. After studying them for a minute or two Okonkwo picked one card. It was the ace of spades and so he won. So it went on until Okonkwo and Okeke won one hundred pounds between them.

"E do now," said the host, as the hundredth pound was being handed over to Okonkwo and Okeke. "E do now. You be lucky people. Tomorrow you go get lorry."

So they stopped playing and the people left. The host also went to bed after showing Okonkwo and Okeke a place to sleep in the parlour.

When he thought that Okonkwo and Okeke would be asleep, their host opened the door quietly and peered in. The haversack was chained to a chair. He shut the door. But soon he was back again unable to resist the anticipation of the money he would trick them out of the next day. Okonkwo and Okeke snored. They were the greenest things he'd ever come across, he thought. He already felt the seven hundred and fifty pounds in the haversack in his palms. Tomorrow, tomorrow, he thought and, shutting the door gently, went to bed a rich man. . . . But when he went to greet his guests in the morning, the room was empty!

In the lavatory of the "Up Limited" train, Okonkwo and Okeke were grooming themselves.

"Free food, free lodging, and a gift of a hundred pounds!" Okonkwo was saying, as he washed his face.

"When he was peeping in again and again, I thought he was going to be tough," said Okeke, as he rubbed his chin before the mirror.

"They'll never learn," said Okonkwo, as he wiped his face. They are green as green peas, the whole batch of them. See how they left the door only bolted."

So they bantered on as the train jugged along. Swaying on the handle of the door was their haversack now emptied of the stones and old rags that had won them the hundred pounds.

The Will of Allah

DAVID OWOYELE

There had been a clear moon. Now the night was dark. Dogo glanced up at the night sky. He saw that scudding black clouds had obscured the moon. He cleared his throat. "Rain tonight," he observed to his companion. Sule, his companion, did not reply immediately. He was a tall powerfully-built man. His face, as well as his companion's, was a stupid mask of ignorance. He lived by thieving as did Dogo, and just now he walked with an unaccustomed limp. "It is wrong to say that," Sule said after a while, fingering the long, curved sheath-knife he always wore on his upper left arm when, in his own words, he was "on duty". A similar cruel-looking object adorned the arm of his comrade. "How can you be sure?" "Sure?" said Dogo, annoyance and impatience in his voice. Dogo is the local word for tall. This man was thickset, short and squat, anything but tall. He pointed one hand up at the scurrying clouds. "You only want to look up there. A lot of rain has fallen in my life: those up there are rain clouds."

They walked on in silence for a while. The dull red lights of the big town glowed in crooked lines behind them. Few people were abroad, for it was already past midnight. About half a mile ahead of them the native town, their destination, sprawled in the night. Not a single electric light bulb glowed on its crooked streets. This regrettable fact suited the books of the two men perfectly. "You are not Allah," said Sule at last. "You may not assert."

Sule was a hardened criminal. Crime was his livelihood, he had told the judge this during his last trial that had earned him a short stretch in jail. "Society must be protected from characters like you," he could still hear the stern judge intoning in the hushed courtroom. Sule had stood in the dock, erect, unashamed, unimpressed; he'd heard it all before. "You and your type constitute a threat to life and property and this court will always see to it that you get your just deserts, according to the Law." The judge had then fixed him with a stern gaze, which Sule coolly returned: he had stared into too many so-called judges' eyes to be easily intimidated. Besides, he feared nothing and no one except Allah. The judge thrust his legal chin forward. "Do you never pause to consider that the road of crime leads only to frustration, punishment and suffering? You look fit enough for anything. Why don't you try your hand at earning an honest living for a change?" Sule had shrugged his broad shoulders. "I earn my living the only way I know," he said. "The only way I've chosen." The judge had sat back, dismayed. Then he leaned forward to try again. "Is it beyond you to see anything wrong in thieving, burglary, crime?" Again Sule had shrugged. "The way I earn my living I find quite satisfactory." "Satisfactory!" exclaimed the judge, and a wave of whispering swept over the court. The judge stopped this with a rap of his gavel. "Do you find it satisfactory to break the law?" "I've no choice," said Sule. "The law is a nuisance. It keeps getting in one's way." "Constant arrest and imprisonment—do you find it satisfactory to be a jailbird?" queried the judge, frowning most severely. "Every calling has its hazards," replied Sule philosophically. The judge mopped his face. "Well, my man, you cannot break the law. You can only attempt to break it. And you will only end up by getting broken." Sule nodded. "We have a saying like that," he remarked conversationally. "He who attempts to shake a stump only shakes himself." He glanced up at the frowning judge. "Something like a thick stump—the law, eh?" The judge had given him three months. Sule had shrugged. "The will of Allah be done. . . ."

A darting tongue of lightning lit up the overcast sky for a second. Sule glanced up. "Sure it looks like rain. But you do not say: It will rain. You are only a mortal. You only say: If it is the will of Allah, it will rain." Sule was a deeply religious man, according to his lights. His religion forbade being dogmatic or prophetic about the future, about anything. His fear of Allah was quite genuine. It was his firm conviction that Allah left the question of a means of livelihood for each man to decide for himself. Allah, he was sure, gives some people more than they need so that others with too little could help themselves to some of it. It could certainly not be the intention of Allah that some stomachs remain empty while others are overstuffed.

Dogo snorted. He had served prison sentences in all the major towns in the country. Prison had become for him a home from home. Like his companion in crime, he feared no man; but unlike him, he had no religion other than self-preservation. "You and your religion," he said in derision. "A lot of good it has done you." Sule did not reply. Dogo knew from experience that Sule was touchy about his religion, and the first intimation he would get that Sule had lost his temper would be a blow on the head. The two men never pretended that their partnership had anything to do with love or friendship or any other luxurious idea: they operated together when their prison sentences allowed because they found it convenient. In a partnership that each believed was for his own special benefit, there could be no fancy code of conduct. "Did you see the woman tonight?" Dogo asked, changing the subject, not because he was afraid of Sule's displeasure but because his grasshopper mind had switched to something else. "Uh-huh," granted Sule. "Well?" said Dogo, when he did not go on. "Bastard!" said Sule, without any passion. "Who? Me?" said Dogo thinly. "We were talking about the woman," replied Sule.

They got to a small stream. Sule stopped, washed his arms and legs, his clean-shaven head. Dogo squatted on the bank, sharpening his sheath-knife on a stone. "Where do you think you are going?" "To yonder village," said Sule, rinsing out his mouth. "Didn't know you had a sweetheart there," said Dogo. "I'm not going to any woman," said Sule. "I am going to collect stray odds and ends—if it is the will of Allah."

"To steal, you mean?" suggested Dogo.

"Yes," conceded Sule. He straightened himself, pointed a brawny arm at Dogo: "You are a burglar, too . . . and a bastard besides."

Dogo, calmly testing the edge of the knife on his arm, nodded. "Is that part of your religion, washing in midnight streams?" Sule didn't reply until he had climbed on to the farther bank, "Wash when you find a stream; for when you cross another is entirely in the hands of Allah." He limped off, Dogo following him. "Why did you call her a bastard?" Dogo asked. "Because she is one." "Why?" "She told me she sold the coat and the black bag for only fifteen shillings." He glanced down and sideways at his companion. "I suppose you got on to her before I did and told her what to say?" "I've not laid eyes on her for a week," protested Dogo. "The coat is fairly old. Fifteen shillings sounds all right to me. I think she had done very well indeed." "No doubt," said Sule. He didn't believe Dogo. "I'd think the same way if I'd already shared part of the proceeds with her. . . ."

Dogo said nothing. Sule was always suspicious of him, and he returned the compliment willingly. Sometimes their suspicion of each other was groundless, other times not. Dogo shrugged. "I don't know what you are talking about." "No. I don't suppose you would," said Sule drily. "All I'm interested in is my share," went on Dogo. "Your second share, you mean," said Sule. "You'll both get your share—you cheating son without a father, as well as that howling devil of a woman." He paused before he added, "She stabbed me in the thigh—the bitch." Dogo chuckled softly to himself. "I've been wondering about that limp of yours. Put a knife in your thigh, did she? Odd, isn't it?" Sule glanced at him sharply. "What's odd about it?" "You getting stabbed just for asking her to hand over the money." "Ask her? I didn't ask her. No earthly use asking anything of characters like that." "Oh?" said Dogo. "I'd always thought all you had to do was ask. True, the coat wasn't yours. But you asked her to sell it. She's an old 'fence' and ought to know that you are entitled to the money." "Only a fool would be content with fifteen shillings for a coat and a bag," said Sule. "And you are not a fool, eh?" chuckled Dogo. "What did you do about it?" "Beat the living daylight out of her," rasped Sule. "And quite right, too," commented Dogo. "Only snag is you seem to have got more than you gave her." He chuckled again. "A throbbing wound is no joke," said Sule testily. "And who's joking? I've been stabbed in my time, too. You can't go around at night wearing a knife and not expect to get stabbed once in a while. We should regard such things as an occupational hazard." "Sure," grunted Sule. "But that can't cure a wound." "No, but the hospital can," said Dogo. "I know. But in the hospital they ask questions before they cure you."

They were entering the village. In front of them the broad path diverged into a series of tracks that twined away between the houses. Sule paused, briefly, took one of the paths. They walked along on silent feet, just having a look around. Not a light showed in any of the crowded mud houses. Every little hole of a window was shut or plugged, presumably against the threatening storm. A peal of languid thunder rumbled over from the east. Except for a group of goats and sheep, which rose startled at their approach, the two had the village paths to themselves. Every once in a while Sule would stop by a likely house; the two would take a careful look around; he'd look inquiringly down at his companion, who would shake his head, and they would move on.

They had been walking around for about a quarter of an hour when a brilliant flash of lightning almost burned out their eyeballs. That decided them. "We'd better hurry," whispered Dogo. "The storm's almost here." Sule said nothing. A dilapidated-looking house stood a few yards away. They walked up to it. They were not put off by its appearance. Experience had taught them that what a house looked like was no indication of what it contained. Some stinking hovels had yielded rich hauls. Dogo nodded at Sule. "You stay outside and try to keep awake," said Sule. He nodded at a closed window. "You might stand near that."

Dogo moved off to his post. Sule got busy on the crude wooden door. Even Dogo's practised ear did not detect any untoward sound, and from where he stood he couldn't tell when Sule gained entry into the house. He remained at his post for what seemed ages—it was actually a matter of minutes. Presently he saw the window at his side open slowly. He froze against the wall. But it was Sule's muscular hands that came through the window, holding out to him a biggish gourd. Dogo took the gourd and was surprised at its weight. His pulse quickened. People around here trusted gourds like this more than banks. "The stream," whispered Sule through the open window. Dogo understood. Hoisting the gourd on to his head, he made off at a fast trot for the stream. Sule would find his way out of the house and follow him.

He set the gourd down carefully by the stream, took off its carved lid. If this contained anything of value, he thought, he and Sule did not have to share it equally. Besides, how did he know Sule had not helped himself to a little of its contents before passing it out through the window? He thrust his right hand into the gourd and next instant he felt a vicious stab on his wrist. A sharp exclamation escaped from him as he jerked his arm out. He peered at his wrist closely then slowly and steadily he began to curse. He damned to hell and glory everything under the sun in the two languages he knew. He sat on the ground, holding his wrist, cursing softly. He heard Sule approaching and stopped. He put the lid back on the gourd and waited. "Any trouble?" he asked, when the other got to him. "No trouble," said Sule. Together they stooped over the gourd. Dogo had to hold his right wrist in his left hand but he did it so Sule wouldn't notice. "Have you opened it?" Sule asked. "Who? Me? Oh, no!" said Dogo. Sule did not believe him and he knew it. "What can be so heavy?" Dogo asked curiously. "We'll see," said Sule.

He took off the lid, thrust his hand into the gaping mouth of the gourd and felt a sharp stab on his wrist. He whipped his hand out of the gourd. He stood up. Dogo, too, stood up and for the first time Sule noticed Dogo's wrist held in the other hand. They were silent for a long time, glaring at each other. "As you always insisted, we should go fifty-fifty in everything," said Dogo casually. Quietly, almost inaudibly, Sule started speaking. He called Dogo every name known to obscenity. Dogo for his part was holding up his end quite well. They stopped when they had run out of names. "I am going home," Dogo announced. "Wait!" said Sule. With his uninjured hand he rummaged in his pocket, brought out a box of matches. With difficulty he struck one, held the flame over the gourd, peered in. He threw the match away. "It is not necessary," he said. "Why not?" Dogo demanded. "That in there is an angry cobra," said Sule. The leaden feeling was creeping up his arm fast. The pain was tremendous. He sat down. "I still don't see why I can't go home," said Dogo. "Have you never heard the saying that what the cobra bites dies at the foot of the cobra? The poison is that good: just perfect for sons of swine like you. You'll never make it home. Better sit down and die here." Dogo didn't agree but the throbbing pain forced him to sit down.

They were silent for several minutes while the lightning played around them. Finally Dogo said, "Funny that your last haul should be a snake-charmer's gourd. "I think it's funnier still that it should contain a cobra, don't you?" said Sule. . . . He groaned. "I reckon funnier things will happen before the night is done," said Dogo. "Uh!" he winced with pain. "A couple of harmless deaths, for instance," suggested Sule. "Might as well kill the bloody snake," said Dogo. He attempted to rise and pick up a stone from the stream; he couldn't. "Ah, well," he said, lying on his back. "It doesn't matter anyway."

The rain came pattering down. "But why die in the rain?" he demanded angrily. "Might help to die soaking wet if you are going straight to hell from here," said Sule. Teeth clenched, he dragged himself to the gourd, his knife in his good hand. Closing his eyes, he thrust knife and hand into the gourd, drove vicious thrusts into the reptile's writhing body, breathing heavily all the while. When he crawled back to lie down a few minutes later the breath came whistling out of his nostrils; his arm was riddled with fang-marks; but the reptile was dead. "That's one snake that has been charmed for the last time," said Sule. Dogo said nothing.

Several minutes passed in silence. The poison had them securely in its fatal grip, especially Sule, who couldn't suppress a few groans. It was only a matter of seconds now. "Pity you have to end up this way," mumbled Dogo, his senses dulling. "By and large, it hasn't been too bad—you thieving scoundrel!" "I'm soaked in tears on account of you," drawled Sule, unutterably weary. "This seems the end of the good old road. But you ought to have known it had to end some time, you rotten bastard!" He heaved a deep sigh. "I shan't have to go up to the hospital in the morning after all," he mumbled, touching the wound in his thigh with a trembling hand. "Ah," he breathed in resignation, "the will of Allah be done." The rain came pattering down.

Rain

RICHARD RIVE

Rain poured down, blotting out all sound with its sharp and vibrant tattoo. Dripping neon signs reflecting lurid reds and yellows in mirror-wet streets. Swollen gutters. Water overflowing and squelching on to pavements. Gurgling and sucking at stormwater drains. Table Mountain cut off by a grey film of mist and rain. A lost City Hall clock trying manfully to chime nine over an indifferent Cape Town. Baleful reverberations through a spluttering all-consuming drizzle.

Yellow light filters through from Solly's Grand Fish and Chips Palace. Door tight-shut against the weather. Inside stuffy with heat, hot bodies, steaming clothes and the nauseating smell of stale fish-oil. Misty patterns on the plate-glass windows and a messy pool where rain has filtered beneath the door and mixed with the sawdust.

Solly himself in shirt-sleeves, sweating, vulgar and moody. Bellowing at a dripping woman who has just come in.

"Shut 'e damn door. Think you live in a tent?"

"Ag, Solly."

"Don't ag me. You Coloured people can never shut blarry doors."

"Don' bloomingwell swear at me."

"I bloomingwell swear at you, yes."

"Come. Gimme two pieces 'e fish. Tail cut."

"Two pieces 'e fish."

"Raining like hell outside," the woman said to no one.

"Mmmmmm. Raining like hell," a thin befezzed Malay cut in.

"One an' six. Thank you. An' close 'e door behin' you."

"Thanks. Think you got 'e on'y door in Hanover Street?"

"Go to hell!" Solly cut the conversation short and turned to another customer.

Rain

The north-wester sobbed heavy rain squalls against the window-panes. The Hanover Street bus screeched to a slithery stop and passengers darted for shelter in a cinema entrance. The street lamps shone blurredly.

Solly sweated as he wrapped parcels of fish and chips in a newspaper. Fish and chips. Vinegar? Wrap? One an' six, please. Thank you. Next. Fish and chips. No? Two fish. No chips? Salt? Vinegar? One an' six, please. Thank you! Next. Fish an' chips.

"Close 'e blarry door!" Solly glared daggers at a woman who had just come in. She half-smiled apologetically at him.

"You Coloured people are worse than Kaffirs."

She struggled with the door and then stood dripping in a pool of wet sawdust. Solly left the counter to add two presto-logs to the furnace. She moved out of the way. Another customer showed indignation at Solly's remark.

"You blooming Jews are always making Coloured people out."

"Go to hell!" Solly dismissed the attack on his race. Fish an' chips. Vinegar? Salt? One an' six. Thank you.

"Yes, madam?"

"Could you tell me when the bioscope comes out?"

"Am I the blooming manager?"

"Please."

"Half pas' ten," the Malay offered helpfully.

"Thank you. Can I stay here till then? It's raining outside."

"I know it's blarrywell raining, but this is not a Salvation Army."

"Please, Baas!"

This caught Solly unawares. He had had his shop in that corner of District Six since most could remember and had been called a great many unsavoury things down the years. Solly didn't mind. But this caught him unawares.

Please, Baas.

This felt good. His imagination adjusted a black bow-tie to an evening suit. Please, Baas.

"Okay, stay fer a short while. But when 'e rain stops you go!"

She nodded dumbly and tried to make out the blurred name of the cinema opposite, through the misted windows.

"Waitin' fer somebody?" Solly asked.

No response.

"I ask if yer waitin' fer somebody!"

The figure continued to stare.

"Oh, go to hell," said Solly, turning to another customer.

Through the rain blur Siena stared at nothing in particular. Dim visions of slippery wet cars. Honking and wheezing in the rain. Spluttering buses. Heavy, drowsy voices in the Grand Fish and Chips Palace. Her eyes travelled beyond the street and the water cascades of Table Mountain, beyond the winter of Cape Town to the summer of the Boland. Past the green grapelands of Stellenbosch and Paarl, and the stuffy wheat district of Malmesbury to the lazy sun and laughter of Teslaarsdal. A tired sun here. An uninterested sun. Now it seemed that the sun was weary of the physical effort of having to rise, to shine, to comfort and to set.

Inside the nineteenth-century gabled mission church she had first met Joseph. The church is still there, and beautiful, and the ivy climbs over it and makes it more beautiful. Huge silver oil-lamps suspended from the roof, polished and shining. It was in the flicker of the lamps that she had first become aware of him. He was visiting from Cape Town. She sang that night like she had never sung before. Her favourite psalm.

"*Al ging ik ook in een dal der schaduw des doods.* . . . Though I walk through the valley of the shadow of death. . . . *Der schaduw des doods.*"

And then he had looked at her. Everyone had looked at her for she was good in solos.

"*Ik zoude geen kwaad vreezen.* . . . I will fear no evil."

And she had not feared but loved. Had loved him. Had sung for him. For the wide eyes, the yellow skin, the high cheek-bones. She had sung for a creator who could create a man like Joseph.

"*Want gij zijt met mij; Uw stok en Uw staf, die vertroosten mij.*"

Those were black and white polka-dot nights when the moon did a gollywog cake-walk across a banjo-strung sky. Nights of sweet remembrances when he had whispered love to her and told her of Cape Town. She had giggled coyly at his obscenities. It was fashionable, she hoped, to giggle coyly at obscenities. He lived in one of those streets off District Six and was, he boasted, quite a one amongst the girls. She heard of Molly and Miena and Sophia and a sophisticated Charmaine who was almost a school-teacher and always spoke English. But he told her that he had only found love in Teslaarsdal. She wasn't sure whether to believe him. And then he had felt her richness and the moon darted behind a cloud.

The loud screeching of the train to Cape Town. Screeching loud enough to drown the protest of her family. The wrath of her father. The icy stares of Teslaarsdal matrons. Loud and confused screechings to drown her hysteria, her ecstasy. Drowned and confused in the roar of a thousand cars and a hundred thousand lights and a summer of carnival evenings which is Cape Town. Passion in a tiny room off District Six. Desire surrounded by four bare walls, and a rickety chair and a mounted cardboard tract that murmured, "Bless this House".

And the agony of the nights when he came home later and later and sometimes not at all. The waning of his passion and whispered names of others. Molly and Miena and Sophia. Charmaine. The helpless knowledge that he was slipping from her. Faster and faster. Gathering momentum.

"Not that I'm saying so but I only heard . . ."

"Why don't you go to bioscope one night and see for yourself. . . ."

"Marian's man is searching for Joseph. . . ."

Searching for Joseph. Looking for Joseph; knifing for Joseph. Joseph! Joseph!! JOSEPH!! Molly! Miena! Sophia! Names! Names! Names! Gossip. One-sided desire. Go to bioscope and see. See what? See why? When! Where!

And after he had been away a week she decided to see. Decided to go through the rain and stand in a sweating fish and chips shop owned by a blaspheming Jew. And wait for the cinema to come out.

The rain had stopped sobbing against the plate-glass window. A skin-soaking drizzle now set in. Continuous. Unending. Filming everything with dark depression. A shivering, weeping neon sign flickered convulsively on and off. A tired Solly shooting a quick glance at a cheap alarm clock.

"Half pas' ten, bioscope out soon."

Siena looked more intently through the misty screen. No movement whatsoever in the deserted cinema foyer.

"Time it was bloomingwell out." Solly braced himself for the wave of after-show customers who would invade his Palace.

"Comin' out late tonight, Missus."

"Thank you, Baas."

Solly rubbed sweat out of his eyes and took in her neat and plain figure. Tired face but good legs. A few late stragglers catching colds in the streets. Wet and squally outside.

"Your man in bioscope?"

She was intent on a khaki-uniformed usher struggling to open the door.

"Man in bioscope, Missus?"

The cinema had to come out some time or other. An usher opening the door, adjusting the outside gate. Preparing for the crowds to pour out. Vomited and spilt out.

"Man in bioscope?"

No response.

"Oh, go to hell!"

They would be out now. Joseph would be out. She rushed for the door, throwing words of thanks to Solly.

"Close the blarry door!"

She never heard him. The drizzle had stopped. An unnatural calm hung over the empty foyer, over the deserted street. Over her empty heart. She took up her stand on the bottom step. Expectantly. Her heart pounding.

Then they came. Pouring, laughing, pushing, jostling. She stared with fierce intensity but faces passed too fast. Laughing, roaring, gay. Wide-eyed, yellow-skinned, high cheek-boned. Black, brown, ivory, yellow. Black-eyed, laughing-eyed, gay, bouncing. No Joseph. Palpitating heart that felt like bursting into a thousand pieces. If she should miss him. She found herself searching for the wrong face. Solly's face. Ridiculously searching for hard blue eyes and a sharp white chin in a sea of ebony and brown. Solly's face. Missing half a hundred faces and then again searching for the familiar high cheek-bones. Solly. Joseph. Molly. Miena. Charmaine.

The drizzle restarted. Studying the overcoats instead of faces. Longing for the pale blue shirt she had seen in the shop at Solitaire. A bargain at £1.50. She had scraped and scrounged to buy it for him. A week's wages. Collecting her thoughts and continuing the search for Joseph. And then the thinning out of the crowd and the last few stragglers. The ushers shutting the iron gates. They might be shutting Joseph in. Herself out. Only the ushers left. And the uncompromising iron gates.

"Please is Joseph inside?"

"Who's Joseph?"

"Is Joseph still inside?"

"Joseph who?"

They were teasing her. Laughing behind her back. Preventing her from finding him.

"Joseph is inside!" she shouted frenziedly.

"Look, merrim, it's raining cats an' dogs. Go home."

Go home. To whom? To what? An empty room? An empty bed? A tract that shrieked its lie, "Bless this House"?

And then she was aware of the crowd on the corner. Maybe he was there. Running and peering into every face. Joseph. The crowd in the drizzle. Two battling figures. Joseph. Figures locked in struggle slithering in the wet gutter. Muck streaking down clothes through which wet bodies were silhouetted. Joseph. A blue shirt. And then she wiped the rain out of her eyes and saw him. Fighting for his life. Desperately kicking in the gutter. Joseph. The blast of a police-whistle. A pick-up van screeching to a stop.

"Please, sir, it wasn't him. They all ran away. Please, sir, he's Joseph. He done nothing. He done nothing, my Baas. Please, sir, he's my Joseph. Please, Baas!"

"*Maak dat jy weg kom.* Get away. *Voetsak!*"

"Please, sir, it wasn't him. They ran away! *Asseblief,* Baas."

Alone. An empty bed. An empty room.

Solly's Grand Fish and Chips Palace crowded out. People milling inside. Rain once more squalling and sobbing against the door and windows. Swollen gutters unable to cope with the giddy rush of water. Solly sweating to deal with the after-cinema rush.

Fish an' chips. Vinegar? Salt? One an' six. Thank you. Sorry, no fish. Wait five minutes. Chips on'y. Vinegar? Ninepence. Tickey change. Thank you. Sorry, no fish. Five minutes' time. Chips? Ninepence. Thank you. Solly paused for breath and stirred the fish.

"What's 'e trouble outside?"

"Bioscope, Solly."

"No, man, outside!"

"I say, bioscope."

"What were 'e police doin'? Sorry, no fish yet, sir. Five minutes' time. What were 'e police doin'?"

"A fight in 'e bloomin' rain."

"Jeesus, in 'e rain?"

"*Ja.*"

"Who was fightin'?"

"Joseph an' somebody."

"Joseph?"

"*Ja*, fellow in Arundel Street."

"Yes, I know Joseph. Always in trouble. Chucked him outta here a'reddy."

"Well, that chap."

"An' who?"

"Dinno."

"Police get them?"

"Got Joseph."

"Why were 'ey fightin'? Fish in a minute, sir."

"Over a dame."

"Who?"

"You know Miena who work by Patel? Now she. Her boy-friend caught 'em."

"In bioscope?"

"*Ja.*"

Solly chuckled deeply, suggestively.

"See that woman an' 'e police?"

"What woman?"

"Dame cryin' to 'e police."

"They say it's Joseph's dame."

"Joseph always got plenty 'e dames. F-I-S-H—R-E-A-D-Y!!! Two pieces for you, sir? One an' six. Shilling change. Fish an' chips? One an' six? Thank you. Fish on'y? Vinegar? Salt? Ninepence. Tickey change. Thank you!

"What you say about 'e woman?"

"They say Joseph's girl was crying to 'e police."

"Oh, he got plenty 'e girls."

"This one was living with him."

"Oh, what she look like? Fish, sir?"

"Okay. Nice legs."

Hmmmmm," said Solly. "Hey, close 'e damn door. Oh, you again."

Siena came in. A momentary silence. Then a buzzing and whispering.

"Oh," said Solly, nodding as someone whispered over the counter to him, "I see. She was waiting here. Mussta been waitin' for him."

A young girl in jeans giggled.

"Fish an' chips costs one an' six, madam."

"Wasn't it one an' three before?"

"Before the Boer War, madam. Price of fish go up. Potatoes go up an' you expect me to charge one an' three?"

"Why not?"

"Oh, go to hell! Next, please!"

"Yes, that's 'e one, Solly."

"Mmmm. Excuse me, madam." Turning to Siena, "Like some fish an' chips? Free of charge, never min' 'e money."

"Thank you, my Baas."

The rain now sobbed wildly as the shop emptied and Solly counted the cash in his till. Thousands of watery horses charging down the street. Rain drilling into cobbles and pavings. Miniature waterfalls down the sides of buildings. Blurred lights through unending streams. Siena listlessly holding the newspaper parcel of fish and chips.

"You can stay here till it clears up," said Solly.

She looked up tearfully. Solly grinned showing his yellow teeth.

"It's quite okay."

A smile flickered across her face for a second.

"It's quite okay by me."

She looked down and hesitated for a moment. Then she struggled against the door. It yielded with a crash and the north-wester howled into Solly's Palace.

"Close 'e blarry door!" he said, grinning.

"Thank you, my Baas," she said, as she shivered out into the rain.

Feather Woman of the Jungle

AMOS TUTUOLA

From the Town of Famine
to the Town of the Water People
The entertainment of the fifth night
(My Fourth Journey)

In the fourth night, when the people gathered in the front of my house and the drinks were served as they were dancing and singing with great joy. Then I stopped them and I addressed them first as follows: "I am very happy indeed to see all of you again in front of me and I thank every one of you for the true affection you have on me, although I am the head of the village. And I wonder greatly, too, to see that you are increased again this night more than 90 per cent. But (all sat quietly and paid great attention to me) when I first saw the whole of you, I was afraid, but after I thought it over again my fear was expelled. Because I first thought within myself that where to get sufficient planks to make coffins for every one of you when you die because you are too many. But when I thought it over again, I remembered that not the whole of you would need coffins to bury you when you die. Because many of you would be killed and eaten up by the wild animals. Many would die in the rivers, many would be burnt into ashes by the fire, many would be kidnapped and so many of you would be fallen into the wells. So, therefore, coffins would not be required for those who died such death, and so many would not die in their homes but where their people would not see their bodies to bury with coffins." But the people were greatly annoyed when they heard like that from me. All were snapping their fingers on heads and saying that they would not die in the rivers or in the fire or in the wells or eaten up by the wild animals, but they would die in their homes, villages, etc., and they would be buried with coffins. But after a while, when their noises went down, I explained to them that they must not misunderstand me, because there was nobody on earth who could know the real place and real time he or she is going to die, or if anyone knew, let him or her tell me. And if anyone knew it, it meant I was guilty of what I had said. Having said so, I hesitated to hear the reply, but there was none of the people who could reply but they admitted at last.

After they danced and drank some of their palm-wine, I started to tell them the story as follows:

One fine morning, after six months that I had returned from my third journey, I took my usual gun, hunting-bag and matchet. I bade good-bye to my father, mother, sister and brother and all my friends and my neighbours. Some of the people cautioned me very seriously not to go for any treasure again. They said that all I had brought were enough. But I told them that I must try more for we knew of today but we did not know of tomorrow.

Then I left my village that bright day and I was going to the north this time. Having travelled for several days, I came to a town. This town was very big and famous. It was near a very wide and deep river. Immediately I entered the town I was greatly shocked first with fear when I saw the terrible appearances of the people or the inhabitants. Every one of them was so leaned that he had no more muscle on his body. Every one of them was as thin as a dried stick. The legs and arms were just like sticks. The eyes were seeing faintly in the skull except the head, which was so big that the thin neck could not even carry it. Both upper and lower jaws had already dried up like a roasted meat. The stomach was no more seen except the breast and exposed ribs.

When I first saw them in that appearances, I thought within myself and cried out unnoticed: "Ah, how people were created so terribly like this?" Because in the first instance I did not know that they were in famine and that they were starved until when they had leaned to that state. And they were so starved that the breasts of the women had dried up. The king, too, was so bitterly starved that he was unable to put on his crown whenever he went out. And it was a great pity that the hunger had forced the people of the town not to respect the king or chiefs again except one who brought food to them.

But, according to the custom of that town, I was first taken to the king and when he approved of my staying there, then I lodged in the house of the paramount chief which was almost next to the palace of the king. When it was night I tried to sleep but I was unable to fall asleep because of hunger. So hardly in the morning when I went to the king and told him: "Please, King, I am badly hungry, will you give me something to eat now?" But he said at the same time: "Is that so? Sorry, we are in great famine since past few years, therefore, I have no food to give you except cold water which is our main food in this town at present!"

Then I went back to my room, I sat and I was expecting that the paramount chief would soon send food to me as the king had failed to give it to me. Having waited for many hours and yet he did not send anything to me. Then I sold my shame and I went to him. Without shame, I told him that I wanted to eat. But he said that their main food was cold water. He said furthermore, that the famine was so serious they they had money but it was useless. They had plenty of costly clothes but the hunger did not let them wear them and even the clothes were oversized them because they had leaned too much. And again, this paramount chief advised me that I should be drinking the cold water.

Having heard like that as well from him, then without hesitation I started to drink the cold water. But when it was not yet daybreak when I was woken by hunger in the following morning. I hardly got up when I went to the king's attendants, I complained to them again that since I had come to the town I had nothing to eat except cold water which I was drinking. I complained to them perhaps they might help me. But I was very surprised that they did not allow me to tell them all of my complaints when they interrupted immediately they heard the word "hunger" from me. They naked themselves and told me to look how every one of them was leaned. They told me further that I, too, would soon become bones if I kept longer in that town.

Having failed again to get food from the attendants, I shook my head with surprise before I left them. When I returned to my room,

I sat down quietly and I began to think how to get food by all means. I first thought to go back to my village to be bringing the foodstuffs to this town for sale. But I remembered that my village was too far away from there and again, there was no real road on which to be travelled always.

As I was still suggesting within myself of what to do, it came to my mind to go to the big river which was near this town, perhaps I might get fishes from there. And without hesitation, I went to that river. Luckily, I found many canoes tied up to the trees on the bank and I loosened one. I put my matchet in it and then I pushed it on the river. I started to find fishes about to kill. But there was none to be found. But, of course, as I was still paddling along, I came to the swampy bush at about twelve o'clock p.m. In that swampy bush there were many palm-trees. When I stopped the canoe I climbed one palm-tree but unfortunately, there was no fruits on it. But when I climbed the third one, I found two ripen bunches of palm-fruits on top of it. So I drove all the birds which were eating them away first and then I cut both down.

After I had put them in the canoe, I first ate of them to my satisfaction and then I took the rest to the town. But I was nearly torn into pieces by the hungry people as I was carrying them along in the town to the king. However, I carried them to the king at last. With great wonder and admiration, he took them from me and thanked me greatly. Having eaten as many fruits as he could then he distributed the rest to his people.

After the people had gone back to their houses the king invited me to one of his property rooms. He showed me all his money and many other property as gold, silver, costly beads and diamonds. He promised me that if I could be getting such palm-fruits for him and his people till when the famine was finished, he would give me a lot of money, gold, silver, diamond and beads as rewards. Having promised me like that, I replied with a smile that I would try my best to be supplying him the fruits till when the famine was finished and then I went back to my room, in the paramount chief's house.

In the following morning I went to the river again. I tried all my efforts in climbing so many palm-trees. Luckily after a while, I got one bunch of palm-fruits and I brought it to the king. After he had eaten of the fruits to his satisfaction he distributed the rest to his people. It was so I brought the fruits to the king and his people for the period of five months. But unfortunately, as the famine was not stopped in time and the season of the palm-fruits came to an end, therefore, I could not get anything for the king any more. I tried all my best to get the fruits, but it was in vain.

When it was the third day that I had not eaten except to drink the cold water from morning till night, I was so weak that I thought that I would die soon. I thought of going back to my village that time, but I could not trek the distance of about one mile when I would fall down. This, my fourth journey, was so bad and hopeless that I said within myself that if I returned to my village this time I would never attempt to go for any treasure again.

Having failed in all my efforts to get food, then I went back to the palm-trees perhaps I might get some fruits which probably had fallen to the bottoms of the palm-trees during the season. So I started to search the bottom of every palm-tree and I found only one over-ripen fruit when it was about three o'clock in the afternoon. I hastily picked it up. But as I held it, I said to myself sorrowfully that what a single palm-fruit could do for me. It could not satisfy my hunger.

Anyhow, I went in the canoe. But as I was paddling it along on the river and when I came to the deepest part of it, this palm-fruit was mistakenly fallen into the water. And this was affected me so badly that I threw the paddle in the canoe and then jumped in the water without hesitation. But as I was swimming here and there just to pick up the fruit, someone held my both feet and was pulling me down into the bottom of the river. Having tried all my best to take my feet from him and failed, then I left myself to him. After a while he pulled me into the water and it was then I saw who was pulling me. He held one coffin, with left hand. The lid of that coffin was glass and he hardly pushed that lid to one side when he pushed me in it and he entered it as well and then covered it with that glass lid at the same time. As I was inside the coffin with him, I was breathing in and out quite easily and I saw plainly that this man covered his body from the knee to the waist with the leather of big fish. He had no hair on head but small scales instead, his arms were very short and were as strong as iron, but there were fingers on each arm and they were resembled that of human being. Although he had two eyes like myself but each was as round as full moon.

But to my fear, he had fins on shoulders, elbows, knees and ankles and there were a number of moustache on his upper jaw, which was that of a big fish. His mouth was flat but the nose was round. As the coffin was taking us deeply into the river, this man began to threat me badly. Sometime, he would scratch my face with his sharp nails, sometime he would slap me on the ear and sometime he would be frightening by pointing a sharp iron on my eyes. It was like that he was ill-treating me until the coffin took us to the bottom of the river. Then he pushed the lid of the coffin to one side, he came down and then pulled me out. When I came down, I noticed that we were on the land and not in the water as before. The river was seen no more. Then he pushed me in front of him and told me to be going along on one road which led to a very beautiful house. As I was going along it so he was following me as fast as he could.

On both sides of that road there were beautiful trees and flowers. Having travelled on that road for a while I was seeing several men similar to this one, they lined up on both sides of the road as if they were policemen or soldiers. Having travelled farther, we came to the front of that beautiful house. And it was then I saw it clearly that it was a mighty palace. As he was escorting me along in it and as we were going from one place to another, I was seeing the costly decorations which were hung on every corner. Again, I noticed that the sun was so dull that there was only little difference from the full moon of the dry season. The air was a little thicker than my village's air and the sands on the ground were as white as white cloth. The sky was almost cloudy throughout the day.

After a while, that man escorted me to the beautiful sitting-room in which one beautiful lady sat in royal state. Without hesitation I stood before her and bowed down as the man who had escorted me in stood at back. But when I stood for a few minutes, I simply walked to one of the seats and then sat on it. Hardly crossed my legs when I started to glance at every decorations which were on the walls and on the floor. Now it was revealed to me that the inhabitants of this town were the water people and that beautiful lady was the nymph of that river, so they were belonged to the fish race. The nymph and her attendants and guardsmen were very surprised as I was not afraid of them at all, but they did not know that I had surrendered myself to all what might happened to me that time.

The decorations on the walls were stuffed goldfishes, polished large sea shells, skulls of the sea animals, etc., and every part of that walls was twinkling like stars. The seats were also stuffed fishes and were as fresh as if they were still alive. The ruler or the nymph herself was dressed in the skins of beautiful fishes. The skins were so highly refined that they were as smooth as very costly clothes. Some were shining like gold, some were twinkling like the bright stars and the top ones were shining steadily like diamonds. She sat on an armchair which had many carved sea creatures on top. She stretched feet on a well-polished skull of a big whale. Many big sea tortoises were walking about on the floor and the crown on her head was full of small beautiful sea shells.

As far as I saw her, she was about thirty years old. Her eyes were very clear and the face was very fresh as the face of a fifteen-year-old girl. There were no scars or pimples on her cheeks or face and the hair of her head was not so much dark but, of course, probably the climate of that town had turned the hair to be like that. Her teeth were very white and very closely to each other. Her nose was quite pointed like that of an image, the slippers on her feet were made from the soft leather of crocodile. She had clear and lovely voice and her face always seemed as if she was kind and merciful.

As I was still noticing these things, a number of another set of guardsmen walked in and those whom I met in there walked out and those who were just come in took over the duty. Again, I noticed these new set of the guardsmen that everyone of them was a man of strong body, stout and fearful to see. The skull of shark was on everyone's head, and wore the apron which was the skin of fish, but the scaly skins of fishes were their purtises and gloves. Many of them held the tails of big fishes. Each of that tails was about four feet long and the width was about six inches and very thick indeed and sharp thorns were lined up on both edges. Some of those who held the long spears were shielded their breasts with the very big sea tortoise back shells. All of these were their uniforms. Every one of them was a giant-like and cynical.

As I sat on the chair facing the nymph or the queen of the river, and I was still looking at the decorations and thinking also in mind that no doubt I would leave this town with much wealths, the man who had brought me in there started to complain to the nymph that he brought me before her for punishment because I struck his head when I jumped on the river when the only palm-fruit which I could find had fallen into the river. That man hardly complained to the nymph when all her guardsmen gathered at my back and ready to hold me. But the nymph hastily rang the bell on her side, to them to leave me. Then with a very cool voice, she asked from me: "Why did you strike him on the head?" So before I started to reply, I first crossed my feet and seated very easy as if I was in my house and then I said: "In fact, I jumped on the river when the only palm-fruit that I could get, had fallen in the water. But I did not know whether I had struck him on the head, but if it was so then it was by a mistake." She asked again: "Why did you jump into the river in respect of one palm-fruit?" And as those guardsmen were in attention and got ready to hold me if the nymph gave them the order to do so. So I replied: "My work was to find the palm-fruits to the people of the town of famine because they had nothing to eat since the famine had started in their town and they had already leaned to the bones." But when she heard like that from me, she was so wondered that she sat up and then asked again: "The famine was so serious that only the palm-fruits the people eat?" I said: "Yes. Even the palm-fruits were not easily to get." Then she and her guardsmen breathed out with wonder and as she hesitated and was looking at me the guardsmen looked at each other's eyes with great wonder and then stood easy and that showed me that they were in sympathy with me. So the nymph said suddenly: "Oh, no wonder, your appearance even shows that you are in a great famine because you are too lean." But I hastily interrupted: "That town is not mine but I went there to find the treasure."

But as she was about to ask me another question, one beautiful lady walked in that moment. She put one big basin in front of her and then she bowed down for her and walked out. When she removed the lid of that basin, it was roasted fish and then she started to eat it as a refreshment. But as I was very hungry even before I was brought before her, so I stood up, I walked to her and without excuse, I took some slices and then I walked back to me seat and there I started to eat the fish bit by bit with greediness. But as the nymph was kind and merciful, she rang the bell on her side and after a few seconds, one attendant walked in. Then she told her to take me to the dining-room and give me food. So I walked out with that attendant. She (attendant) gave me the nice food which I ate to my entire satisfaction. After that I went back to the nymph. Having discussed with me about the famine for a while, she stood up and walked into one room opposite that sitting-room. After a while she came back with one round box. It was very big but one man could carry it from one place to another. It was sealed round. She gave it to me and then explained to me that, "This sealed box (she pointed finger to it) will supply food and drinks of all kinds to you and the people of the town of famine throughout the period of the famine. But you and the people must be very careful not to break the delicate box. If you break it it will not be able to supply anything to you any more and all of you will be punished for it. Furthermore, if it is stolen away from you, all of you will be punished as well. And again, you must put in your mind always that you must not come back to me for anything as from today!"

Having warned me like that she rang the bell and the man (the water-man) who had brought me to her, walked in. As he stood before her, she told him to take me back to where he had caught me. Then I put thc box on head, I thanked her greatly before I followed the water-man and some of the guardsmen led us to a short distance before they went back. After a while we came to where that coffin was. Having put that box in it and I went inside it, the water-man pushed it on to the river and then he entered it. But to my surprise, he hardly covered it with its lid when the coffin started to run furiously on the water and within a few seconds it floated on the very part of that river from which he had caught me before.

As my canoe was still driven here and there by the tides. Then as soon as the coffin stopped closely to it, I put that box in it and then I started to paddle it along to the town of famine. But the water-man did not talk to me until when he had brought me back to that river and returned to the nymph.

When I paddled the canoe for about two hours I reached the bank of that river. Having tied up the canoe, I carried the box direct to the king. In the presence of the paramount chief the king removed the lid of it. To their surprise, they met several basins of variety of food and one small spoon in it. But they did not believe me when I told them that the food would be sufficient to feed the whole people till whenever the famine was finished.

Anyhow, the king put the box in his strong-room and he choose me to be serving the food to the people and to himself. Then I first served him and the paramount chief and they had first satisfied their hunger, then the whole people in the town were invited to the palace. The king told them that everyone of them should go back to his or her house and bring the plate and spoon. Then the people ran back to their houses and they returned with all these things after a few minutes. Then I began to serve each of them. But the people ate and drank to their satisfaction and yet the food and the drinks remained in that box as if I had not served from them.

It was so the people and the king were eating and drinking to their satisfaction for three times daily for three months and yet the food and the drinks remained as if nothing had touched them. And within a few weeks more, the people had forgotten the famine. They had enough muscles on bodies, they became as powerful as before the famine had started. They were able to walk about easily in the town, singing, dancing and laughing with great joy. They were so satisfied that they determined not to work again for their living.

But as the news of that wonderful box had spread to many towns and villages and many people from those towns and villages had come to witness that box. So one midnight, a gang of night marauders came from one of those towns to the palace. When they came in and as they were trying to break and enter into the strong-room to steal the box away to their town. The king's bugle-blowers who were keeping watch of the gate of the palace, started to blow the bugles just to wake the king and the rest people in the palace. When the people and the king woke, they took clubs, cudgels, matchets, axes, bows and arrows, etc. They rushed to the marauders and I followed them with my matchet in my hand. Then all of us started to beat them, but they beat us so mercilessly in return that everyone got wounds all over the body. They beat me until I fell down unconsciously. Every part of my body was bleeding continuously. But at last, when the arrows were shot to them continuously for a few minutes then they ran away for their lives.

After the marauders had escaped, the king and some of the rest people took me from the floor to one room. The king started to treat my wounds with medicine and all were healed within a few days. And the marauders did not attempt to come to the palace for some weeks, but one of them whom we did not recognize at all, came to the bugle-blowers. He tried all his possible best and made friends with them. He was so kind to them that they did not suspect him as one of the marauders. He was sitting with them from morning till the evening. He was just spying the easiest way to get into the strong-room in which the wonderful box was kept always.

Having satisfied himself, then he went back to his members and told them to be ready for another attempt to steal the box. In the very night that they were coming, he had come to the bugle-blowers before his members. He was playing with them as he was usually doing. But he hid one bottle of thick honey under his dress. When he noticed that the bugle-blowers went to the palace to take their supper, he hastily filled their bugles with that thick honey and then hung them back on their usual rack before they came back.

When they returned he ate and drank with them, after that he told them that he was going to visit another man in the next house. But not knowing that immediately he had left them, he went direct to the rest marauders. He told them that it was time to go and burgle the strong-room. Then all of them came to the town and entered the palace through the other gate. As they were splitting the door of the strong-room with axes, the bugle-blowers woke and hastily took their bugles from the rack. But when they put them in the mouths just to be blowing them as a warning to the king and the people in the palace that the night marauders came again. The thick honey started to run from their bugles into their mouths. Therefore, they were unable to blow the bugles, but they were licking the honey and enjoying it as it was running into their mouths and it was so the marauders were breaking the strong-room as hastily as they could.

It was like that the room was broken into and the wonderful box together with the king's property were taken and then they left the town as quickly as possible. And they had gone far away before the bugle-blowers were able to blow their bugles after they had licked the honey in their bugles. Anyhow, the king and the rest people took up the fighting weapons. Then we chased the marauders to catch and then to take the box back from them. But they had gone too far away, we did not see any trace of them.

Then we came back to the palace. The king cast down on his throne and was thinking sorrowfully of what to eat in the morning. In the morning, when the people gathered in the front of the palace and were waiting for their breakfast, the king and his paramount chief told me to go back to the nymph for another wonderful box. But when I explained to the king that the nymph had warned me already not to come back to her for anything and she had warned me as well that if the box was split or stolen away, we would be punished for it. The hungry people shouted at a time: "Don't tell us a lie! But you must go back to her and if you explain to her how the box was stolen from the strong-room, she would not refuse to give you another one!" Again, I insisted to go back, but that time the king and the paramount chief said that if I refused to go back to the nymph it meant I disobeyed their order and therefore, they would punish me and the punishment was to behead me.

Anyhow, I went back to that river and as I was paddling the canoe along, I came to the same spot from where the water-man had taken me to the nymph the other day. Then I wilfully threw the paddle in the water with the hope that it would sink like that palm-fruit. But when the paddle did not sink, I jumped into the water and I hardly dived when the same water-man held my both feet and pulled me deeply into the water before he put me inside the same coffin and within a few minutes it took us to the town of the nymph. Then the water-man took me before her like the first time. He complained to her that he caught me again when I struck his head with my feet.

But the nymph grew annoyed when she saw me there again. Instead to say anything to the complaint of the water-man, she asked me: "Had I not told you last time not to come here again?" I replied with trembling voice: "In fact you had told me not to come to you again. But I come back to take another wonderful box in which everlasting food and drinks are kept!" Having heard like that from me, she became more anger and asked: "By the way, what has happened to the one which I had given to you the other day?" I replied that the night marauders had stolen it away from the king's strong-room a few days ago. Then she remarked with fearful voice: "Is that how you people are careless? I had warned you that you should keep the box so savely that it might not be stolen. All right, I shall send another thing to the king which will teach all of you sense!"

Then she stood up and entered the same room opposite the sitting-room and I was very happy when she told me that she would send another thing to us which would teach us sense. After a while, she returned with one huge sealed pot. When gave it to me, she told me that I should open it when the whole people and the king gathered into one place. Then I thanked her greatly for I believed that this pot was going to supply the food and drinks like that box. So when I was ready to leave, she rang the bell to the same water-man and he walked in at the same time. As he bowed down for her, she told him to take me back with the same coffin. Having taken me back to where he had caught me, then I put the pot in my canoe and I paddled it to the bank and from there I carried the pot to the town.

The hungry people and the king who had already gathered in the front of the palace and were waiting for my return, shouted greatly with joy when they saw the pot on my head. But when I gave it to the king and he put it in the middle of the people, then I told him how he would open it. So he first told the people to bring their plates nearer and then he forced it open. But uncountable of bees, wasps and all kinds of the stinging insects rushed out from it instead of food and drinks. Without hesitation, these insects started to sting all of us. Within a few minutes many people were stung to death, that place was disordered at the same time. Everyone was running skelter-helter for his or her life. And at last, as the king was running away for his life, the crown fell off from his head but he was unable to wait and take it back. So almost all the people of the town of famine had run away for their lives and when the town was empty, then I took my gun, hunting-bag and matchet, and I started to go back to my village at the same time. I could not wait to tell the king to fulfil his promise but, of course, he too was nowhere to be found.

After a few days' travel, I reached my village and I entered my father's house very quietly, but not as joyfully as my last three journeys which had profited me greatly. Then the people rushed to my house to honour my return, but they were greatly shocked when they noticed that I did not bring anything this time. Having told them all what had happened to me in the town of famine, some cautioned me not to go any journey again and some advised me not to give up my adventures because time was not always as straight as a straight line and that one who was finding goodness about must endanger his life and must be able to endure all hardships as well. Then I thanked them greatly. After that I sent for drinks and all of us drank together till the midnight.

"That was the end of my fourth journey. It was so many journeys were not profitable in those days. One journey might prove to be a better one from beginning but might be the worst towards the end. But I was not discouraged at all as my fourth journey was vanity at last. I thank you for your listening. Good night to you all." Then after the people of my village had danced, sung and drunken for a few minutes they went back to their houses.

The Dube Train

CAN THEMBA

The morning was too cold for a summer morning, at least, to me, a child of the sun. But then on all Monday mornings I feel rotten and shivering, with a clogged feeling in the chest and a nauseous churning in the stomach. It debilitates my interest in the whole world around me.

The Dube Station with the prospect of congested trains, filled with sour-smelling humanity, did not improve my impression of a hostile life directing its malevolence plumb at me. All sorts of disgruntledties darted through my brain: the lateness of the trains, the shoving savagery of the crowds, the grey aspect around me; even the announcer over the loudspeaker gave confused directions. I suppose it had something to do with the peculiar chemistry of the body on Monday morning. But for me all was wrong with the world.

Yet, by one of those flukes that occur in all routines, the train I caught was not full when it came. I usually try to avoid seats next to the door, but sometimes it cannot be helped. So it was that Monday morning when I hopped into the Third Class carriage. As the train moved off, I leaned out of the paneless window and looked lacklustrely at the leaden platform churning away beneath me like a fast conveyance belt.

Two or three yards away, a door had been broken and repaired with masonite so that it would be an opening door no more. Moreover, just there a seat was missing, and there was a kind of a hall.

I was sitting across a hulk of a man. His hugeness was obtrusive to the sight when you saw him and to the mind when you looked away. His head tilted to one side in a half-drowsy position, with flaring nostrils and trembling lips. He looked like a kind of genie, pretending to sleep but watching your every nefarious intention. His chin was stubbled with crisp, little black barbs. The neck was thick and corded, and the enormous chest was a live barrel that heaved forth and back. The overall he wore was open almost down to the navel, and he seemed to have nothing else underneath. I stared, fascinated, at his large breasts with their winking, dark nipples.

With the rocking of the train as it rolled towards Phefeni Station, he swayed slightly this way and that, and now and then he lazily chanted a township ditty. The titillating bawdiness of the words excited no humour or lechery or significance. The words were words, the tune was just a tune.

Above and around him, the other passengers, looking Monday-bleared, had no enthusiasm about them. They were just like the lights of the carriage—dull, dreary, undramatic. Almost as if they, too, felt that they should not be alit during the day.

Phefeni Station rushed at us with human faces blurring past. When the train stopped, in stepped a girl. She must have been a mere child. Not just *petite*, but juvenile in structure. Yet her manner was all adult, as if she knew all about "this sorry scheme of things entire" and with a scornful toss relegated it. She had the premature features of the township girls, pert, arrogant, live. There was that about her that petrifies grown-ups who think of asking for her seat. She sat next to me.

The train slid into Phomolong. Against the red-brick waiting-room, I saw a *tsotsi* lounging, for all the world not a damn interested in taking the train. But I knew the type, so I watched him in grim anticipation. When the train started sailing out of the platform, he turned round nonchalantly and trippled along backwards towards an open door. It amazes me no end how these boys know exactly where the edge of the platform comes when they run like that backwards. But just at the drop he caught the ledge of the train and heaved himself in gracefully.

He swaggered towards us and stood between our seats with his back to the outside, his arms gripping the frame of the paneless window. He noticed the girl and started teasing her. All township love-making is rough.

"*Hê*, rubberneck!"—he clutched at her pear-like breast jutting from her sweater—"how long did you think you'll duck me?"

She looked round in panic: at me, at the old lady opposite her, at the hulk of a man opposite me. Then she whimpered: "Ah, *Au-boetie*, I don't even know you."

The *tsotsi* snarled: "You don't know me, eh? You don't know me when you're sitting with your student friends. You don't know last night, too, *nê*? You don't know how you ducked me?"

Some woman, reasonably out of reach, murmured: "The children of today . . ." in a drifting sort of way.

Mzimhlophe, the dirty-white station.

The *tsotsi* turned round and looked out of the window on to the platform. He recognized some of his friends there and hailed them.

"O, Zigzagza, it's how there?"

"It's jewish!"

"*Hela*, Tholo, my ma hears me, I want that ten-'n-six!"

"Go get it in hell!"

"Weh, my sister, don't lissen to that guy. Tell him Shakespeare nev'r said so!"

The gibberish exchange was all in exuberant superlatives.

The train left the platform in the echoes of its stridency. A washer-woman had just got shoved into it by ungallant males, bundle and all. People in the train made sympathetic noises, but too many passengers had seen too many tragedies to be rattled by this incident. They just remained bleared.

As the train approached New Canada, the confluence of the Orlando and the Dube train lines, I looked over the head of the girl next to me. It must have been a crazy engineer who had designed this crossing. The Orlando train comes from the right. It crosses the Dube train overhead just before we reach New Canada. But when it reaches the station it is on the right again, for the Johannesburg train enters ex-treme left. It is a curious kind of game.

Moreover, it has necessitated cutting the hill and building a bridge. But just this quirk of an engineer's imagination has left a spectacularly beautiful scene. After the drab, chocolate-box houses of the township, monotonously identical for row upon row, this gash of man's imposi-tion upon nature never fails to intrigue me.

Our caveman lover was still at the girl while people were changing from our train to the Westgate train in New Canada. The girl wanted to get off, but the *tsotsi* would not let her. When the train left the station, he gave her a vicious slap across the face so that her beret went flying. She flung a leg over me and rolled across my lap in her hurtling escape. The *tsotsi* followed, and as he passed me he reeled with the sway of the train.

To steady himself, he put a full paw in my face. It smelled sweaty-sour. Then he ploughed through the humanity of the train, after the girl. Men gave way shamelessly, but one woman would not take it. She burst into a spitfire tirade that whiplashed at the men.

"Lord, you call yourself men, you poltroons! You let a small ruffian insult you. Fancy, he grabs at a girl in front of you—might be your daughter—this thing with the manner of a pig! If there were real men here, they'd pull his pants off and give him such a leathering he'd never sit down for a week. But, no, you let him do this here; tonight you'll let him do it in your homes. And all you do is whimper: 'The children of today have never no respect!' *Sies!*"

The men winced. They said nothing, merely looked round at each other in shy embarrassment. But those barbed words had brought the little thug to a stop. He turned round, scowled at the woman, and with cold calculation cursed her anatomically, twisted his lips to give the words the full measure of its horror.

It was like the son of Ham finding a word for his awful discovery. It was like an impression that shuddered the throne of God Almighty. It was both a defilement and a defiance.

"Hela, you street-urchin, that woman is your mother," came the shrill voice of the big hulk of a man, who had all the time sat quietly opposite me, humming his lewd little township ditty. Now he moved towards where the *tsotsi* had stood rooted.

There was menace in every one swing of his clumsy movements, and the half-mumbled tune of his song sounded like under-breath cursing for all its calmness. The carriage froze into silence.

Suddenly, the woman shrieked, and men scampered on to seats. The *tsotsi* had drawn a sheath-knife, and he faced the big man.

There is something odd that a knife in a crowd does to various people. Most women go into pointless clamour, sometimes even hugging, round the arms, the men who might fight for them. Some men make gangway, stampeding helter-skelter. But with that hulk of a man the sight of the gleaming blade in the *tsotsi's* hand, drove him berserk. The splashing people left a sort of arena. There was an evil leer in his eye, much as if he was experiencing satanic satisfaction.

Croesus Cemetery flashed past.

Seconds before the impact, the *tsotsi* lifted the blade and plunged it obliquely. Like an instinctual, predatory beast, he seemed to know exactly where the vulnerable jugular was and he aimed for it. The jerk of the train deflected his stroke, though, and the blade slit a long cleavage along the big man's open chest.

With a demoniacal scream, the big man reached out for the boy, crudely and careless now of the blade that made another gash in his arm. He caught the boy by the upper arm with the left hand, and between the legs with the right, he lifted him bodily. Then he hurled him towards me. The flight went clean through the paneless window, and only a long cry trailed in the wake of the crushing train.

It was so sudden that the passengers were galvanized into action, darting to the windows; the human missile was nowhere to be seen. It was not a fight proper, not a full-blown quarrel. It was just an incident in the morning Dube train.

The big man, bespattered with blood, got off at Langlaagte Station. Only after we had left the station did the stunned passengers break out into a cacophony of chattering.

Odd, that no one expressed sympathy for the boy or man. They were just greedily relishing the thrilling episode of the morning.